THE THIRD F
GREAT HO

Also in Fontana

The Fontana Book of Great Horror Stories
The 3rd Fontana Book of Great Horror Stories
The 4th Fontana Book of Great Horror Stories
Ed. Christine Bernard

The 5th Fontana Book of Great Horror Stories
The 6th Fontana Book of Great Horror Stories
The 7th Fontana Book of Great Horror Stories
The 8th Fontana Book of Great Horror Stories
The 9th Fontana Book of Great Horror Stories
The 10th Fontana Book of Great Horror Stories
Ed. Mary Danby

London Tales of Terror
Ed. Jacquelyn Visick

Scottish Tales of Terror
Ed. Angus Campbell

Irish Tales of Terror
Ed. Jim McGarry

Cornish Tales of Terror
Ed. R. Chetwynd-Hayes

European Tales of Terror
Ed. J. J. Strating

THE THIRD FONTANA BOOK OF GREAT

Horror Stories

Edited by Christine Bernard

Collins · Fontana

First published by Fontana Books 1968
Ninth Impression May 1977

Made and printed in Great Britain by
William Collins Sons and Co Ltd Glasgow

CONTENTS

ACKNOWLEDGMENTS

The editor gratefully acknowledges permission to reprint copyright material to the following:

R. C. Cook for *Green Fingers.* © Copyright 1968 by R. C. Cook
Stanley Ellin and T. V. Boardman & Co. for *The Speciality of the House*
The Owner of the Copyright and A. P. Watt & Son for *The Room in the Tower*
David Ely and Thomas Bohen for *The Academy,* which originally appeared in *Playboy* Magazine, © Copyright 1965 by David Ely.
The Estate of J. D. Beresford and Sidgwick & Jackson Ltd for *Cut-throat Farm*
Roald Dahl and Michael Joseph Ltd for *Poison*
H. R. Wakefield and Curtis Brown Ltd for *Lucky's Grove*
R. Chetwynd-Hayes and London Authors for *Housebound*
H. P. Lovecraft, August Derleth and Victor Gollancz Ltd for *The Shuttered Room*
Mrs. G. Bambridge and Macmillan and Co. Ltd for *At the End of the Passage*

GREEN FINGERS

R. C. Cook

Widow Bowen was getting old. She was seventy-five, perhaps, or eighty. No one in Breth Common really knew. But then, it didn't really matter. She looked the same trim little person that she had always been, even while her husband, Ernest, had been alive, and he had died ten years ago.

The little grey stone cottage on the hill lane up to the common was half hidden by damson trees from the road, and wrapped snugly, as if in a woollen comforter, by the flowering creeper which grew up beside the door. The round hawthorn hedge at the bottom of the garden by the road was neatly trimmed and looked like a long green sponge roll.

At times, the villagers expressed surprise and a little pride in the old lady when they saw how well kept the garden still was. It was a lot of work for an old woman, and a house-proud woman at that. Widow Bowen would just smile when the baker remarked on how strong and green her shallots were growing, or when Nurse Foley called up from the road, with her laughing red face, to say that the broad beans looked a picture. Widow Bowen would say, and her blue eyes would twinkle, " I think I must have green fingers. Everything grows well here." And she thought she was being rather modest at that, for she could not remember anything that had not grown for her when she planted it.

She would say the same thing to Mrs. Beddoe at the farm when, in summer, she took down a basketful of long runner beans to help pay for the milk she fetched. " I must have green fingers," she would say and smile into Mrs. Beddoe's sceptical face. Mrs. Beddoe didn't quite know what to think. She didn't really want the vegetables that Widow Bowen brought in her basket, and yet, neither did she want to show the old lady how mercenary she was by asking for money instead, so she just looked down at the white bobbed hair and placed the jug of milk carefully into the thin hands.

Often when Widow Bowen knelt polishing the red-tiled step at her front door she would pause and smile to herself because the brass edge on the step and the kettle on the hob in the kitchen gleamed so brightly. There could not have been a brighter house on the common than hers, for Ernest and she had never had children, and she was a spotless housekeeper. But most of all she was pleased with the garden behind her. Not a weed showing itself, and everything so very green and growing. "Really, I must be very clever," she thought. She was not superstitious, and wasn't sure at times that there was in fact a God in the sky—often she would look up when it was blue and couldn't see even a trace of him—but she felt that, in some way, she must have a gift. She would trot on her small feet round into the shade at the back of the house and plant another cutting from the rose tree near the lavatory which had a seat scrubbed white as snow.

"I think I could make just anything grow," she said to herself once, and to prove it she broke a twig off the old apple tree and stuck it into the ground. It was February, and the buds were still hard. Sure enough, in a week, the buds began to show green. She examined the twig each morning, and soon there were slender green shoots bursting out with a flare of leaf at their tips.

She felt it was all so very simple. Indeed, they were only ordinary things that she planted, such as anyone on the common might grow. It wasn't enough for a person with really green fingers. So, when the gardener from the big house in the valley walked by, up the hill, one Sunday afternoon, she stopped him at her gate and asked him in a quiet little voice if he would do her the kindness of bringing her a few bits of the tropical plants from the hothouses. He smiled at her, thinking that she couldn't possibly have anywhere to plant them, but promised. "It'd be a pleasure, Mrs. Bowen," he said, touching his cap. "I'll find something for you." And on the following Sunday he brought a chip basket to her door filled with queer little bits of dark shiny leaves and pieces of cactus.

"Won't you come in and have a cup of tea?" she asked, smiling up at him, and though he was anxious to be off to his sister's house at the corner of the coppice, he took off his cap and bowed his head to go in under the low doorway. He blushed and mumbled, "Thank you, kindly," when she brought him sweet milky tea in a china cup with blackberries painted on it. He wet his finger on his tongue and dabbed up all the crumbs of the piece of faintly scented cake she placed by his arm.

"I can make those plants grow," she said, smoothing her hands on her black apron.

"Are you going to have them in pots indoors, then?" he asked.

"Oh, no," she laughed, carelessly. "In the garden. They'll grow all right."

"I think you'll find it's too cold for 'em out there," he said. "I could've brought you some proper outdoor plants if you'd said, only . . ."

"No. These are just what I want. I want to try something really difficult for a change."

He was puzzled a little, and when he had gone down the path and the gate had clicked behind him she fetched her broom and tidied up the dust his boots had brought in.

"How are they growing?" he asked with a secret sort of smile when he came up on the following Sunday. "I've brought you a few more."

"Very nicely," she said, with a rather straight face, because she could see that he didn't quite believe. "The grey woolly one is in flower," she added, looking up at him from under her eyebrows. She watched his eyes open just a little wider. "Come and see," she said, and took him along to the corner of the house.

There they were against the wall: dark shiny blue-green leaves, coloured fancy-patterned leaves, and on the grey woolly plant a deep wine-coloured flower. He lifted his cap and scratched his head thoughtfully, trying to work out how he had made a mistake, but he left his new lot of cuttings and took away his old basket and determined to find something she wouldn't be able to grow for next week.

Widow Bowen chuckled to herself as he went through the gate, and knelt down on the path to sort out the plants. "They shall grow!" she said with her mouth held rather tight, and she puddled them into the soil with a little pot of rain water. When she looked at them next morning they had already begun to perk up and look settled. Fern fronds and spiky leaves reached out towards the wall of the house, and the narrow border had begun to look like a section of tropical jungle. "I'll show that gardener what he knows about growing things," she muttered as she scrubbed at the lavatory seat, and it was with a little high-pitched laugh of triumph that she met him at the gate at the weekend.

When he had gone, Widow Bowen wondered if she could have offended him because he made no promise to bring anything more. She did not press him. She thought that perhaps it was as well that she had finished with him. His plants grew so very easily. She even had a sense of having wasted time, and she pressed the roots of the delicate trailing creeper he had brought into the ground with an offhand dig of her thin fingers. She said to Mrs. Beddoe the next morning when she went to fetch her jug of milk, "You know, I really believe I could make a stick of firewood grow."

The woman looked at her with uncertain eyes and felt that perhaps Widow Bowen was going a little dotty in her old age. It was not altogether surprising after losing her husband and living on her own all the time. The old lady understood the look, but she did not care very deeply. Mrs. Beddoe's thoughts did not worry her, and as she sat knitting by her fire in the evening she said, "Well, and why not? A stick of firewood had to grow at one time or another." And she decided to try it. No harm could come of it, after all. "If it doesn't grow, perhaps it will stop me being a conceited old woman for a bit." But in spite of this she laughed in her throat as she thought of the gardener and his tropical plants. "Oh! the look on his face!" She laughed until a tear fell on her knitting.

She had been buying bundles of chopped firewood from the shop up the hill for more than a month. Her tree prunings had all been used up, and she was too nervous of the dark coppice to fetch sticks from there, so it was a piece of the shop firewood that she took out into the garden the following morning. She shook her head over it as she carried it round to the back of the house. "I really am stupid," she thought. "It looks as dead as a doornail." She couldn't decide what sort of wood it was, either. The grain was very straight and soft—nothing like apple or damson wood. As she bent down to press it into the ground she looked round carefully for fear someone might be watching her. "Then they would think I'm mad!" she said loudly to make herself feel better. She stood back and looked at the stick in the ground, holding her soiled hands away from her sides. It stuck up out of the earth like a long thin bar of yellow soap cut off smartly at the top. For a moment she seriously considered the possibility that she might be going mad, and then she hurried away to put the potatoes on for dinner.

The delicate creeper grew just as if she had planted it with the utmost care, just as though it were in its native climate, and she stopped bothering about her tropical plants. When no one was passing up the lane and she thought she was unobserved she would hurry round to the back of the house, up past the rainwater butt, to look at her piece of firewood. Each time she went she felt more and more silly. After three days had gone by and she couldn't see any change she was tempted to pull it up and have done with the whole business. But then it rained hard for three or four days so that she was hardly able to go out of the house at all. She sat at her window and watched the mist of rain sweeping up the valley. When she got tired of that she would put on the headphones of Ernest's crystal set and sit listening to the radio programme. And she cleaned and polished the house from top to bottom until she could see her wrinkled little face in the shine on the floor tiles.

Only when the rain had stopped and she was able to go out into the garden again did she realise how long she had been cooped up. Little specks of chickweed and groundsel were dotting the spaces between her rows of peas and onions. She put on her leather-topped clogs and went to work with the rake. The piece of firewood was completely forgotten. It was only when she took a steaming hot bucket of water and a scrubbing brush up the steps outside the back door to scour the lavatory seat that it came to mind. When she saw it she set down her bucket with a clank. Flaky brown bark had covered up the yellow wood, and the chopped-off top was now a beautifully pointed spear, a shoot, reaching nearly a foot high, with a small arrow head of pale green pine needles at its top. Then she said, " Well of course, I knew it would," and picked up her bucket and went into the lavatory to scrub the seat. But when she had finished and dried the woodwork off with a steaming cloth she examined her new plant carefully.

It was a little thick round the base, perhaps, but a very pretty little tree for all that. She looked about to see if anyone was watching, but the house was a perfect screen from the road, and the damson trees in the top corner of the orchard hid her effectively from all the cottages higher up the hill. A sudden feeling of elation filled her so that she picked up her bucket and almost danced down the steps into her small kitchen. Over and over again she sang, "I've got green fingers," to a tune that came into her head, and she got out a small pot of honey for tea.

Next morning while she was washing in the kitchen she studied her face in the mirror. "Your hair wants cutting!" she said suddenly, noticing some stray pieces that had become rather long. Before she coiled her hair into its bob and pinned it she fetched her best scissors from her sewing basket in the window and cut the wisps of hair carefully. "Really, you still look quite pretty," she said to the glass and twisted the corners of her mouth into a mocking little smile. For a few seconds she stood daydreaming with the puffs of white hair in her hand. Then, coming to with a start, she went out to the dark little patch of earth at the back and pressed the hair together in a little tuft in the ground.

The tree was growing fast. It was many inches higher, and shoots had begun to press out all round the sides of it. Suddenly she was worried in case it should become a large tree because the small kitchen window needed all the light it could get. "If it grows too big," she said firmly, "I shall have to chop it down." And with that she went back into the house and put on the kettle for her morning cup of tea.

She began to say less and less to Mrs. Beddoe when she went down for her milk. She took money now and refrained from offering the woman vegetables. She knew that if she mentioned her garden now she wouldn't be believed. The tuft of hair was growing tall and bushy, and new sprouts of golden brown were coming up from the bottom. She couldn't possibly tell Mrs. Beddoe that. By the middle of summer she was becoming a little uneasy. The tropical creeper was growing all up the end wall of the house and was beginning to push back her own wistaria. She had tried to cut it back, but it only seemed to shoot out more strongly. The bush of hair needed trimming every few days or it hung over the path in great curling locks. And the piece of firewood was now a strong tree over seven feet tall. She was worried, too, by the little accidents she had been having. They depressed her. The first had happened when she clipped back the climbing plant. Being a tiny woman she was unable to reach the higher tentacles it shot out, and she fetched a chair to stand on. As she reached high to cut the last spray the chair tipped sideways, and she fell, twisting her ankle, so that for a few days it was swollen and painful. While she was hobbling about with this she tried to twist off one of the branches of the young tree because it was reaching out in front of the lavatory door. A tuft of pine needles caught her in the eye so that she believed for a few painful moments that it had blinded her. She had hardly recovered from these injuries when she scratched her leg deeply with the point of the shears while she was clipping the bush of hair. As she said to the baker when he called, "I've been knocking myself about lately."

But pushing things into the ground had become a habit with her. Any little pieces of wood or vegetable peelings she had she pressed into the ground behind the house. In time, they all began to grow, and the small hidden patch of earth was becoming a flourishing little garden of mixed odds and ends. She wondered at times whether the lack of sun behind the house might not prevent some of her experiments from doing well, but the various growths seemed to prefer the shade. Thinking of the hair that had grown, she pushed into the soil one day a piece of broken finger nail that she had cut off. It grew up like a long slender leaf, milky white and swaying in the wind. At times, when she stood and watched it, there seemed to be something mocking and truculent about it. She had the feeling that it, and the other things too, were returning a challenge that she had thrown down by sticking them into the soil. It increased her uneasiness, but she couldn't stop herself doing it. She swung between moods of triumphant success and timid disgust.

It was about the time when her leg had finally healed that she noticed something sticking out of her little plot of earth that had not been there a few days before. She racked her brains to remember what she could possibly have planted, but she could think of nothing, and she couldn't quite see what it was that was growing. It wasn't green certainly. It seemed to be a small brown knob covered with a thin greyish slime "Oh, a toadstool, I expect," she said and went off up the road to the shop. But on the way back with her groceries and firewood a thought suddenly struck her. The gamekeeper from the big house had brought her a rabbit the week before, and rather than suffer the smell of burning the bones, she had buried them.

"But I never meant those to be planted!" she said aloud as she hurried down the lane. "Not to grow!" Without stopping to put her shopping basket indoors she hastened round to the back of the house and peered closely again at the new thing. At last she decided that it was in fact one of the rabbit bones, but rather high out of the ground, and looking very sticky and wet. It was ugly, too, and she drew her hand back quickly when she realised that she had just been about to touch it.

The next day she refused to look at it as she went past. Indeed, for a few days she managed to half convince herself that if she ceased to show any more interest in her experiments they would stop growing. "After all," she said, "it's me that has the green fingers—not them!" But at last she could not curb her curiosity, and she went to examine the thing. There was more of it out of the ground by this time. The slimy covering had dried a little, and there were thin red lines running criss-cross all over it. Right down near the ground a fine grey mould had begun to form.

Gradually she accommodated herself to the idea. There were soon three more shoots near the first, all beginning to reach up to the same height. The grey mould had become thick and fluffy, growing nearly to the tops of the stems, which were beginning to spread out so much in the manner of tall toadstools that she began to think her first idea had been the right explanation. And yet their centres remained pink and milky, unlike any toadstool she had ever seen.

When her damsons were ripe Widow Bowen spent all her time picking and packing them off to market. She refused all the offers of the menfolk of the village to help with the ladder work. And so, for a few weeks, her secret garden was forgotten. By the beginning of October many of her plants had died off, and the leaves on the various young trees had turned yellow. Even the bush of hair had begun to slow in its growth, and she was able to gather up handfuls of the trailing fronds and lay them back from the path on to the garden. The four grey plants had spread right out at the top until they met, and were growing one thick bulbous blob on top of them all.

"There's no doubt about it," she said quietly as she stood looking at it. "It's them rabbit bones. What would that smarty gardener say if I showed him this?" She couldn't imagine. It was the last thing in the world she would have dreamt of mentioning to anyone. By the time winter came, all signs of pink in the peculiar animal plant had been covered up by the grey fur, and the rough form of the animal had become apparent. Widow Bowen was not always sure in the dull light of the late afternoons whether she imagined it or whether the form did actually twitch as it appeared to do.

At last, in early January, the snow came and hung in sheets on the branches of the pine tree. The whole of her cottage was lit up with the whiteness of the snow outside. Only the top of the rabbit plant was visible, but short ears had begun to sprout, and now, definitely, she noticed that there was some movement in the snow. It was this that disturbed her far more than the growth itself, though she did not know why. For nearly a fortnight she woke each morning to find it had snowed in the night, and she would stand at her bedroom window and look out across the valley with its fields, trees, everything, covered in white. Then she would look down sadly at her paths and know that she must put on stockings over her shoes and go out with tingling fingers to sweep.

One morning the snow was marked with black dots leading down to the hedge. She knew at once what they were, and because she knew she was shocked. She hurried out to the back of the house with a fearful choking in her throat. It was gone. There was a black hole in the snow and four imprints in the damp earth beneath. She stood a long time too dazed to think. When at last she was able to think her thoughts frightened her so much that she ran back into the house and did not venture out again all day. She sat huddled in her chair by the empty fireplace too frightened to move and did not think of eating. She slept there that night.

Next morning the sun shone fiercely and the snow began to melt. Widow Bowen stirred herself and laid the fire. The sunlight shone into her room and everything seemed cheerful once more. She thought carefully about her fears, and the more she thought the more silly they appeared. "It's gone. I'm well rid of it." With that she began to clean up the house and sweep the slushy snow away from her door. By afternoon nearly all the snow had gone. "I've been worried more than enough by all these growing things," she said firmly. "I'm the one with the green fingers, and I'm going to have my own way with them." She fetched out the shears and oiled them and cut back the hair bush. She trimmed the creeper and the frond of white nail back to decent limits with a sharp kitchen knife. "And now," she announced loudly to herself, "I'm going to lay my axe at the butt of that tree. It's darkened my window long enough."

The axe was heavy and sharp. Milk-white chips of wood jumped out on to the earth as she chopped at the small V-shaped cut she had made in the trunk, and after a few minutes she was very hot and tired. She stood up with the branches all about her head, looking at her little cottage. For the first time in many years she wished that Ernest was still alive. Chopping this small tree down would have been nothing to him. It was less than four inches across at the bottom, but she had made very little progress.

At her second attempt she steadied herself by resting her left hand low down on the trunk, and swung the axe slowly with one hand, letting the weight of the head do the work. The chips were smaller now, and the neat V had become a ragged notch in the white wood. She felt that she was going to expend all her energy without cutting more than halfway through it, and with a burst of determination she began to hack fiercely at it so that the blood came to her bowed head making her feel a little dizzy. The end of the haft caught her bent knee as she swung the axe. With a sickening pain the blade swung up into her hand on the trunk. She fell down in a faint with the blood spurting from the stump of her forefinger. When her vision cleared she knew what had happened. She felt weak and knew that the bleeding must be stopped. There was no pain now, only a dull numbness all up her arm. She crawled shakily to her feet and tottered uncertainly down the steps into her kitchen. She found a piece of white cloth and wrapped it round her bleeding hand. She felt old, very old, and wanted to die.

Soon the blood was soaking through the cloth, and she realised that she needed a doctor or she would indeed die very soon. She stirred herself and went down to the front gate, holding her bandaged hand up in front of her like a dog with a lame paw. Her neighbour's little boy was circling in the lane on his bicycle, and she called weakly to him to ride down the hill and ask the nurse to come quickly in her little car.

When the nurse came, Widow Bowen was leaning on the gate for support with the blood dripping from her bandage. Nurse Foley took one look at the hand and carried the old lady into the back of her car. Then she set off for the town hospital.

It was only when they were driving back in the dark that Widow Bowen truly woke up to what had happened to her. A huge white pad of bandage held her mutilated hand firmly bound.

"You must take things easy for a week or so," said Nurse Foley, half turning her red face to the back seat. "You've lost a lot of blood, you know. I asked them if they could keep you in for a few days, but they just haven't got a bed to spare." Widow Bowen smiled weakly and said she felt very well, considering. But there was something troubling her at the back of her mind. "Shall I ask Mrs. Jones to come in and help you get your tea?" the nurse asked when she had taken the old lady in and lit the lamp for her.

"I think I can manage well enough one-handed," said Widow Bowen, and her blue eyes twinkled a little again now that she was back home. To prove it she made a cup of tea for herself and the nurse and sat gazing at the big round-faced woman in her sitting-room. The tea made her feel a lot better, and she brought out some scones and put a light to the laid fire in the grate. She felt quite safe with the house round her.

At last the nurse went, promising to call in the morning, and the old woman sat thinking in her chair. Her fingers, her precious green fingers, were irrevocably damaged. Slowly she got up and walked, carrying the lamp, out through the kitchen to the back of the house. Little splashes of blood had dried in a trail across the kitchen floor. She stood in the wavering light of the lamp, looking at the hacked tree with the chips of white wood lying all round it, and felt very sorry that she had tried to cut it down. She could sympathise now that the axe had cut her too. The axe lay at the foot of the tree with a little stain of blood on the blade. Suddenly, in the chippings, she saw her finger, bent and white. Her stomach lurched, and she felt a bit dizzy again. Wondering, she stooped and set her lamp down and picked up the finger and looked at it. It looked so old and wrinkled and white. Many times she had pressed holes into the earth with it for seedlings, and now it was cut off. She held it against her breast, crying a little. It looked so forlorn. " And you'll never plant another thing!" she sobbed sadly to it, as though it were a dead child. The frustrated maternal instincts of years welled up in her small bent body, and she nursed this small part of her close in the warmth of her dress.

After standing there a long while, with the lamp at her feet throwing up the shadows all around her, she said with sudden determination, " You shan't die! I'll put you in the ground and you shall grow." In spite of her resolve her heart was beating rapidly as she stepped on to the garden and crouched down in the darkness behind the rose bush at the side of the lavatory. With tears pooling in her eyes she made a hole in the ground and placed her finger in it. For minutes she crouched brooding over this strange child of her body until her old legs ached with cramp, and then she went into the house and up to bed.

Many times in the night she woke crying with the pain in her hand, and when the morning came she was pale and worn out. Nurse Foley suggested that a woman should come in and look after her for a few days, but the old woman refused fiercely. The nurse sighed and said, " Very well." She tucked the stray ends of her grey hair into her cap and left. Widow Bowen went round to the back of the house to look at her finger. The dew of the night had taken all the limpness out of it. It pointed straight up at the sky and had a tinge of colour again around the knuckles. A wave of defiant will flowed through her, and then left her feeling weary and apathetic.

She was no longer surprised. It was difficult for her even to think clearly about it. The thing was growing. She only felt that at all costs she must prevent anyone from ever seeing it. In a few days there were the tips of other fingers showing.

The old lady nodded her white head tiredly when she saw them. She felt it was out of her control now. In a fortnight a full hand had appeared. Fear began to fill the old widow. She wandered about her cottage in a vague dream. The brass door knob began to discolour and the kettle grew tarnished and blackened. Crumbs of food lay on the floors, and a fine film of dust was thickening on her sideboard. Out in the garden the unplanted earth had a thin carpet of weeds, and the hedge at the roadside grew woolly. Often she forgot to go for her milk, and cried peevishly one morning when Mrs. Beddoe brought it up to her. For many days at a time she was too frightened to go and look at the growing thing in the shadows behind her house, but eventually she would have to go, and would stand staring at it with a glaze over her blue eyes. A wrist and an arm had appeared, with the skin wrinkled lightly like her own, and by the time the cherries blossomed the crest of a white head had begun to appear, like the top of a large horse mushroom. She would spend hours staring at it with a terrible fascination. The fear that anyone should see it became an obsession with her. She began to meet the baker at the gate to prevent him walking up to the house, and she covered the naked head and shoulders over with brown potato sacks. The eyes of the figure were closed, but on the face and the bare shoulders were the wrinkles and freckles that resembled her own in the minutest detail. Night after night she lay tossing in a half stupor of sleep while horrible dreams flashed through her frightened mind.

By the time the damsons were ripe the white body was out of the ground to its knees, bent slightly forward as she herself stood. Widow Bowen let her damsons rot on the trees. Birds settled in screaming crowds, pecking at the decaying fruit, and as the season passed over shrivelled brown drops remained to hang like tiny bats from all the branches. The cottage was now thick in dirt, and the forest of weeds in the garden had already begun to die down. The hawthorn hedge had sprung up unchecked, hiding the house from the view of the villagers, and, but for her occasional dishevelled appearance at the gate to wait for the baker, they would have believed her to be dead. At first they had enquired whether they might lend a hand in the house or garden, but she answered them with such hysterical outbursts that they stopped asking, and hurried past her gate with heads down whenever she happened to be standing there.

As December passed the snow came again, bearing down the tall raggedness of the hedge, and settling like a mantle on the sack-covered shoulders of the growing figure behind the house. Mornings would come, and the old lady would wake from her fitful sleep to find the room flooded with white light from the blanket of snow outside. She dreaded it. Each morning she expected to see a dark trail leading across the garden from the back of the house as she had done the year before. But each morning the snow stretched, untouched, down to the hedge, startlingly white. Every day she would take a quick frightened look behind the rambling rose tree beside the lavatory to be sure the figure still stood there. At times it would sway slightly, and Widow Bowen would stand, rigid with horror, until it was still again.

The lavatory seat was no longer white. Cobwebs and dusty bits of newspaper littered its once-scrubbed surface. Widow Bowen was almost too frightened to go in there for fear of the figure standing close outside.

The snow still covered the ground in a hard frozen layer when she came out of the lavatory late one afternoon and took her usual hurried look behind the rose bush. Her heart stopped beating for a second, and the breath choked in her throat. Two black patches of soil were all that remained to show where it had been. She looked wildly about her. There were no tracks in the snow. It was frozen far too hard. With a terrified scream she stumbled down the steps into her kitchen and slammed the door behind her. She bolted it at top and bottom with dithering fingers, and scurried into the sitting-room to lock the front door.

There in her chair sat the figure, staring at her. She stood with her back against the door, unable to move. The other did not move either. It was her exact double, from the white hair to the twinkling blue eyes, but clothed, almost demurely, in sacks. The old lady stared at the white thin hands spread out on the arms of the chair. The fingers were complete, whole. Widow Bowen looked up into the eyes again, and they looked into hers with a faint mocking smile, as though they could see into the deepest corners of her mind. She was rigid with terror. The blood began to leave her head. A gradual blackness clouded out her sight, and she sank to the floor unconscious.

Nurse Foley came down the hill in her car next morning. The snow had almost melted in the night, and the sun was shining. Catching sight of the old lady, she stopped and put her head out. "I'm glad to see you trimming your hedge," she said. "It had begun to look untidy."

The old lady smiled, holding the shears in front of her. "Yes," she said, "the whole place is in a terrible mess. I've been dying to get started on it, but the snow held me up, you know." Her blue eyes twinkled brightly.

"I suppose you've heard the news," said the nurse, pushing her head further out of the window.

"No, I haven't. What's that, then?"

"Oh, my dear! I've been up there for hours. They found a body in the coppice, you know. Little Chris Bradley found it first—at least, a piece of it. Horrible it is—all chopped to pieces with an axe or something. The police are there now. They think it's probably an old woman, but it's so wickedly smashed about that they can't recognise anything."

"What a nasty thing!"

"Oh, terrible! Yes. Still, you don't want to bother your head about that. You've had enough trouble. How is your hand going on?" She looked from one hand to the other, confused between left and right, but there was no missing finger.

"Oh, beautifully," said the old lady, smiling and nodding her head. "Everything grows well here. I think I must have green fingers."

THE SPECIALTY OF THE HOUSE

Stanley Ellin

"And this," said Laffler, "is Sbirro's." Costain saw a square brownstone façade identical with the others that extended from either side into the clammy darkness of the deserted street. From the barred windows of the basement at his feet a glimmer of light showed behind heavy curtains.

"Lord," he observed, "it's a dismal hole, isn't it?"

"I beg you to understand," said Laffler stiffly, "that Sbirro's is the restaurant without pretensions. Besieged by these ghastly, neurotic times, it has refused to compromise. It is perhaps the last important establishment in this city lit by gas jets. Here you will find the same honest furnishing, the same magnificent Sheffield service, and possibly, in a far corner, the very same spider webs that were remarked by the patrons of a half-century ago!"

"A doubtful recommendation," said Costain, "and hardly sanitary."

"When you enter," Laffler continued, "you leave the insanity of this year, this day, and this hour, and you find yourself for a brief span restored in spirit, not by opulence, but by dignity, which is the lost quality of our time."

Costain laughed uncomfortably. "You make it sound more like a cathedral than a restaurant," he said.

In the pale reflection of the street lamp overhead, Laffler peered at his companion's face. "I wonder," he said abruptly, "whether I have not made a mistake in extending this invitation to you."

Costain was hurt. Despite an impressive title and large salary, he was no more than clerk to this pompous little man, but he was impelled to make some display of his feelings. "If you wish," he said coldly, "I can make other plans for my evening with no trouble."

With his large, cowlike eyes turned up to Costain, the mist drifting into the ruddy, full moon of his face, Laffler seemed strangely ill at ease. Then " No, no," he said at last, " absolutely not. It's important that you dine at Sbirro's with me." He grasped Costain's arm firmly and led the way to the wrought-iron gate of the basement. " You see, you're the sole person in my office who seems to know anything at all about good food. And on my part, knowing about Sbirro's but not having some appreciative friend to share it, is like having a unique piece of art locked in a room where no one else can enjoy it."

Costain was considerably mollified by this. " I understand there are a great many people who relish that situation."

" I'm not one of that kind!" Laffler said sharply. " And having the secret of Sbirro's locked in myself for years has finally become unendurable." He fumbled at the side of the gate and from within could be heard the small, discordant jangle of an ancient pull-bell. An interior door opened with a groan, and Costain found himself peering into a dark face whose only discernible feature was a row of gleaming teeth.

" Sair?" said the face.

" Mr. Laffler and a guest."

" Sair," the face said again, this time in what was clearly an invitation. It moved aside and Costain stumbled down a single step behind his host. The door and gate creaked behind him, and he stood blinking in a small foyer. It took him a moment to realise that the figure he now stared at was his own reflection in a gigantic pier glass that extended from floor to ceiling. " Atmosphere," he said under his breath and chuckled as he followed his guide to a seat.

He faced Laffler across a small table for two and peered curiously around the dining-room. It was no size at all, but the half-dozen guttering gas jets which provided the only illumination threw such a deceptive light that the walls flickered and faded into uncertain distance.

There were no more than eight or ten tables about, arranged to ensure the maximum privacy. All were occupied, and the few waiters serving them moved with quiet efficiency. In the air was a soft clash and scrape of cutlery and a soothing murmur of talk. Costain nodded appreciatively.

Laffler breathed an audible sigh of gratification. " I knew you would share my enthusiasm," he said. " Have you noticed, by the way, that there are no women present?"

Costain raised inquiring eyebrows.

"Sbirro," said Laffler, "does not encourage members of the fair sex to enter the premises. And, I can tell you, his method is decidedly effective. I had the experience of seeing a woman get a taste of it not long ago. She sat at a table for not less than an hour waiting for service which was never forthcoming."

"Didn't she make a scene?"

"She did." Laffler smiled at the recollection. "She succeeded in annoying the customers, embarrasing her partner, and nothing more."

"And what about Mr. Sbirro?"

"He did not make an appearance. Whether he directed affairs from behind the scenes, or was not even present during the episode, I don't know. Whichever it was, he won a complete victory. The woman never reappeared nor, for that matter, did the witless gentleman who by bringing her was really the cause of the entire contretemps."

"A fair warning to all present," laughed Costain.

A waiter now appeared at the table. The chocolate-dark skin, the thin, beautifully moulded nose and lips, the large liquid eyes, heavily lashed, and the silver white hair so heavy and silken that it lay on the skull like a cap, all marked him definitely as an East Indian. The man arranged the stiff table linen, filled two tumblers from a huge, cut glass pitcher, and set them in their proper places.

"Tell me," Laffler said eagerly, "is the special being served this evening?"

The waiter smiled regretfully and showed teeth as spectacular as those of the majordomo. "I am so sorry, sair. There is no special this evening."

Laffler's face fell into lines of heavy disappointment. "After waiting so long. It's been a month already, and I hoped to show my friend here . . ."

"You understand the difficulties, sair."

"Of course, of course." Laffler looked at Costain sadly and shrugged. "You see, I had in mind to introduce you to the greatest treat that Sbirro's offers, but unfortunately it isn't on the menu this evening."

The waiter said: "Do you wish to be served now, sair?" and

Laffler nodded. To Costain's surprise the waiter made his way off without waiting for any instructions.

"Have you ordered in advance?" he asked.

"Ah," said Laffler, "I really should have explained. Sbirro's offers no choice whatsoever. You will eat the same meal as everyone else in this room. To-morrow evening you would eat an entirely different meal, but again without designating a single preference."

"Very unusual," said Costain, "and certainly unsatisfactory at times. What if one doesn't have a taste for the particular dish set before him?"

"On that score," said Laffler solemnly, "you need have no fears. I give you my word that, no matter how exacting your tastes, you will relish every mouthful you eat in Sbirro's."

Costain looked doubtful, and Laffler smiled. "And consider the subtle advantages of the system," he said. "When you pick up the menu of a popular restaurant, you find yourself confronted with innumerable choices. You are forced to weigh, to evaluate, to make uneasy decisions which you may instantly regret. The effect of all this is a tension which, however slight, must make for discomfort.

"And consider the mechanics of the process. Instead of a hurly-burly of sweating cooks rushing about a kitchen in a frenzy to prepare a hundred varying items, we have a chef who stands serenely alone, bringing all his talents to bear on one task, with all the assurance of a complete triumph!"

"Then you have seen the kichen?"

"Unfortunately, no," said Laffler sadly. "The picture I offer is hypothetical, made of conversational fragments I have pieced together over the years. I must admit, though, that my desire to see the functioning of the kitchen here comes very close to being my sole obsession nowadays."

"But have you mentioned this to Sbirro?"

"A dozen times. He shrugs the suggestion away."

"Isn't that a rather curious foible on his part?"

"No, no," Laffler said hastily, "a master artist is never under the compulsion of petty courtesies. Still," he sighed, "I have never given up hope."

The waiter now reappeared bearing two soup bowls which

he set in place with mathematical exactitude, and a small tureen from which he slowly ladled a measure of clear, thin broth. Costain dipped his spoon into the broth and tasted it with some curiosity. It was delicately flavoured, bland almost to the verge of tastelessness. Costain frowned, tentatively reached for the salt and pepper cellars, and discovered there were none on the table. He looked up, saw Laffler's eyes on him, and although unwilling to compromise with his own tastes, he hesitated to act as a damper on Laffler's enthusiasm. Therefore he smiled and indicated the broth.

"Excellent," he said.

Laffler returned his smile. "You do not find it excellent at all," he said coolly. "You find it flat and badly in need of condiments. I know this," he continued as Costain's eyebrows shot upward, "because it was my own reaction many years ago, and because like yourself I found myself reaching for salt and pepper after the first mouthful. I also learned with surprise that condiments are not available in Sbirro's."

Costain was shocked. "Not even salt!" he exclaimed.

"Not even salt. The very fact that you require it for your soup stands as evidence that your taste is unduly jaded. I am confident that you will now make the same discovery that I did: by the time you have nearly finished your soup your desire for salt will be non-existent."

Laffler was right; before Costain had reached the bottom of his plate he was relishing the nuances of the broth with steadily increasing delight. Laffler thrust aside his own empty bowl and rested his elbows on the table. "Do you agree with me now?"

"To my surprise," said Costain, "I do."

As the waiter busied himself clearing the table, Laffler lowered his voice significantly. "You will find," he said, "that the absence of condiments is but one of several noteworthy characteristics which mark Sbirro's. I may as well prepare you for these. For example, no alcoholic beverages of any sort are served here, nor for that matter any beverage except clear, cold water, the first and only drink necessary for a human being."

"Outside of mother's milk," suggested Costain dryly.

"I can answer that in like vein by pointing out that the

average patron of Sbirro's has passed that primal stage of his development."

Costain laughed. "Granted," he said.

"Very well. There is also a ban on the use of tobacco in any form."

"But, good heavens," said Costain, "doesn't that make Sbirro's more a teetotaller's retreat than a gourmet's sanctuary?"

"I fear," said Laffler solemnly, "that you confuse the words, *gourmet* and *gourmand*. The gourmand, through glutting himself, requires a wider and wider latitude of experience to stir his surfeited senses, but the very nature of the gourmet is simplicity. The ancient Greek in his coarse chiton savouring the ripe olive; the Japanese in his bare room contemplating the curve of a single flower stem—these are the true gourmets."

"But an occasional drop of brandy, or pipeful of tobacco," said Costain dubiously, "are hardly over-indulgences."

"By alternating stimulant and narcotic," said Laffler, "you seesaw the delicate balance of your taste so violently that it loses its most precious quality: the appreciation of fine food. During my years as a patron of Sbirro's I have proved this to my satisfaction."

"May I ask," said Costain, "why you regard the ban on these things as having such deep aesthetic motives? What about such mundane reasons as the high cost of a liquor licence, or the possibility that patrons would object to the smell of tobacco in such confined quarters?"

Laffler shook his head violently. "If and when you meet Sbirro," he said, "you will understand at once that he is not the man to make decisions on a mundane basis. As a matter of fact, it was Sbirro himself who first made me cognisant of what you call 'aesthetic' motives."

"An amazing man," said Costain, as the waiter prepared to serve the entrée.

Laffler's next words were not spoken until he had savoured and swallowed a large portion of meat. "I hesitate to use superlatives," he said, "but to my way of thinking Sbirro represents man at the apex of his civilisation!"

Costain cocked an eyebrow and applied himself to his roast

which rested in a pool of stiff gravy ungarnished by green or vegetable. The thin steam rising from it carried to his nostrils a subtle, tantalising odour which made his mouth water. He chewed a piece as slowly and thoughtfully as if he were analysing the intricacies of a Mozart symphony. The range of taste he discovered was really extraordinary, from the pungent nip of the crisp outer edge to the peculiarly flat yet soul-satisfying ooze of blood which the pressure of his jaws forced from the half-raw interior.

Upon swallowing, he found himself ferociously hungry for another piece, and then another, and it was only with an effort that he prevented himself from wolfing down all his share of the meat and gravy without waiting to get the full voluptuous satisfaction from each mouthful. When he had scraped his platter clean, he realised that both he and Laffler had completed the entire course without exchanging a single word. He commented on this, and Laffler said: "Can you see any need for words in the presence of such food?"

Costain looked round at the shabby, dimly lit room, the quiet diners, with a new perception. "No," he said humbly, "I cannot. For any doubts I had I apologise unreservedly. In all your praise of Sbirro's there was not a single word of exaggeration."

"Ah," said Laffler delightedly. "And that is only part of the story. You heard me mention the special which unfortunately was not on the menu to-night. What you have just eaten is as nothing when compared to the absolute delights of that special!"

"Good lord!" cried Costain; "What is it? Nightingales' tongues? Fillet of unicorn?"

"Neither," said Laffler. "It is lamb."

"Lamb?"

Laffler remained lost in thought for a minute. "If," he said at last, "I were to give you in my own unstinted words my opinion of this dish you would judge me completely insane. That is how deeply the mere thought of it affects me. It is neither the fatty chop, nor the too solid leg; it is, indeed, a select portion of the rarest sheep in existence and is named after the species—lamb Amirstan."

Costain knit his brows. "Amirstan?"

"A fragment of desolation almost lost on the border which

separates Afghanistan and Russia. From chance remarks dropped by Sbirro, I gather it is no more than a plateau which grazes the pitiful remnants of a flock of superb sheep. Sbirro, through some means or other, obtained rights to the traffic in this flock and is, therefore, the sole restaurateur ever to have lamb Amirstan on his bill of fare. I can tell you that the appearance of this dish is a rare occurrence indeed, and luck is the only guide in determining for the clientele the exact date when it will be served."

"But surely," said Costain, "Sbirro could provide some advance knowledge of this event."

"The objection to that is simply stated," said Laffler. "There exists in this city a large number of professional gluttons. Should advance information slip out, it is quite likely that they will, out of curiosity, become familiar with the dish and thenceforth supplant the regular patrons at these tables."

"But you don't mean to say," objected Costain, "that these few people present are the only ones in the entire city, or for that matter, in the whole wide world, who know of the existence of Sbirro's!"

"Very nearly. There may be one or two regular patrons who, for some reason, are not present at the moment."

"That's incredible."

"It is done," said Laffler, the slightest shade of menace in his voice, "by every patron making it his solemn obligation to keep the secret. By accepting my invitation this evening, you automatically assume that obligation. I hope you can be trusted with it."

Costain flushed. "My position in your employ should vouch for me. I only question the wisdom of a policy which keeps such magnificent food away from so many who would enjoy it."

"Do you know the inevitable result of the policy *you* favour?" asked Laffler bitterly. "An influx of idiots who would nightly complain that they are never served roast duck with chocolate sauce. Is that picture tolerable to you?"

"No," admitted Costain, "I am forced to agree with you."

Laffler leaned back in his chair wearily and passed his hand over his eyes in an uncertain gesture. "I am a solitary man," he said quietly, "and not by choice alone. It may sound strange to you, it may border on eccentricity, but I feel to my depths that this restaurant, this warm haven in a coldly insane world, is both family and friend to me."

And Costain, who to this moment had never viewed his companion as other than tyrannical employer or officious host, now felt an overwhelming pity twist inside his comfortably expanded stomach.

By the end of two weeks the invitations to join Laffler at Sbirro's had become something of a ritual. Every day, at a few minutes after five, Costain would step out into the office corridor and lock his cubicle behind him; he would drape his overcoat neatly over his left arm, and peer into the glass of the door to make sure his Homburg was set at the proper angle. At one time he would have followed this by lighting a cigarette, but under Laffler's prodding he had decided to give abstinence a fair trial. Then he would start down the corridor, and Laffler would fall in step at his elbow, clearing his throat. "Ah, Costain. No plans for this evening, I hope."

"No," Costain would say, "I'm foot-loose and fancy-free," or "At your service," or something equally inane. He wondered at times whether it would not be more tactful to vary the ritual with an occasional refusal, but the glow with which Laffler received his answer, and the rough friendliness of Laffler's grip on his arm, forestalled him.

Among the treacherous crags of the business world, reflected Costain, what better way to secure your footing than friendship with one's employer. Already, a secretary close to the workings of the inner office had commented publicly on Laffler's highly favourable opinion of Costain. That was all to the good.

And the food! The incomparable food at Sbirro's! For the first time in his life, Costain, ordinarily a lean and bony man, noted with gratification that he was certainly gaining weight; within two weeks his bones had disappeared under a layer of sleek firm flesh, and here and there were even signs of incipient plumpness. It struck Costain one night, while surveying himself in his bath, that the rotund Laffler himself might have been a spare and bony man before discovering Sbirro's.

So there was obviously everything to be gained and nothing to be lost by accepting Laffler's invitations. Perhaps after testing the heralded wonders of lamb Amirstan and meeting Sbirro, who thus far had not made an appearance, a refusal or two might be in order. But certainly not until then.

That evening, two weeks to a day after his first visit to Sbirro's, Costain had both desires fulfilled: he dined on lamb Amirstan, and he met Sbirro. Both exceeded all his expectations.

When the waiter leaned over their table immediately after seating them and gravely announced: "To-night is special, sair," Costain was shocked to find his head pounding with expectation. On the table before him he saw Laffler's hands trembling violently. "But it isn't natural," he thought suddenly: "Two full-grown men, presumably intelligent and in the full possession of their senses, as jumpy as a pair of cats waiting to have their meat flung to them!"

"This is it!" Laffler's voice startled him so that he almost leaped from his seat. "The culinary triumph of all times! And faced by it you are embarrassed by the very emotions it distils."

"How did you know that?" Costain asked faintly.

"How? Because a decade ago I underwent your embarrassment. Add to that your air of revulsion and it's easy to see how affronted you are by the knowledge that man has not yet forgotten how to slaver over his meat."

"And these others," whispered Costain, "do they all feel the same thing?"

"Judge for yourself."

Costain looked furtively around at the nearby tables. "You are right," he finally said. "At any rate, there's comfort in numbers."

Laffler inclined his head slightly to the side. "One of the numbers," he remarked, "appears to be in for a disappointment."

Costain followed the gesture. At the table indicated a grey-haired man sat conspicuously alone, and Costain frowned at the empty chair opposite him.

"Why, yes," he recalled, "that very stout, bald man, isn't it? I believe it's the first dinner he's missed here in two weeks."

"The entire decade more likely," said Laffler sympathetically. "Rain or shine, crisis or calamity, I don't think he's missed an evening at Sbirro's since the first time I dined here. Imagine his expression when he's told that on his very first defection lamb Amirstan was the *plat du jour*."

Costain looked at the empty chair again with a dim discomfort. "His very first?" he murmured.

"Mr. Laffler! And friend! I am so pleased. So very, very pleased. No, do not stand; I will have a place made." Miraculously a seat appeared under the figure standing there at the table. "The lamb Amirstan will be an unqualified success, hurr? I myself have been stewing in the miserable kitchen all the day, prodding the foolish chef to do everything just so. The just so is the important part, hurr? But I see your friend does not know me. An introduction, perhaps?"

The words ran in a smooth, fluid eddy. They rippled, they purred, they hypnotised Costain so that he could do no more than stare. The mouth that uncoiled this sinuous monologue was alarmingly wide, with thin mobile lips that curled and twisted with every syllable. There was a flat nose with a straggling line of hair under it; wide-set eyes, almost oriental in appearance, that glittered in the unsteady flare of gaslight; and long, sleek hair that swept back from high on the unwrinkled forehead—hair so pale that it might have been bleached of all colour. An amazing face surely, and the sight of it tortured Costain with the conviction that it was somehow familiar. His brain twitched and prodded but could not stir up any solid recollection.

Laffler's voice jerked Costain out of his study. "Mr. Sbirro. Mr. Costain, a good friend and associate." Costain rose and shook the proffered hand. It was warm and dry, flint-hard against his palm.

"I am so very pleased, Mr. Costain. So very, very pleased," purred the voice. "You like my little establishment, hurr? You have a great treat in store, I assure you."

Laffler chuckled. "Oh, Costain's been dining here regularly for two weeks," he said. "He's by way of becoming a great admirer of yours, Shirro."

The eyes were turned on Costain. "A very great compliment. You compliment me with your presence and I return same with my food, hurr? But the lamb Amirstan is far superior to anything of your past experience, I assure you.

All the trouble of obtaining it, all the difficulty of preparation, is truly merited."

Costain strove to put aside the exasperating problem of that face. "I have wondered," he said, "why with all these difficulties you mention, you even bother to present lamb Amirstan to the public. Surely your dishes are excellent enough to uphold your reputation."

Sbirro smiled so broadly that his face became perfectly round. "Perhaps it is a matter of the psychology, hurr? Someone discovers a wonder and must share it with others. He must fill his cup to the brim, perhaps, by observing the so evident pleasure of those who explore it with him. Or," he shrugged, "perhaps it is just a matter of good business."

"Then in the light of all this," Costain persisted, "and considering all the conventions you have imposed on your customers, why do you open the restaurant to the public instead of operating it as a private club?"

The eyes abruptly glinted into Costain's, then turned away. "So perspicacious, hurr? Then I will tell you. Because there is more privacy in a public eating place than in the most exclusive club in existence! Here no one inquires of your affairs; no one desires to know the intimacies of your life. Here the business is eating. We are not curious about names and addresses or the reasons for the coming and going of our guests. We welcome you when you are here; we have no regrets when you are here no longer. That is the answer, hurr?"

Costain was startled by this vehemence "I had no intention of prying," he stammered.

Sbirro ran the tip of his tongue over his thin lips. "No, no," he reassured, "you are not prying. Do not let me give you that impression. On the contrary, I invite your questions."

"Oh, come, Costain," said Laffler. "Don't let Sbirro intimidate you. I've known him for years and I guarantee that his bark is worse than his bite. Before you know it, he'll be showing you all the privileges of the house—outside of inviting you to visit his precious kitchen, of course."

"Ah," smiled Sbirro, "for that, Mr. Costain may have to wait a little while. For everything else I am at his beck and call."

Laffler slapped his hand jovially on the table. " What did I tell you!" he said. " Now let's have the truth, Sbirro. Has anyone, outside of your staff, ever stepped into the sanctum sanctorum?"

Sbirro looked up. " You see on the wall above you," he said earnestly, " the portrait of one to whom I did the honour. A very dear friend and a patron of most long standing, he is evidence that my kitchen is not inviolate."

Costain studied the picture and started with recognition. " Why," he said excitedly, " that's the famous writer—you know the one, Laffler—he used to do such wonderful short stories and cynical bits and then suddenly took himself off and disappeared in Mexico!"

" Of course!" cried Laffler, " and to think I've been sitting under his portrait for years without even realising it!" He turned to Sbirro. " A dear friend, you say? His disappearance must have been a blow to you."

Sbirro's face lengthened. " It was, it was, I assure you. But think of it this way, gentlemen: he was probably greater in his death than in his life, hurr? A most tragic man, he often told me that his only happy hours were spent here at this very table. Pathetic, is it not? And to think the only favour I could ever show him was to let him witness the mysteries of my kitchen, which is, when all is said and done, no more than a plain, ordinary kitchen."

" You seem very certain of his death," commented Costain. " After all, no evidence has ever turned up to substantiate it."

Sbirro contemplated the picture. " None at all," he said softly. " Remarkable, hurr?"

With the arrival of the entrée Sbirro leaped to his feet and set about serving them himself. With his eyes alight he lifted the casserole from the tray and sniffed at the fragrance from within with sensual relish. Then, taking great care not to lose a single drop of gravy, he filled two platters with chunks of dripping meat. As if exhausted by this task, he sat back in his chair, breathing heavily. " Gentlemen," he said, " to your good appetite."

Costain chewed his first mouthful with great deliberation and swallowed it. Then he looked at the empty tines of his fork with glazed eyes.

" Good God!" he breathed.

"It is good, hurr? Better than you imagined?"

Costain shook his head dazedly. "It is as impossible," he said slowly, "for the uninitiated to conceive the delights of lamb Amirstan as for mortal man to look into his own soul."

"Perhaps," Sbirro thrust his head so close that Costain could feel the warm, fetid breath tickle his nostrils, "perhaps you have just had a glimpse into your soul, hurr?"

Costain tried to draw back slightly without giving offence. "Perhaps," he laughed, "and a gratifying picture it made: all fang and claw. But without intending any disrespect, I should hardly like to build my church on *lamb en casserole*."

Sbirro rose and laid a hand gently on his shoulder. "So perspicacious," he said. "Sometimes when you have nothing to do, nothing, perhaps, but sit for a very little while in a dark room and think of this world—what it is and what it is going to be—then you must turn your thoughts a little to the significance of the Lamb in religion. It will be so interesting. And now," he bowed deeply to both men, "I have held you long enough from your dinner. I was most happy"—he nodded to Costain—"and I am sure we will meet again." The teeth gleamed, the eyes glittered, and Sbirro was gone down the aisle of tables.

Costain twisted around to stare after the retreating figure. "Have I offended him in some way?" he asked.

Laffler looked up from his plate. "Offended him? He loves that kind of talk. Lamb Amirstan is a ritual with him; get him started and he'll be back at you a dozen times worse than a priest making a conversion."

Costain turned to his meal with the face still hovering before him. "Interesting man," he reflected. "Very."

It took him a month to discover the tantalising familiarity of that face, and when he did, he laughed aloud in his bed. Why, of course! Sbirro might have sat as the model for the Cheshire cat in *Alice*!

He passed this thought on to Laffler the very next evening as they pushed their way down the street to the restaurant against a chill, blustering wind. Laffler only looked blank.

"You may be right," he said, "but I'm not a fit judge. It's a far cry back to the days when I read the book. A far cry, indeed."

As if taking up his words, a piercing howl came ringing down the street and stopped both men short in their tracks. "Someone's in trouble there," said Laffler. "Look!"

Not far from the entrance to Sbirro's two figures could be seen struggling in the near darkness. They swayed back and forth and suddenly tumbled into a writhing heap on the sidewalk. The piteous howl went up again, and Laffler, despite his girth, ran toward it at a fair speed with Costain tagging cautiously behind.

Stretched out full length on the pavement was a slender figure with the dusky complexion and white hair of one of Sbirro's servitors. His fingers were futilely plucking at the huge hands which encircled his throat, and his knees pushed weakly up at the gigantic bulk of a man who brutally bore down with his full weight.

Laffler came up panting. "Stop this!" he shouted. "What's going on here?"

The pleading eyes almost bulging from their sockets turned toward Laffler. "Help, sair. This man—drunk——"

"Drunk am I, ya dirty——" Costain saw now that the man was a sailor in a badly soiled uniform. The air around him reeked with the stench of liquor. "Pick me pocket and then call me drunk, will ya!" He dug his fingers in harder, and his victim groaned.

Laffler seized the sailor's shoulder. "Let go of him, do you hear! Let go of him at once!" he cried, and the next instant was sent careening into Costain, who staggered back under the force of the blow.

The attack on his own person sent Laffler into immediate and berserk action. Without a sound he leaped at the sailor, striking and kicking furiously at the unprotected face and flanks. Stunned at first, the man came to his feet with a rush and turned on Laffler. For a moment they stood locked together, and then as Costain joined the attack, all three went sprawling to the ground. Slowly Laffler and Costain got to their feet and looked down at the body before them.

"He's either out cold from liquor," said Costain, "or he struck his head going down. In any case, it's a job for the police."

"No, no, sair!" The waiter crawled weakly to his feet, and

stood swaying. "No police, sair. Mr. Sbirro do not want such. You understand, sair." He caught hold of Costain with a pleading hand, and Costain looked at Laffler.

"Of course not," said Laffler. "We won't have to bother with the police. They'll pick him up soon enough, the murderous sot. But what in the world started all this?"

"That man, sair. He make most erratic way while walking, and with no meaning I push against him. Then he attack me, accusing me to rob him."

"As I thought." Laffler pushed the waiter gently along. "Now go on in and get yourself attended to."

The man seemed ready to burst into tears. "To you, sair, I owe my life. If there is anything I can do——"

Laffler turned into the areaway that led to Sbirro's door. "No, no, it was nothing. You go along, and if Sbirro has any questions send him to me. I'll straighten it out."

"My life, sair," were the last words they heard as the inner door closed behind them.

"There you are, Costain," said Laffler, as a few minutes later he drew his chair under the table: "civilised man in all his glory. Reeking with alcohol, strangling to death some miserable innocent who came too close."

Costain made an effort to gloss over the nerve-shattering memory of the episode. "It's the neurotic cat that takes to alcohol," he said. "Surely there's a reason for that sailor's condition."

"Reason? Of course there is. Plain atavistic savagery!" Laffler swept his arm in an all-embracing gesture. "Why do we all sit here at our meat? Not only to appease physical demands, but because our atavistic selves cry for release. Think back, Costain. Do you remember that I once described Sbirro as the epitome of civilisation? Can you now see why? A brilliant man, he fully understands the nature of human beings. But unlike lesser men he bends all his efforts to the satisfaction of our innate natures without resultant harm to some innocent bystander."

"When I think back on the wonder of lamb Amirstan," said Costain, "I quite understand what you're driving at. And, by the way, isn't it nearly due to appear on the bill of fare? It must have been over a month ago that it was last served."

The waiter, filling the tumblers, hesitated. " I am so sorry, sair. No special this evening."

" There's your answer," Laffler grunted, " and probably just my luck to miss out on it altogether the next time."

Costain stared at him. " Oh, come, that's impossible."

" No, blast it." Laffler drank off half his water at a gulp and the waiter immediately refilled the glass. " I'm off to South America for a surprise tour of inspection. One month, two months, Lord knows how long."

" Are things that bad down there?"

" They could be better." Laffler suddenly grinned. " Mustn't forget it takes very mundane dollars and cents to pay the tariff at Sbirro's."

" I haven't heard a word of this around the office."

" Wouldn't be a surprise tour if you had. Nobody knows about this except myself—and now you. I want to walk in on them completely unsuspected. Find out what flimflammery they're up to down there. As far as the office is concerned, I'm off on a jaunt somewhere. Maybe recuperating in some sanatorium from my hard work. Anyhow, the business will be in good hands. Yours, among them."

" Mine?" said Costain, surprised.

" When you go in to-morrow you'll find yourself in receipt of a promotion, even if I'm not there to hand it to you personally. Mind you, it has nothing to do with our friendship either ; you've done fine work, and I'm immensely grateful for it."

Costain reddened under the praise. " You don't expect to be in to-morrow. Then you're leaving to-night?"

Laffler nodded. " I've been trying to wangle some reservations. If they come through, well, this will be in the nature of a farewell celebration."

" You know," said Costain slowly, " I devoutly hope that your reservations don't come through. I believe our dinners here have come to mean more to me than I ever dared imagine."

The waiter's voice broke in. " Do you wish to be served now, sair?" and they both started.

" Of course, of course," said Laffler sharply, " I didn't realise you were waiting."

" What bothers me," he told Costain as the waiter turned

away, "is the thought of the lamb Amirstan I'm bound to miss. To tell you the truth, I've already put off my departure a week, hoping to hit a lucky night, and now I simply can't delay any more. I do hope that when you're sitting over your share of lamb Amirstan, you'll think of me with suitable regrets."

Costain laughed. "I will indeed," he said as he turned to his dinner.

Hardly had he cleared the plate when a waiter silently reached for it. It was not their usual waiter, he observed; it was none other than the victim of the assault.

"Well," Costain said, "how do you feel now? Still under the weather?"

The waiter paid no attention to him. Instead, with the air of a man under great strain, he turned to Laffler. "Sair," he whispered. "My life. I owe it to you. I can repay you!"

Laffler looked up in amazement, then shook his head firmly. "No," he said; "I want nothing from you, understand? You have repaid me sufficiently with your thanks. Now get on with your work and let's hear no more about it."

The waiter did not stir an inch, but his voice rose slightly. "By the body and blood of your God, sair, I will help you even if you do not want! *Do not go into the kitchen, sair.* I trade you my life for yours, sair, when I speak this. To-night or any night of your life, do not go into the kitchen at Sbirro's!"

Laffler sat back, completely dumbfounded. "Not go into the kitchen? Why shouldn't I go into the kitchen if Mr. Sbirro ever took it into his head to invite me there? What's all this about?"

A hard hand was laid on Costain's back, and another gripped the waiter's arm. The waiter remained frozen to the spot, his lips compressed, his eyes downcast.

"What is all *what* about, gentlemen?" purred the voice. "So opportune an arrival. In time as ever, I see, to answer all the questions, hurr?"

Laffler breathed a sigh of relief. "Ah, Sbirro, thank heaven you're here. This man is saying something about my not going into your kitchen. Do you know what he means?"

The teeth showed in a broad grin. "But of course. This good man was giving you advice in all amiability. It so happens that my too emotional chef heard some rumour that I might have a guest into his precious kitchen, and he flew into a fearful rage. Such a rage, gentlemen! He even threatened to give notice on the spot, and you can understand what that should mean to Sbirro's, hurr? Fortunately, I succeeded in showing him what a signal honour it is to have an esteemed patron and true connoisseur observe him at his work first hand, and now he is quite amenable. Quite, hurr?"

He released the waiter's arm. "You are at the wrong table," he said softly. "See that it does not happen again."

The waiter slipped off without daring to raise his eyes and Sbirro drew a chair to the table. He seated himself and brushed his hand lightly over his hair. "Now I am afraid that the cat is out of the bag, hurr? This invitation to you, Mr. Laffler, was to be a surprise; but the surprise is gone, and all that is left is the invitation."

Laffler mopped beads of perspiration from his forehead. "Are you serious?" he said huskily. "Do you mean that we are really to witness the preparation of your food to-night?"

Sbirro drew a sharp fingernail along the tablecloth, leaving a thin, straight line printed in the linen. "Ah," he said, "I am faced with a dilemma of great proportions." He studied the line soberly. "You, Mr. Laffler, have been my guest for ten long years. But our friend here——"

Costain raised his hand in protest. "I understand perfectly. This invitation is solely to Mr. Laffler, and naturally my presence is embarrassing. As it happens, I have an early engagement for this evening and must be on my way anyhow. So you see there's no dilemma at all, really."

"No," said Laffler, "absolutely not. That wouldn't be fair at all. We've been sharing this until now, Costain, and I won't enjoy this experience half as much if you're not along. Surely Sbirro can make his conditions flexible, this one occasion."

They both looked at Sbirro, who shrugged his shoulders regretfully.

Costain rose abruptly. "I'm not going to sit here, Laffler, and spoil your great adventure. And then too," he bantered, "think of that ferocious chef waiting to get his cleaver on you. I prefer not to be at the scene. I'll just say good-bye," he went on, to cover Laffler's guilty silence, "and leave you to

Sbirro. I'm sure he'll take pains to give you a good show." He held out his hand and Laffler squeezed it painfully hard.

"You're being very decent, Costain," he said. "I hope you'll continue to dine here until we meet again. It shouldn't be too long."

Sbirro made way for Costain to pass. "I will expect you," he said. "*Au 'voir*."

Costain stopped briefly in the dim foyer to adjust his scarf and fix his Homburg at the proper angle. When he turned away from the mirror, satisfied at last, he saw with a final glance that Laffler and Sbirro were already at the kitchen door; Sbirro holding the door invitingly wide with one hand, while the other rested, almost tenderly, on Laffler's meaty shoulders.

THE ROOM IN THE TOWER

E. F. Benson

It is probable that everybody who is at all a constant dreamer has had at least one experience of an event or a sequence of circumstances which have come to his mind in sleep being subsequently realised in the material world. But, in my opinion, so far from this being a strange thing, it would be far odder if this fulfilment did not occasionally happen, since our dreams are, as a rule, concerned with people whom we know and places with which we are familiar, such as might very naturally occur in the awake and daylit world.

All my life I have been a habitual dreamer: the nights are few when I do not find on awaking in the morning that some mental experience has been mine, and sometimes, all night long apparently, a series of the most dazzling adventures befall me. Almost without exception these adventures are pleasant, though often merely trivial. It is of an exception that I am going to speak.

It was when I was about sixteen that a certain dream first came to me, and this is how it befell. It opened with my being set down at the door of a big red-brick house, where, I understood, I was going to stay. The servant who opened the door told me that tea was going on in the garden, and led me through a low dark-panelled hall, with a large open fireplace, on to a cheerful green lawn set round with flower beds. There were grouped about the tea-table a small party of people, but they were all strangers to me except one, who was a school-fellow called Jack Stone, clearly the son of the house, and he introduced me to his mother and father and a couple of sisters. I was, I remember, somewhat astonished to find myself here, for the boy in question was scarcely known to me, and I rather disliked what I knew of him: moreover, he had left school nearly a year before. The afternoon was very hot, and an intolerable oppression reigned. On the far side of the lawn ran a red-brick wall, with an iron gate in its centre, outside which stood a walnut-tree. We sat in the shadow of the house opposite a row of long windows, inside which I could see a table with cloth laid, glimmering with glass and silver. This garden front of the house was very long, and at one end of it stood a tower of three storeys, which looked to me much older than the rest of the building.

Before long, Mrs. Stone, who, like the rest of the party, had sat in absolute silence, said to me, "Jack will show you your room: I have given you the room in the tower."

Quite inexplicably my heart sank at her words. I felt as if I had known that I should have the room in the tower, and that it contained something dreadful and significant. Jack instantly got up, and I understood that I had to follow him. In silence we passed through the hall, and mounted a great oak staircase with many corners, and arrived at a small landing with two doors set in it. He pushed one of these open for me to enter, and without coming in himself, closed it behind me. Then I knew that my conjecture had been right: there was something awful in the room, and with the terror of nightmare growing swiftly and enveloping me, I awoke in a spasm of terror.

Now that dream or variations on it occurred to me intermittently for fifteen years. Most often it came in exactly this form, the arrival, the tea laid out on the lawn, the deadly silence succeeded by that one deadly sentence, the mounting with Jack Stone up to the room in the tower where horror dwelt, and it always came to a close in the nightmare of terror at that which was in the room, though I never saw what it was. At other times I experienced variations on this same theme. Occasionally, for instance, we would be sitting at dinner in the dining-room, into the windows of which I had looked on the first night when the dream of this house visited me, but wherever we were, there was the same silence, the same sense of dreadful oppression and foreboding. And the silence I knew would always be broken by Mrs. Stone saying to me, "Jack will show you your room: I have given you the room in the tower." Upon which (this was invariable) I had to follow him up the oak staircase with many corners, and enter the place that I dreaded more and more each time that I visited it in sleep. Or, again, I would find myself playing cards still in silence in a drawing-room lit with immense chandeliers, that gave a blinding illumination. What the game was I have no idea; what I remember, with a sense of miserable anticipation, was that soon Mrs. Stone would get up and say to me, "Jack will show you your room: I have given you the room in the tower." This drawing-room where we played cards was next to the dining-room, and, as I have said, was always brilliantly illuminated, whereas the rest of the house was full of dusk and shadows. And yet, how often, in spite of those bouquets of lights, have I not pored over the cards that were dealed to me, scarcely able for some reason to see them. Their designs, too, were strange: there were no red suits, but all were black, and among them there were certain cards which were black all over. I hated and dreaded those.

As this dream continued to recur, I got to know the greater part of the house. There was a smoking-room beyond the drawing-room, at the end of a passage with a green baize door. It was always very dark there, and as often as I went there I passed somebody whom I could not see in the doorway coming out. Curious developments, too, took place in the characters that peopled the dream as might happen to living persons. Mrs. Stone, for instance, who, when I first saw her, had been black haired, became grey, and instead of rising briskly, as she had done at first when she said, "Jack will show you your room: I have given you the room in the tower," got up very feebly, as if the strength was leaving her limbs. Jack also grew up, and became a rather ill-looking young man, with a brown moustache, while one of the sisters ceased to appear, and I understood she was married.

Then it so happened that I was not visited by this dream for six months or more, and I began to hope, in such inexplicable dread did I hold it, that it had passed away for good. But one night after this interval I again found myself being shown out on to the lawn for tea, and Mrs. Stone was not there, while the others were all dressed in black. At once I guessed the reason, and my heart leaped at the thought that perhaps this time I should not have to sleep in the room in the tower, and though we usually all sat in silence, on this occasion the sense of relief made me talk and laugh as I had never yet done. But even then matters were not altogether comfortable, for no one else spoke, but they all looked secretly at each other. And soon the foolish stream of my talk ran dry, and gradually an apprehension worse than anything I had previously known gained on me as the light slowly faded.

Suddenly a voice which I knew well broke the stillness, the voice of Mrs. Stone, saying, " Jack will show you your room: I have given you the room in the tower." It seemed to come from near the gate in the red-brick wall that bounded the lawn, and looking up, I saw that the grass outside was sown thick with gravestones. A curious greyish light shone from them, and I could read the lettering on the grave nearest me, and it was, " In evil memory of Julia Stone." And as usual Jack got up, and again I followed him through the hall and up the staircase with many corners. On this occasion it was darker than usual, and when I passed into the room in the tower I could only just see the furniture, the position of which was already familiar to me. Also there was a dreadful odour of decay in the room, and I woke screaming.

The dream, with such variations and developments as I have mentioned, went on at intervals for fifteen years. Sometimes I would dream it two or three nights in succession ; once, as I have said, there was an intermission of six months, but taking a reasonable average, I should say that I dreamed it quite as often as once in a month. It had, as is plain, something of nightmare about it, since it always ended in the same appalling terror, which so far from getting less, seemed to me to gather fresh fear every time that I experienced it. There was, too, a strange and dreadful consistency about it. The characters in it, as I have mentioned, got regularly older, death and marriage visited this silent family, and I never in the dream, after Mrs. Stone had died, set eyes on her again. But it was always her voice that told me that the room in the tower was prepared for me, and whether we had tea out on the lawn, or the scene was laid in one of the rooms overlooking it, I could always see her gravestone standing just outside the iron gate. It was the same, too, with the married daughter ; usually she was not present, but once or twice she returned again, in company with a man, whom I took to be her husband. He, too, like the rest of them, was always silent. But, owing to the constant repetition of the dream, I had ceased to attach, in my waking hours, any significance to it. I never met Jack Stone again during all those years, nor did I ever see a house that resembled this dark house of my dream. And then something happened.

I had been in London in this year, up till the end of July, and during the first week in August went down to stay with a friend in a house he had taken for the summer months, in the Ashdown Forest district of Sussex. I left London early, for John Clinton was to meet me at Forest Row Station, and we were going to spend the day golfing, and go to his house in the evening. He had his motor with him, and we set off, about five in the afternoon, after a thoroughly delightful day, for the drive, the distance being some ten miles. As it was still so early we did not have tea at the clubhouse, but waited till we should get home. As we drove, the weather, which up till then had been, though hot, deliciously fresh, seemed to me to alter in quality, and become very stagnant and oppressive, and I felt that indefinable sense of ominous apprehension that I am accustomed to before thunder. John, however, did not share my views, attributing my loss of lightness to the fact that I had lost both my matches. Events proved, however, that I was right, though I do not think that the thunderstorm that broke that night was the sole cause of my depression.

Our way led through deep high-banked lanes, and before we had gone very far I fell asleep, and was only awakened by the stopping of the motor. And with a sudden thrill, partly of fear but chiefly of curiosity, I found myself standing in the doorway of my house of dream. We went, I half wondering whether or not I was dreaming still, through a low oak-panelled hall, and out on to the lawn, where tea was laid in the shadow of the house. It was set in flower beds, a red-brick wall, with a gate in it, bounded one side, and out beyond that was a space of rough grass with a walnut-tree. The façade of the house was very long, and at one end stood a three-storeyed tower, markedly older than the rest.

Here for the moment all resemblance to the repeated dream ceased. There was no silent and somehow terrible family, but a large assembly of exceedingly cheerful persons, all of whom were known to me. And in spite of the horror with which the dream itself had always filled me, I felt nothing of it now that the scene of it was thus reproduced before me. But I felt the intensest curiosity as to what was going to happen.

Tea pursued its cheerful course, and before long Mrs.

Clinton got up. And at that moment I think I knew what she was going to say. She spoke to me, and what she said was:

"Jack will show you your room: I have given you the room in the tower."

At that, for half a second, the horror of the dream took hold of me again. But it quickly passed, and again I felt nothing more than the most intense curiosity. It was not very long before it was amply satisfied.

John turned to me.

"Right up at the top of the house," he said, "but I think you'll be comfortable. We're absolutely full up. Would you like to go and see it now? By Jove, I believe that you are right, and that we are going to have a thunderstorm. How dark it has become."

I got up and followed him. We passed through the hall, and up the perfectly familiar staircase. Then he opened the door, and I went in. And at that moment sheer unreasoning terror again possessed me. I did not know for certain what I feared: I simply feared. Then like a sudden recollection, when one remembers a name which has long escaped the memory, I knew what I feared. I feared Mrs. Stone, whose grave with the sinister inscription, "In evil memory," I had so often seen in my dream, just beyond the lawn which lay below my window. And then once more the fear passed so completely that I wondered what there was to fear, and I found myself, sober and quiet and sane, in the room in the tower, the name of which I had so often heard in my dream, and the scene of which was so familiar.

I looked round it with a certain sense of proprietorship, and found that nothing had been changed from the dreaming nights in which I knew it so well. Just to the left of the door was the bed, lengthways along the wall, with the head of it in the angle. In a line with it was the fireplace and a small bookcase; opposite the door the outer wall was pierced by two lattice-paned windows, between which stood the dressing-table, while ranged along the fourth wall was the washing-stand and a big cupboard. My luggage had already been unpacked, for the furniture of dressing and undressing lay orderly on the washstand and toilet-table, while my dinner clothes were spread out on the coverlet of the bed. And then, with a sudden start of unexplained dismay, I saw that there were two rather conspicuous objects which I had not seen before in my dreams: one a life-sized oil-painting of Mrs. Stone, the other a black-and-white sketch of Jack Stone, representing him as he had appeared to me only a week before in the last of the series of these repeated dreams, a rather secret and evil-looking man of about thirty. His picture hung between the windows, looking straight across the room to the other portrait, which hung at the side of the bed. At that I looked next, and as I looked I felt once more the horror of nightmare seize me.

It represented Mrs. Stone as I had seen her last in my dreams: old and withered and white haired. But in spite of the evident feebleness of body, a dreadful exuberance and vitality shone through the envelope of flesh, the whole face was instinct with some secret and appalling mirth, while the hands, clasped together on the knee, seemed shaking with suppressed and nameless glee. Then I saw also that it was signed in the left-hand bottom corner, and wondering who the artist could be, I looked more closely, and read the inscription, "Julia Stone by Julia Stone."

There came a tap at the door, and John Clinton entered.

"Got everything you want?" he asked.

"Rather more than I want," said I, pointing to the picture.

He laughed.

"Hard-featured old lady," he said. "By herself, too, I remember. Anyhow she can't have flattered herself much."

"But don't you see?" said I. "It's scarcely a human face at all. It's the face of some witch, of some devil."

He looked at it more closely.

"Yes; it isn't very pleasant," he said. "Scarcely a bedside manner, eh? Yes; I can imagine getting the nightmare, if I went to sleep with that close by my bed. I'll have it taken down if you like."

"I really wish you would," I said.

He rang the bell, and with the help of a servant we detached the picture and carried it out on to the landing, and put it with its face to the wall.

"By Jove, the old lady is a weight," said John, mopping his forehead. "I wonder if she had something on her mind."

The extraordinary weight of the picture had struck me too. I was about to reply, when I caught sight of my own hand.

There was blood on it, in considerable quantities, covering the whole palm.

"I've cut myself somehow," said I.

John gave a little startled exclamation.

"Why, I have too," he said.

Simultaneously the footman took out his handkerchief and wiped his hand with it. I saw that there was blood also on his handkerchief.

John and I went back into the tower room and washed the blood off; but neither on his hand nor or mine was there the slightest trace of a scratch or cut. It seemed to me that, having ascertained this, we both, by a sort of tacit consent, did not allude to it again. Something in my case had dimly occurred to me that I did not wish to think about. It was but a conjecture, but I fancied that I knew the same thing had occurred to him.

The heat and oppression of the air, for the storm we had expected was still undischarged, increased very much after dinner, and for some time most of the party, among whom were John Clinton and myself, sat outside on the path bounding the lawn, where we had had tea. The night was absolutely dark, and no twinkle of star or moon ray could penetrate the pall of cloud that overset the sky. By degrees our assembly thinned, the women went up to bed, men dispersed to the smoking- or billiard-room, and by eleven o'clock my host and I were the only two left. All the evening I thought that he had something on his mind, and as soon as we were alone he spoke.

"The man who helped us with the picture had blood on his hand, too, did you notice?" he said. "I asked him just now if he had cut himself, and he said he supposed he had, but that he could find no mark of it. Now where did that blood come from?"

By dint of telling myself that I was not going to think about it, I had succeeded in not doing so, and I did not want, especially just at bedtime, to be reminded of it.

"I don't know," said I, "and I don't really care so long as the picture of Mrs. Julia Stone is not by my bed."

He got up.

"But it's odd," he said. "Ha! Now you'll see another odd thing."

A dog of his, an Irish terrier by breed, had come out of the house as we talked. The door behind us into the hall was open, and a bright oblong of light shone across the lawn to the iron gate which led on to the rough grass outside, where the walnut-tree stood. I saw that the dog had all his hackles up, bristling with rage and fright; his lips were curled back from his teeth, as if he was ready to spring at something, and he was growling to himself. He took not the slightest notice of his master or me, but stiffly and tensely walked across the grass to the iron gate. There he stood for a moment, looking through the bars and still growling. Then of a sudden his courage seemed to desert him: he gave one long howl, and scuttled back to the house with a curious crouching sort of movement.

"He does that half a dozen times a day," said John. "He sees something which he both hates and fears."

I walked to the gate and looked over it. Something was moving on the grass outside, and soon a sound which I could not instantly identify came to my ears. Then I remembered what it was: it was the purring of a cat. I lit a match, and saw the purrer, a big blue Persian, walking round and round in a little circle just outside the gate, stepping high and ecstatically, with tail carried aloft like a banner. Its eyes were bright and shining, and every now and then it put its head down and sniffed at the grass.

I laughed.

"The end of that mystery, I am afraid," I said. "Here's a large cat having Walpurgis night all alone."

"Yes, that's Darius," said John. "He spends half the day and all night there. But that's not the end of the dog mystery, for Toby and he are the best of friends, but the beginning of the cat mystery. What's the cat doing there? And why is Darius pleased, while Toby is terror-stricken?"

At that moment I remembered the rather horrible details of my dreams when I saw through the gate, just where the cat was now, the white tombstone with the sinister inscription. But before I could answer the rain began, as suddenly and heavily as if a tap had been turned on, and simultaneously the big cat squeezed through the bars of the gate, and came leaping across the lawn to the house for shelter. Then it sat in the doorway, looking out eagerly into the dark. It spat and struck at John with its paw, as he pushed it in, in order to close the door.

Somehow, with the portrait of Julia Stone in the passage outside, the room in the tower had absolutely no alarm for me, and as I went to bed, feeling very sleepy and heavy, I had nothing more than interest for the curious incident about our bleeding hands, and the conduct of the cat and dog. The last thing I looked at before I put out my light was the square empty space by my bed where the portrait had been. Here the paper was of its original full tint of dark red: over the rest of the walls it had faded. Then I blew out my candle and instantly fell asleep.

My awaking was equally instantaneous, and I sat bolt upright in bed under the impression that some bright light had been flashed in my face, though it was now absolutely pitch dark. I knew exactly where I was, in the room which I had dreaded in dreams, but no horror that I ever felt when asleep approached the fear that now invaded and froze my brain. Immediately after a peal of thunder crackled just above the house, but the probability that it was only a flash of lightning which awoke me gave no reassurance to my galloping heart. Something I knew was in the room with me, and instinctively I put out my right hand, which was nearest the wall, to keep it away. And my hand touched the edge of a picture-frame close to me.

I sprang out of bed, upsetting the small table that stood by it, and I heard my watch, candle, and matches clatter on to the floor. But for the moment there was no need of light, for a blinding flash leaped out of the clouds, and showed me that by my bed again hung the picture of Mrs. Stone. And instantly the room went into blackness again. But in that flash I saw another thing also, namely a figure that leaned over the end of my bed, watching me. It was dressed in some close-clinging white garment, spotted and stained with mould, and the face was that of the portrait.

Overhead the thunder cracked and roared, and when it ceased and the deathly stillness succeeded, I heard the rustle of movement coming nearer me, and, more horrible yet, perceived an odour of corruption and decay. And then a hand was laid on the side of my neck, and close beside my ear I heard quick-taken, eager breathing. Yet I knew that this thing, though it could be perceived by touch, by smell, by eye and by ear, was still not of this earth, but something that had passed out of the body and had power to make itself manifest. Then a voice, already familiar to me, spoke.

"I knew you would come to the room in the tower," it said. "I have been long waiting for you. At last you have come. To-night I shall feast; before long we will feast together."

And the quick breathing came closer to me; I could feel it on my neck.

At that the terror, which I think had paralysed me for the moment, gave way to the wild instinct of self-preservation. I hit wildly with both arms, kicking out at the same moment, and heard a little animal-squeal, and something soft dropped with a thud beside me. I took a couple of steps forward, nearly tripping up over whatever it was that lay there, and by the merest good luck found the handle of the door. In another second I ran out on the landing, and had banged the door behind me. Almost at the same moment I heard a door open somewhere below, and John Clinton, candle in hand, came running upstairs.

"What is it?" he said. "I sleep just below you, and heard a noise as if—Good heavens, there's blood on your shoulder."

I stood there, so he told me afterwards, swaying from side to side, white as a sheet, with the mark on my shoulder as if a hand covered with blood had been laid there.

"It's in there," I said, pointing. "She, you know. The portrait is in there, too, hanging up on the place we took it from."

At that he laughed.

"My dear fellow, this is mere nightmare," he said.

He pushed by me, and opened the door, I standing there simply inert with terror, unable to stop him, unable to move.

"Phew! What an awful smell," he said.

Then there was silence; he had passed out of my sight behind the open door. Next moment he came out again, as white as myself, and instantly shut it.

"Yes, the portrait's there," he said, "and on the floor is a thing—a thing spotted with earth, like what they bury people in. Come away, quick, come away."

How I got downstairs I hardly know. An awful shuddering and nausea of the spirit rather than of the flesh had seized me, and more than once he had to place my feet upon the steps, while every now and then he cast glances of terror and apprehension up the stairs. But in time we came to his dressing-room on the floor below, and there I told him what I have here described.

The sequel can be made short; indeed, some of my readers have perhaps already guessed what it was, if they remember that inexplicable affair of the churchyard at West Fawley, some eight years ago, where an attempt was made three times to bury the body of a certain woman who had committed suicide. On each occasion the coffin was found in the course of a few days again protruding from the ground. After the third attempt, in order that the thing should not be talked about, the body was buried elsewhere in unconsecrated ground. Where is was buried was just outside the iron gate of the garden belonging to the house where this woman had lived. She had committed suicide in a room at the top of the tower in that house. Her name was Julia Stone.

THE ACADEMY

David Ely

The Academy lay in the centre of a valley, its red-brick buildings arranged in a square. Beyond the surrounding athletic and drill fields were thick woods that rose gradually on all sides, forming a shield of privacy that made the Academy seem in fact to be, in the words of the school brochure, "a little world of its own."

Mr. Holston parked his car in the area marked for visitors. Before proceeding toward the administration building, he paused to watch several groups of uniformed cadets marching to and fro on one of the fields. There was an atmosphere of regularity and tradition that he found quite pleasing. The buildings were old and solid, their bricks weathered to a pale hue, and the stone steps worn down by generations of cadets. The concrete walkways were scrubbed clean and bordered by grass meticulously clipped and weeded. Even the trees of the forest stood in formation.

In front of the administration building was the statue of an elderly man in military dress, one hand resting benignly on the stone shoulder of a young cadet, the other arm extended in a pointing gesture. Mr. Holston supposed this might represent the Academy's founder, perhaps a retired Civil War general, but the legend inscribed on the base was so faded that he could not read it. The symbolism of the man and boy was conventional, of course—the firm but kindly teacher indicating the horizon of manhood to his youthful charge—although Mr. Holston noted that the figures were facing so that the stone commander was pointing toward the school, rather than in the direction of the outside world, which would have been more appropriate.

In the lobby of the administration building, Mr. Holston gave his name to the cadet at the reception desk, and was at once ushered down a hallway to the Director's office.

The office was as spare and neat as everything else Mr.

Holston had observed about the Academy. It contained a filing cabinet, a single chair for visitors, and a desk, behind which the Director himself was in the process of rising.

The Director was a strongly built man whose white hair was closely cut in military fashion, and his handshake was vigorous. He wore the grey uniform of the school, with a single star on each shoulder to denote his rank.

"Well, Mr. Holston," he said, after the customary exchange of amenities, "I've studied your boy's transcript and test records, and I've discussed them with the Admissions Committee, and without beating around the bush, sir, we're prepared to look favourably on a formal application, if you care to make one."

"I see," said Mr. Holston, who had not expected such an immediate response. "That's very encouraging to hear." Feeling slightly ill at ease under the Director's gaze, he glanced around at the walls, which, however, were absolutely bare.

"So," continued the Director, "the only question that remains is whether you want your son to be enrolled here. I'm assuming there's no special financial problem involved, naturally."

"Oh, no. We have that all worked out." Mr. Holston hesitated, thinking that such an important matter should not be disposed of so simply. "I would like to ask about one thing," he said. "Your catalogue mentioned a policy of not having any home visits the first year."

The Director nodded. "Yes. Well, we've worked out our system over a long period of time, and we've found that home visits just don't fit into the picture until the cadet is thoroughly oriented to our way of doing things. We say 'a year' merely as a general guide Sometimes it's longer than that. Parents can visit here, of course, at specified times." The Director gazed inquiringly at Mr. Holston, who tried to think of some more questions, but could not. "Actually," the Director continued, "the cadets seem to prefer it this way, once they get started. What we're looking for, Mr. Holston, is to motivate them—motivate them to achieve success, which means success in becoming a fully oriented member of this community, and you can see how home visits might cause a little disruption in the process."

"Oh, yes," said Mr. Holston.

"Well," said the Director. "You'll want to see a little more of the Academy before making up your mind, I should imagine. Classrooms, dormitories, and so forth."

"If it isn't too much trouble."

"No trouble at all." The Director rose and escorted Mr. Holston out to the hall. "Nothing special about our classrooms," the Director remarked, stopping at one of the doors. He opened it. The instructor, a grey-haired man, roared "*Attention!*" and the entire class leaped up smartly, as the instructor did a left-face and saluted the Director. "At ease, Grimes," said the Director, returning the salute. "Proceed with instruction."

"Very good, sir."

The Director closed the door again, so that Mr. Holston had only a glimpse of the class—a roomful of grey uniformed figures, heads so closely cropped that they were almost shaven, with nothing much to distinguish one cadet from the next.

"Those were big fellows," remarked Mr. Holston, as they continued along the hallway. "I suppose they're your seniors."

"We don't go by the usual class designations, Mr. Holston. Each cadet is placed according to his needs and capacities. Our purpose is to build men, sir, and you simply can't find a formula to satisfy the requirements of every case. Now here," said the Director, pushing open a pair of swinging doors, "is our cafeteria, which is staffed by the cadets themselves. Part of our community work programme."

It was the middle of the afternoon, and the cafeteria was empty, except for a few men who were mopping the floor and scrubbing the serving counters. They, too, snapped to attention when the visitors appeared, until the Director motioned for them to continue their work, as he escorted Mr. Holston on into the kitchen, where several male cooks were busy preparing food for the evening meal.

"At ease," the Director called out, for the cooks, too, had come to attention. "All modern equipment, Mr. Holston, as you can see," he said, indicating the gleaming ranges, the sinks and the neat rows of cleavers, knives, and other implements hanging on the white walls. "You will understand," he added, "that we can't run a military establishment in a sloppy fashion. We try to be thorough, sir. We have, as I say, a little world here, and it's a world that happens to be organized along military lines." He turned to an elderly cook. "Looks good, Carson."

"Thank you, sir." Carson saluted.

Mr. Holston and the Director left the kitchen by the rear door, passing into the square formed by the Academy buildings. "I suppose," said Mr. Holston, "that you find a lot of employees who like the military way. Old Army men, say."

The Director was busy returning the salute of an instructor who was marching a platoon of cadets nearby. He stood silently watching the ranks pass by. "Drill," he declared finally. "Sometimes I think it's the greatest lesson of all. When a boy knows drill, Mr. Holston, then he knows something about life, don't you think?"

"Ah, yes," said Mr. Holston, a bit uncertainly. "Of course, it's a splendid training, especially when a boy goes on to have a career in the services."

"Not only there, sir, if you'll permit me. Drill has important values in civilian pursuits as well, in my opinion. And I don't mean only physical drill," the Director added, as he and his guest walked on. "We use drill techniques in classroom work, to instill habits of mental discipline and personal courtesy. We've been given hopeless cases, Mr. Holston, but we've managed in every single one, sir, to find the right answer. And the key to it has been drill, whether on the parade ground or in the classroom. Of course," he said, ushering Mr. Holston into the next building, "in some instances it takes more time than in others, and I don't meant to imply that the Academy deals primarily with so-called problem boys. Not at all. The great majority are like your own son—good, decent young fellows from fine upstanding homes." He opened a door. "This is one of our dormitories, Mr. Holston."

The room ran the length of the building. The wall was lined with beds spaced out to accommodate lockers, chairs and desks. The few cadets who were then studying in the room sprang from their chairs.

"Maybe you'd like to chat with one of the boys," the Director said to Mr. Holston, after he had put the cadets at ease. "Here," he said, as they approached the nearest student, who was taller than either of the men, "it's Cadet Sloan, isn't it?"

"Yes, sir."

"Well, this is Mr. Holston, Sloan, and he'll have a few words with you," said the Director, who then moved off along the row of beds, inspecting the blanket corners and testing here and there for dust.

Mr. Holston, left with Cadet Sloan, did not know quite what to say.

"Well," he began, "how do you like it here?"

"I like it very well, sir."

"That's good. Um, the food and everything . . . you find it all right?"

"Everything is very good, sir."

"Ah," said Mr. Holston, rubbing his hands together, trying to think of additional questions while Cadet Sloan gazed at him with polite attention. "Well, I suppose you're planning on some college or other, aren't you?"

"My plans aren't too definite at present, sir."

"Yes, yes. Well, I can see you're a hard worker on your books, Mr. Sloan," Mr. Holston continued, glancing first at the stack of texts on the desk and then at Cadet Sloan's face, which wore a studious look that was reinforced by little wrinkles of concentration around the eyes and mouth.

"We have plenty to do, sir, that's right."

"Your parents must be proud to have such a hard-working son."

"My parents aren't living, sir."

"Oh—I'm sorry." Mr. Holston regretted his blunder. No wonder Sloan looked drawn.

"That's all right, sir. It's been quite a while."

"Ah, yes. Well." Mr. Holston could not help being struck by the manly demeanour of Cadet Sloan. He put out his hand. "Nice to talk with you, son," he said. "And good luck."

"Thank you, sir."

The Director and his guest walked back toward the administration building. On all sides, Mr. Holston was aware of organized and purposeful activity. Several groups of cadets were marching along the paths on their way from one building to another; a soccer game was in progress on a field nearby, and on the main parade ground, a full company in dress uniform was executing a complex series of drill manœuvres.

"It's all very impressive," said Mr. Holston.

The Director smiled. "We try to keep our young men busy."

"That cadet I talked to back there," Mr. Holston added. "Sloan. He seemed to be a remarkably mature person."

"We strive to build a sense of maturity, Mr. Holston."

"Yes, yes. I can certainly tell that." Mr. Holston saw that they were approaching the stone figures of teacher and student which were turned the wrong way. He gestured toward the statues. "That's quite a piece of sculpture."

"Thank you. We're very proud of it."

Mr. Holston could not repress his curiosity. "It does seem a little—well, unconventional. I mean, the positioning. You know, facing toward the Academy instead of away from it."

The Director nodded. "Yes, most visitors notice that, Mr. Holston. At first glance, it does seem to be a mistake, I agree." He paused beside the figures and gazed approvingly up at the stern features of the teacher. Mr. Holston thought he saw a resemblance between the Director and the statue, which, he reflected further, might be no mere fancy, for the operation of the Academy could very well be a family matter, with the leadership being passed on from one generation to the next.

"For us, you see," said the Director, continuing with his explanation, "the important thing is the Academy. This is our world, Mr. Holston. All that a boy needs is to be found right here. So that the symbolism of the figures, sir, is to represent a welcome to this little world—rather than the more conventional theme of farewell which would be indicated if the man were pointing away from the Academy."

"Of course," said Mr. Holston.

They returned to the Director's office, where an elderly man in green fatigues was polishing the desk and chairs. He stopped as they entered and stood stiffly near the wall.

"At ease, Morgan," said the Director. "That'll be all."

"Very good, sir." The elderly man saluted and hobbled out.

The Director seated himself behind the desk and briefly inspected its top for signs of dust. "Well, Mr. Holston," he said, "now you've seen something of the Academy, and I'm sure you've had an opportunity to consider a little further the question of whether it may be what you're looking for, to help your boy."

"Yes, yes. Of course." Mr. Holston nodded. "You have a fine institution here, I must say. Everything seems to be organized with . . . with real efficiency." He glanced toward the door beyond which he thought he could still hear the shuffling steps of the elderly man in fatigues. "It's a real example of what the military method can achieve," he added, feeling that perhaps he had not sufficiently expressed his admiration for all that the Director had shown him.

The Director took a folder from a drawer and placed it on the desk.

"As for my son," said Mr. Holston, "that's the important question, of course. Whether this would be the right place for him. Or rather," he amended, "whether he would be right for you. I'm sure there are many instances where boys simply don't fit in."

The Director smiled. "We don't believe in failure here, Mr. Holston. When we agree to admit a boy, sir, that means we are laying our reputation on the line." He opened the folder and took out a letter. "And without intending to boast, Mr. Holston, I think I can truthfully say that we have yet to concede defeat." He pushed the letter across the desk. Mr. Holston saw that it was an official notice of acceptance, complete except for his own signature as parent. He felt in his pocket for his fountain pen.

"In some cases, naturally," the Director continued, "we need to have more patience than in others. But patience is built into our system."

"Patience, yes," said Mr. Holston. He laid his pen beside the letter of acceptance. "Boys need patience. You're right there, of course. Some boys need a lot of that, I agree." He moved the letter slightly, so that it was squared off with the edge of the desk. "He's not a bad boy, though. Not at all," he added.

"Mr. Holston, in my experience there is no such thing as a bad boy."

"I mean, he's gotten into a couple of little scrapes—that's

in the records, of course—but nothing really . . ." Mr. Holston cleared his throat.

"Boys will be boys, sir. Lack of proper motivation leads to trouble, even in the best of families. You have nothing to be ashamed of, sir."

"Oh, we're not ashamed. We just feel—my wife and I—we feel that he would be better off in the kind of atmosphere you provide here, especially during the, um, difficult years."

"That's what we're here for, Mr. Holston," said the Director.

"I mean, it's not as though we were trying to avoid our own responsibilities as parents——"

"Far from it, sir," agreed the Director.

"—but in certain situations it seems advisable to, um . . ."

"To place a boy in congenial surroundings under the proper form of supervision," said the Director, helpfully completing Mr. Holston's thought. "You're absolutely right, sir. Believe me, I deal with parents every day of the year, and I know all of the things that pass through their minds." He clasped his hands together and smiled at his visitor.

"Some people think it's a kind of rejection of the child. I mean, getting rid of him——"

"Oh, I've heard plenty of that, Mr. Holston. It's all this modern psychiatric stuff. Guilt feelings!" The Director gave a short laugh and shook his head. "I tell you, when a father and mother are prepared to undergo heavy financial sacrifice in order to see their boy receive a decent chance in life—well, if that's getting rid of him, then it's a pretty conscientious way of doing it!"

"Yes, yes," said Mr. Holston quickly. They smiled at each other. In the brief pause that followed, Mr. Holston heard the commands of the drill instructors faintly in the distance, and the muffled beat of the marching cadets. There was marching in the hallway, too, and he supposed that it was a class, moving in formation from one room to another.

"Perhaps you have some further questions," the Director remarked.

Mr. Holston picked up his pen. "Oh, not at all. No, I think you've covered everything." He tested the point of the pen against his thumb, to be sure it was working.

"This is the time for questions, Mr. Holston," the Director continued. "It's better to ask them now, I mean to say, while the Academy is fresh in your mind. Sometimes it's hard for a parent to remember later on the things he wanted to ask."

"Oh, yes, I can understand that," said Mr. Holston, studying the letter before him.

"For example, you might like to know more about our co-operative work programme for the cadets. The cafeteria was an instance of that."

"It was a very fine cafeteria," said Mr. Holston. "No, I don't really have any questions about it."

"Then there's the academic programme. Perhaps you feel insufficiently informed on that aspect."

"No, the catalogue was quite complete. I really can't think of anything it didn't cover."

"We are great believers in the value of learning by teaching. Let me explain that. The cadets take turns, you see, in the instruction programme——"

"Quite so," said Mr. Holston. "I'm sure it's a remarkably effective feature of your system."

"Oh, it is indeed. That classroom that you saw, for example——"

"Really, I have no questions," said Mr. Holston. He signed his name in the proper place, put his pen in his pocket, and pushed the letter back across the desk.

"Thank you," said the Director, placing the letter carefully in the folder. "Actually, few parents do have questions." He smiled at Mr. Holston who, however, was glancing at his watch and pushing back his chair. "They seem to sense right away whether the Academy is what they really want for their boys. Like yourself, sir, if I am not mistaken."

"Absolutely," said Mr. Holston. He stood up and touched his face with his handkerchief, for the air in the room seemed close.

The Director rose and shook his hand. "Of course, the very best guarantee of satisfaction for the parent is to see the experienced cadet and have a chance to chat with him. As you did with Sloan, I believe."

"Yes, Sloan." Mr. Holston went to the door. "I can find my way out, sir. Don't you bother."

"No bother at all, Mr. Holston," said the Director, accompanying his visitor along the hallway. "Sloan—yes, a fine cadet, Sloan. He's been with us for quite a while now. Let's see——"

"Good-bye, sir," said Mr. Holston, as they reached the front entrance.

"—it must be nearly . . ."

But Mr. Holston did not stay to hear. He went quickly down the worn stone steps, passed by the statues of the man and boy without looking up at them, and hastened to his car. On his way out, he drove by a group of cadets in sweat shirts resting by the road after a session of calisthenics. They got quickly to their feet at the command of their instructor, but Mr. Holston concentrated on his driving, and although it seemed to him that several of the cadets were bald and that others were quite grey, he gave them only a glance, and thought no more about it.

CUT-THROAT FARM

J. D. Beresford

"Ah! Us calls un coot-thro-at farm," said my driver.

"But why?" I asked nervously.

"Yew'll see whoy when yew gets there." And this was all the information I could get from him. So, finding excuse for the driver's ill-temper in the sodden weather, I shielded my strained eyes from the onslaught of the rain and relapsed into silence.

For two miles or thereabouts after leaving Mawdsley we had followed a decent road, but now we were jerking warily down a rutted lane that appeared, so far as I could see through the blur of rain, to creep downwards into a dark, tree-clad valley, the depths of which were obscured in a mass of soaked, depressing verdure. Still the track fell and fell, and on my left I could see a dark slope of trees rising higher and higher above me—a slope that, seen thus dimly, appeared gigantic, overpowering. Then the lane plunged, dipping ever more steeply, into a black wood, and I clung to the side of the swaying cart, expecting catastrophe every moment. I tried desperately to combat the gloom that was overpowering me; I repeated to myself that this was England, that I was within a hundred miles of London, that I was going to spend a delightful summer at the "Valley Farm;" but, despite my efforts, a horror of the place gripped me; I found myself absurdly muttering "The Valley of the Shadow of Death."

The wood ended abruptly, and we came out on the very keel of the valley. "That's un," muttered my driver with a nod; and, shaking the rain from my cap, I discerned a hunched, lop-sided house that crouched in a clearing at the foot of the opposite slope. I pictured it as having slid down the interminable wave of trees that reared its dim crest into the sky beyond, as having slid till brought to a too sudden standstill in the place where it now remained, dislocated, a confusion.

Such was my coming, my first sight of "Cut-throat Farm." If my subsequent experience seems morbid and unaccountable, my final cowardice indefensible, excuse must be found in that first impression which tinged my mind with a gloom and foreboding I could not afterwards throw off.

It was a starveling place. The stock was meagre: a single cow, whose bones were too prominent even for an Alderney, a scatter of ragged, long-legged fowls, three draggled ducks, an old loose-skinned black sow. This was all, save for "my little pig," as I learned fondly to call him, the one bright, cheerful thing in all the valley; a whimsical creature of quaint moods, full of an odd humour that had in it some quality of sadness. Looking back, I see now that his fun was an attempt, largely successful, to make what he could of his short life, to jest in the face of death. . . . My host and his wife were an awe-inspiring couple. He was short and swarthy, the hairiest man I have ever seen, bearded to the cheek bones, with hair low down over his strip of forehead, and great woolly eyebrows. His wife was tall, predatory, with a high-bridged, bony nose and wistfully hungry eyes; she was thinner, more angular even than the emaciated cow: that hastily covered skeleton who stood mournfully ruminant in the dirty yard.

My first morning at the Valley Farm was marked by an incident, not in itself unduly disconcerting, but typical, an incident surcharged, as I see now, with warning. I had had breakfast. I remember that at the time I considered it scanty (later, it became a memory of plenty) and insufficient even for the standard of thirty shillings a week, a sum that covered the whole cost of my entertainment. I considered this price very reasonable when I answered the advertisement.

After breakfast I stood by the window, which was open at the bottom, the top sash being fixed. Outside were clustered the half-dozen gawky chickens, clamorous and excited, straining their stringy necks to look into the room over the low sill. "The poor brutes are hungry," I muttered with some feeling, and I fetched a fragment of crust and threw it to them. Lord! how they fought for those few crumbs! I turned back into the room to get the remainder of the bread left from my breakfast, and, as I turned, a lanky young cockerel, inflamed by a desperate courage, hopped over the sill and followed me. I heard him come, and, interested to note to what lengths he would go, I retreated further into the room. In an instant he was on the table and had seized the chunk of bread from the platter; then, with a frightened squawk, he was out and off across the yard, sprinting away with impetuous, leaping strides, outstretching his fellows, who had immediately set off after him in hot pursuit. On his way he had to pass my little pig (my first sight of him, and how typical), who was sauntering casually in the direction of the yard gate. An inveterate jester, my little pig; he slewed round suddenly as the straining bird came up to him and made a well-timed snap which startled the rooster, intent only upon the hungry crowd behind, into dropping his booty, a morsel something too large for his gaping beak. I can still see the merry twinkle in my little pig's eyes as he ate that piece of bread. It seemed to me that he was unduly deliberate in the doing of it; maybe he chaffed the resentful but intimidated young cockerel, in some Esperanto of the farmyard, as he ate. . . . Nothing else of any account happened that morning; I remember I saw the farmer sharpening his knife, and wondered what he could find to kill with it. . . .

The next morning the young cockerel was not among the expectant group of five that waited under my window; but I met him again at dinner, and as I essayed to gather nourishment from his ill-covered bones, I smiled again over my recollection of his encounter with my little black pig. He is such a neat, quaint little creature, that pig; we have become friends over a few scraps of food, though he allows no liberties as yet. . . .

Among my notes of that stay at the Valley Farm I have found the following; they seem to me so full of suggestion that I append them just as they stand:

"The stock is disappearing; only one old fowl left—the one that has twice provided me with an egg, or so I judge from her ululations. I suppose she will be kept to the last. . . . I was right; there were only two ducks this morning. . . . The ducks are all finished at last (thank Heaven!), but I have a horrible fear upon me. The cow has disappeared! The farmer's wife says they have sold her. Did she buy the suspiciously lean and stringy beef I now live on with the price of her? . . . The sow has gone, and the farmer's wife has bought pork with the money obtained. I may be wrong in thus associating the meat I am given with those vanished animals. Can it be possible that there is some superstition or sentimental affection in buying the flesh of animals similar to those they have just sold? I see points about this theory, but why is the farmer always sharpening his knife? . . . I cannot believe it! He is not there this morning, and yet, surely, no Spanish conquistador of the sixteenth century could have had the brutality to kill my little pig, my whimsical, wayward, humorous little companion, the one living thing in all this accursed valley that could smile in the face of doom. . . . More pork! It *must* be the remains of the old sow; but why has she become so suddenly tender? How is it that she has furnished me with the first satisfying meal I have had for weeks? I cannot believe it, and I dare not ask the farmer's wife. I *will* not believe it until the pork is finished. He must have been sold. I am convinced of it. I hope he has found a happier, less hungry home, poor little chap. . . . I had an egg this morning that went off with a pop when I cracked it. I had a curious sensation when it happened. I have not hitherto been a believer in metempsychosis, but an intuition came to me at that moment that the soul of my little pig had entered into that egg. It would have been so like his whimsical, joking way to go off pop. And I was so hungry. . . . I have been writing a story of two men cast away in an open boat, with very striking patches of what one may call local colour. They suffered horribly from hunger. . . . The old hen has gone at last, and the farmer is still sharpening his knife. Why? Is he going to cut vegetables for me? I don't know where he will find them. In my story of the men in the open boat, one of them, driven to desperation . . . Bread and cheese for dinner. Is this the lull before the storm? I surprised a curious expression in the farmer's eye this afternoon. He was sizing me up with an appraising look. I can't help feeling that he was mentally going through the process I described in my story after the stronger man had . . . The farmer brought me my breakfast of bread and butter this morning. He says his wife is ill, that she it not getting up, that—I don't know what he said. No! Definitely and finally, I cannot, I will not. . . ." (My notes end here.)

After that last breakfast I went for a stroll in the yard, and in an outhouse I saw the farmer sharpening his knife. With an assumed nonchalance worthy of my little pig, I strolled carelessly to the gate; then, with tediously idle steps I sauntered towards the wood. And then—I ran. God, how I ran!

THE ROMANCE OF CERTAIN OLD CLOTHES

Henry James

1

Towards the middle of the eighteenth century there lived in the Province of Massachusetts a widowed gentlewoman, the mother of three children, by name Mrs. Veronica Wingrave. She had lost her husband early in life, and had devoted herself to the care of her progeny. These young persons grew up in a manner to reward her tenderness and to gratify her highest hopes. The first-born was a son, whom she had called Bernard, after his father. The others were daughters—born at an interval of three years apart. Good looks were traditional in the family, and this youthful trio were not likely to allow the tradition to perish. The boy was of that fair and ruddy complexion and that athletic structure which in those days (as in these) were the sign of good English descent—a frank, affectionate young fellow, a deferential son, a patronising brother, a steadfast friend. Clever, however, he was not; the wit of the family had been apportioned chiefly to his sisters. The late Mr. Wingrave had been a great reader of Shakespeare, at a time when this pursuit implied more freedom of thought than at the present day, and in a community where it required much courage to patronise the drama even in the closet: and he had wished to call attention to his admiration of the great poet by calling his daughters out of his favourite plays. Upon the elder he had bestowed the romantic name of Rosalind, and the younger he had called Perdita, in memory of a little girl born between them, who had lived but a few weeks.

When Bernard Wingrave came to his sixteenth year his mother put a brave face upon it and prepared to execute her husband's last injunction. This had been a formal command that, at the proper age, his son should be sent out to England, to complete his education at the university of Oxford, where he himself had acquired his taste for elegant literature. It was Mrs. Wingrave's belief that the lad's equal was not to be found in the two hemispheres, but she had the old traditions of literal obedience. She swallowed her sobs, and made up her boy's trunk and his simple provincial outfit, and sent him on his way across the seas. Bernard presented himself at his father's college, and spent five years in England, without great honour, indeed, but with a vast deal of pleasure and no discredit. On leaving the university he made the journey to France. In his twenty-fourth year he took ship for home, prepared to find poor little New England (New England was very small in those days) a very dull, unfashionable residence. But there had been changes at home, as well as in Mr. Bernard's opinions. He found his mother's house quite habitable, and his sisters grown into two very charming young ladies, with all the accomplishments and graces of the young women of Britain, and a certain native-grown originality and wildness, which, if it was not an accomplishment, was certainly a grace the more. Bernard privately assured his mother that his sisters were fully a match for the most genteel young women in the old country; whereupon poor Mrs. Wingrave, you may be sure, bade them hold up their heads. Such was Bernard's opinion, and such, in a tenfold higher degree, was the opinion of Mr. Arthur Lloyd. This gentleman was a college-mate of Mr. Bernard, a young man of reputable family, of a good person and a handsome inheritance; which latter appurtenance he proposed to invest in trade in the flourishing colony. He and Bernard were sworn friends; they had crossed the ocean together, and the young American had lost no time in presenting him at his mother's house, where he had made quite as good an impression as that which he had received and of which I have just given a hint.

The two sisters were at this time in all the freshness of their youthful bloom; each wearing, of course, this natural brilliancy in the manner that became her best. They were equally dissimilar in appearance and character. Rosalind, the elder—now in her twenty-second year—was tall and white, with calm grey eyes and auburn tresses; a very faint likeness to the Rosalind of Shakespeare's comedy, whom I imagine a brunette (if you will), but a slender, airy creature, full of the softest, quickest impulses. Miss Wingrave, with her slightly lymphatic fairness, her fine arms, her majestic height, her slow utterance, was not cut out for adventures. She would never have put on a man's jacket and hose; and, indeed, being a very plump beauty, she may have had reasons apart from her natural dignity. Perdita, too, might very well have exchanged the sweet melancholy of her name against something more in consonance with her aspect and disposition. She had the cheek of a gipsy and the eye of an eager child, as well as the smallest waist and lightest foot in all the country of the Puritans. When you spoke to her she never made you wait, as her handsome sister was wont to do (while she looked at you with a cold fine eye), but gave you your choice of a dozen answers before you had uttered half your thought.

The young girls were very glad to see their brother once more; but they found themselves quite able to spare part of their attention for their brother's friend. Among the young men their friends and neighbours, the *belle jeunesse* of the Colony, there were many excellent fellows, several devoted swains, and some two or three who enjoyed the reputation of universal charmers and conquerors. But the homebred arts and somewhat boisterous gallantry of these honest colonists were completely eclipsed by the good looks, the fine clothes, the punctilious courtesy, the perfect elegance, the immense information, of Mr. Arthur Lloyd. He was in reality no paragon; he was a capable, honourable, civil youth, rich in pounds sterling, in his health and complacency and his little capital of uninvested affections. But he was a gentleman; he had a handsome person; he had studied and travelled; he spoke French, he played the flute, and he read verses aloud with very great taste. There were a dozen reasons why Miss Wingrave and her sister should have thought their other male acquaintance made but a poor figure before such a perfect man of the world. Mr. Lloyd's anecdotes told our little New England maidens a great deal more of the ways and means of people of fashion in European capitals than he had any idea of doing. It was delightful to sit by and hear him and Bernard talk about the fine people and fine things they had seen. They would all gather round the fire after tea, in the little wainscoted parlour, and the two young men would remind each other, across the rug, of this, that and the other adventure. Rosalind and Perdita would often have given their ears to know exactly what adventure it was, and where it happened, and who was there, and what the ladies had on; but in those days a well-bred young woman was not expected to break into the conversation of her elders, or to ask too many questions; and the poor girls used therefore to sit fluttering behind the more languid—or more discreet—curiosity of their mother.

2

That they were both very fine girls Arthur Lloyd was not slow to discover; but it took him some time to make up his mind whether he liked the big sister or the little sister best. He had a strong presentiment—an emotion of a nature entirely too cheerful to be called a foreboding—that he was destined to stand up before the parson with one of them; yet he was unable to arrive at a preference, and for such a consummation a preference was certainly necessary, for Lloyd had too much young blood in his veins to make a choice by lot and be cheated of the satisfaction of falling in love. He resolved to take things as they came—to let his heart speak. Meanwhile he was on a very pleasant footing. Mrs. Wingrave showed a dignified indifference to his "intentions," equally remote from a carelessness of her daughter's honour and from that sharp alacrity to make him come to the point, which, in his quality of young man of property, he had too often encountered in the worldly matrons of his native islands. As for Bernard, all that he asked was that his friend should treat his sisters as his own; and as for the poor girls themselves, however each may have secretly longed that their visitor should do or say something "marked," they kept a very modest and contented demeanour.

Towards each other, however, they were somewhat more on the offensive. They were good friends enough, and accommodating bedfellows (they shared the same four-poster), betwixt whom it would take more than a day for the seeds of jealousy to sprout and bear fruit; but they felt that the seeds had been sown on the day that Mr. Lloyd came into the house. Each made up her mind that, if she should be slighted, she would bear her grief in silence, and that no one should be any the wiser; for if they had a great deal of ambition, they had also a large share of pride. But each prayed in secret, nevertheless, that upon *her* the selection, the distinction, might fall. They had need of a vast deal of patience, of self-control, of dissimulation. In those days a young girl of decent breeding could make no advances whatever, and barely respond, indeed, to those that were made. She was expected to sit still in her chair, with her eyes on the carpet, watching the spot where the mystic handkerchief should fall. Poor Arthur Lloyd was obliged to carry on his wooing in the little wainscoted parlour, before the eyes of Mrs. Wingrave, her son, and his prospective sister-in-law. But youth and love are so cunning that a hundred signs and tokens might travel to and fro, and not one of these three pairs of eyes detect them in their passage. The two maidens were almost always together, and had plenty of chances to betray themselves. That each knew she was being watched, however, made not a grain of difference in the little offices they mutually rendered, or in the various household tasks they performed in common. Neither flinched nor fluttered beneath the silent battery of her sister's eyes. The only apparent change in their habits was that they had less to say to each other. It was impossible to talk about Mr. Lloyd, and it was ridiculous to talk about anything else. By tacit agreement they began to wear all their choice finery, and to devise such little implements of conquest, in the way of ribbons and top-knots and kerchiefs, as were sanctioned by indubitable modesty. They executed in the same inarticulate fashion a contract of fair play in this exciting game. "Is it better so?" Rosalind would ask, tying a bunch of ribbons on her bosom, and turning about from her glass to her sister. Perdita would look up gravely from her work and examine the decoration. "I think you had better give it another loop," she would say, with great solemnity, looking hard at her sister with eyes that added, "upon my honour!" So they were for ever stitching and trimming their petticoats, and pressing out their muslins, and contriving washes and ointments and cosmetics, like the ladies in the household of the vicar of Wakefield. Some three or four months went by; it grew to be midwinter, and as yet Rosalind knew that if Perdita had nothing more to boast of than she, there was not much to be feared from her rivalry. But Perdita by this time—the charming Perdita—felt that her secret had grown to be tenfold more precious than her sister's.

One afternoon Miss Wingrave sat alone—that was a rare accident—before her toilet-glass, combing out her long hair. It was getting too dark to see; she lit the two candles in their sockets, on the frame of her mirror, and then went to the window to draw her curtains. It was a grey December evening; the landscape was bare and bleak, and the sky heavy with snow-clouds. At the end of the large garden into which her window looked was a wall with a little postern door, opening into a lane. The door stood ajar, as she could vaguely see in the gathering darkness, and moved slowly to and fro, as if someone were swaying it from the lane without. It was doubtless a servant-maid who had been having a tryst with her sweetheart. But as she was about to drop her curtain Rosalind saw her sister step into the garden and hurry along the path which led to the house. She dropped the curtain, all save a little crevice for her eyes. As Perdita came up the path she seemed to be examining something in her hand, holding it close to her eyes. When she reached the house she stopped a moment, looked intently at the object, and pressed it to her lips.

Poor Rosalind slowly came back to her chair and sat down before her glass, where, if she had looked at it less abstractedly, she would have seen her handsome features sadly disfigured by jealousy. A moment afterwards the door opened behind her and her sister came into the room, out of breath, her cheeks aglow with the chilly air.

Perdita started. "Ah," said she, "I thought you were with our mother." The ladies were to go to a tea-party, and on such occasions it was the habit of one of the girls to help their mother to dress. Instead of coming in, Perdita lingered at the door.

"Come in, come in," said Rosalind. "We have more than an hour yet. I should like you very much to give a few strokes to my hair." She knew that her sister wished to retreat, and that she could see in the glass all her movements in the room. "Nay, just help me with my hair," she said, "and I will go to mamma."

Perdita came reluctantly, and took the brush. She saw her sister's eyes, in the glass, fastened hard upon her hands. She had not made three passes when Rosalind clapped her own right hand upon her sister's left, and started out of her chair. "Whose ring is that?" she cried, passionately, drawing her towards the light.

On the young girl's third finger glistened a little gold ring, adorned with a very small sapphire. Perdita felt that she need no longer keep her secret, yet that she must put a bold face on her avowal. "It's mine," she said proudly.

"Who gave it to you?" cried the other.

Perdita hesitated a moment. "Mr. Lloyd."

"Mr. Lloyd is generous, all of a sudden."

"Ah no," cried Perdita, with spirit, "not all of a sudden! He offered it to me a month ago."

"And you needed a month's begging to take it?" said Rosalind, looking at the little trinket, which indeed was not especially elegant, although it was the best that the jeweller of the Province could furnish. "I wouldn't have taken it in less than two."

"It isn't the ring," Perdita answered, "it's what it means!"

"It means that you are not a modest girl!" cried Rosalind. "Pray, does your mother know of your intrigue? does Bernard?"

"My mother has approved my 'intrigue,' as you call it. Mr. Lloyd has asked for my hand, and mamma has given it. Would you have had him apply to you, dearest sister?"

Rosalind gave her companion a long look, full of passionate envy and sorrow. Then she dropped her lashes on her pale cheeks and turned away. Perdita felt that it had not been a pretty scene; but it was her sister's fault. However, the elder girl rapidly called back her pride, and turned herself about again. "You have my very best wishes," she said, with a low curtsey. "I wish you every happiness, and a very long life."

Perdita gave a bitter laugh. "Don't speak in that tone!" she cried. "I would rather you should curse me outright. Come, Rosy," she added, "he couldn't marry both of us."

"I wish you very great joy," Rosalind repeated, mechanically, sitting down to her glass again, "and a very long life, and plenty of children."

There was something in the sound of these words not at all to Perdita's taste. "Will you give me a year to live at least?" she said. "In a year I can have one little boy—or one little girl at least. If you will give me your brush again I will do your hair."

"Thank you," said Rosalind. "You had better go to mamma. It isn't becoming that a young lady with a promised husband should wait on a girl with none."

"Nay," said Perdita good-humouredly, "I have Arthur to wait upon me. You need my service more than I need yours."

But her sister motioned her away, and she left the room. When she had gone poor Rosalind fell on her knees before her dressing-table, buried her head in her arms, and poured out a flood of tears and sobs. She felt very much the better for this effusion of sorrow. When her sister came back she insisted on helping her to dress—on her wearing her prettiest things. She forced upon her acceptance a bit of lace of her own, and declared that now that she was to be married she should do her best to appear worthy of her lover's choice. She discharged these offices in stern silence; but, such as they were, they had to do duty as an apology and an atonement; she never made any other.

Now that Lloyd was received by the family as an accepted suitor nothing remained but to fix the wedding-day. It was appointed for the following April, and in the interval preparations were diligently made for the marriage. Lloyd, on his side, was busy with his commercial arrangements, and with establishing a correspondence with the great mercantile house to which he had attached himself in England. He was therefore not so frequent a visitor at Mrs. Wingrave's as during the months of his diffidence and irresolution, and poor Rosalind had less to suffer than she had feared from the sight of the mutual endearments of the young lovers. Touching his future sister-in-law Lloyd had a perfectly clear conscience. There had not been a particle of love-making between them, and he had not the slightest suspicion that he had dealt her a terrible blow. He was quite at his ease; life promised so well, both domestically and financially. The great revolt of the Colonies was not yet in the air, and that his connubial felicity should take a tragic turn it was absurd, it was blasphemous, to apprehend. Meanwhile, at Mrs. Wingrave's, there was a greater rustling of silks, a more rapid clicking of scissors and flying of needles, than ever. The good lady had determined that her daughter should carry from home the genteelest outfit that her money could buy or that the country could furnish. All the sage women in the Province were convened, and their united taste was brought to bear on Perdita's wardrobe. Rosalind's situation, at this moment, was assuredly not to be envied. The poor girl had an inordinate love of dress, and the very best taste in the world, as her sister perfectly well knew. Rosalind was tall, she was stately and sweeping, she was made to carry stiff brocade and masses of heavy lace, such as belong to the toilet of a rich man's wife. But Rosalind sat aloof, with her beautiful arms folded and her head averted, while her mother and sister and the venerable women aforesaid worried and wondered over their materials, oppressed by the multitude of their resources. One day there came in a beautiful piece of white silk, brocaded with heavenly blue and silver, sent by the bridegroom himself—it not being thought amiss in those days that the husband-elect should contribute to the bride's trousseau. Perdita could think of no form or fashion which would do sufficient honour to the splendour of the material.

"Blue's your colour, sister, more than mine," she said, with appealing eyes. "It's a pity it's not for you. You would know what to do with it."

Rosalind got up from her place and looked at the great shining fabric, as it lay spread over the back of a chair. Then she took it up in her hands and felt it—lovingly, as Perdita could see—and turned about towards the mirror with it. She let it roll down to her feet, and flung the other end over her shoulder, gathering it in about her waist with her white arm, which was bare to the elbow. She threw back her head, and looked at her image, and a hanging tress of her auburn hair fell upon the gorgeous surface of the silk. It made a dazzling picture. The women standing about uttered a little "Look, look!" of admiration. "Yes, indeed," said Rosalind, quietly, "blue is my colour." But Perdita could see that her fancy had been stirred, and that she would now fall to work and solve all their silken riddles. And indeed she behaved very well, as Perdita, knowing her insatiable love of millinery, was quite ready to declare. Innumerable yards of lustrous silk and satin, of muslin, velvet and lace, passed through her cunning hands, without a jealous word coming from her lips. Thanks to her industry, when the wedding-day came

Perdita was prepared to espouse more of the vanities of life than any fluttering young bride who had yet received the sacramental blessing of a New England divine.

It had been arranged that the young couple should go out and spend the first days of their wedded life at the country-house of an English gentleman—a man of rank and a very kind friend to Arthur Lloyd. He was a bachelor; he declared he should be delighted to give up the place to the influence of Hymen. After the ceremony at church—it had been performed by an English clergyman—young Mrs. Lloyd hastened back to her mother's house to change her nuptial robes for a riding-dress. Rosalind helped her to effect the change, in the little homely room in which they had spent their undivided younger years. Perdita then hurried off to bid farewell to her mother, leaving Rosalind to follow. The parting was short; the horses were at the door, and Arthur was impatient to start. But Rosalind had not followed, and Perdita hastened back to her room, opening the door abruptly. Rosalind, as usual, was before the glass, but in a position which caused the other to stand still, amazed. She had dressed herself in Perdita's cast-off wedding veil and wreath, and on her neck she had hung the full string of pearls which the young girl had received from her husband as a wedding-gift. These things had been hastily laid aside, to await their possessor's disposal on her return from the country. Bedizened in this unnatural garb Rosalind stood before the mirror, plunging a long look into its depths and reading heaven knows what audacious visions. Perdita was horrified. It was a hideous image of their old rivalry come to life again. She made a step towards her sister, as if to pull off the veil and the flowers. But catching her eyes in the glass, she stopped.

"Farewell, sweetheart," she said. "You might at least have waited till I had got out of the house!" And she hurried away from the room.

Mr. Lloyd had purchased in Boston a house which to the taste of those days appeared as elegant as it was commodious; and here he very soon established himself with his young wife. He was thus separated by a distance of twenty miles from the residence of his mother-in-law. Twenty miles, in that primitive era of roads and conveyances, were as serious a matter as a hundred at the present day, and Mrs. Wingrave saw but little of her daughter during the first twelvemonth of her marriage. She suffered in no small degree from Perdita's absence; and her affliction was not diminished by the fact that Rosalind had fallen into terribly low spirits and was not to be roused or cheered but by change of air and company. The real cause of the young lady's dejection the reader will not be slow to suspect. Mrs. Wingrave and her gossips, however, deemed her complaint a mere bodily ill, and doubted not that she would obtain relief from the remedy just mentioned. Her mother accordingly proposed, on her behalf, a visit to certain relatives on the paternal side, established in New York, who had long complained that they were able to see so little of their New England cousins. Rosalind was despatched to these good people, under a suitable escort, and remained with them for several months. In the interval her brother Bernard, who had begun the practice of the law, made up his mind to take a wife. Rosalind came home to the wedding, apparently cured of her heartache, with bright roses and lilies in her face and a proud smile on her lips. Arthur Lloyd came over from Boston to see his brother-in-law married, but without his wife, who was expecting very soon to present him with an heir. It was nearly a year since Rosalind had seen him. She was glad—she hardly knew why—that Perdita had stayed at home. Arthur looked happy, but he was more grave and important than before his marriage. She thought he looked "interesting"—for although the word, in its modern sense, was not then invented, we may be sure that the idea was. The truth is, he was simply anxious about his wife and her coming ordeal. Nevertheless, he by no means failed to observe Rosalind's beauty and splendour, and to note how she effaced the poor little bride. The allowance that Perdita had enjoyed for her dress had now been transferred to her sister, who turned it to wonderful account. On the morning after the wedding he had a lady's saddle put on the horse of the servant who had come with him from town, and went out with the young girl for a ride. It was a keen, clear morning in January; the ground was bare and hard, and the horses in good condition—to say nothing of Rosalind, who was charming in her hat and plume, and her dark blue riding coat, trimmed with fur. They rode all the morning, lost their way, and were obliged to stop for dinner at a farm-house. The early winter dusk had fallen when they got home. Mrs. Wingrave met them with a long face. A messenger had arrived at noon from Mrs. Lloyd; she was beginning to be ill, she desired her husband's immediate return. The young man, at the thought that he had lost several hours, and that by hard riding he might already have been with his wife, uttered a passionate oath. He barely consented to stop for a mouthful of supper, but mounted the messenger's horse and started off at a gallop.

He reached home at midnight. His wife had been delivered of a little girl. "Ah, why weren't you with me?" she said, as he came to her bedside.

"I was out of the house when the man came. I was with Rosalind," said Lloyd, innocently.

Mrs. Lloyd made a little moan, and turned away. But she continued to do very well, and for a week her improvement was uninterrupted. Finally, however, through some indiscretion in the way of diet or exposure, it was checked, and the poor lady grew rapidly worse. Lloyd was in despair. It very soon became evident that she was breathing her last. Mrs. Lloyd came to a sense of her approaching end, and declared that she was reconciled with death. On the third evening after the change took place she told her husband that she felt she should not get through the night. She dismissed her servants, and also requested her mother to withdraw—Mrs. Wingrave having arrived on the preceding day. She had had her infant placed on the bed beside her, and she lay on her side, with the child against her breast, holding her husband's hands. The night-lamp was hidden behind the heavy curtains of the bed, but the room was illumined with a red glow from the immense fire of logs on the hearth.

"It seems strange not to be warmed into life by such a fire as that," the young woman said, feebly trying to smile. "If I had but a little of it in my veins! But I have given all *my* fire to this little spark of mortality." And she dropped her eyes on her child. Then raising them she looked at her husband with a long, penetrating gaze. The last feeling which lingered in her heart was one of suspicion. She had not recovered from the shock which Arthur had given her by telling her that in the hour of her agony he had been with Rosalind. She trusted her husband very nearly as well as she loved him; but now that she was called away forever she felt a cold horror of her sister. She felt in her soul that Rosalind had never ceased to be jealous of her good fortune; and a year of happy security had not effaced the young girl's image, dressed in her wedding-garments, and smiling with simulated triumph. Now that Arthur was to be alone, what might not Rosalind attempt? She was beautiful, she was engaging; what arts might she not use, what impression might she not make upon the young man's saddened heart? Mrs. Lloyd looked at her husband in silence. It seemed hard, after all, to doubt of his constancy. His fine eyes were filled with tears; his face was convulsed with weeping; the clasp of his hands was warm and passionate. How noble he looked, how tender, how faithful and devoted! "Nay," thought Perdita, "he's not for such a one as Rosalind. He'll never forget me. Nor does Rosalind truly care for him; she cares only for vanities and finery and jewels." And she lowered her eyes on her white hands, which her husband's liberality had covered with rings, and on the lace ruffles which trimmed the edge of her nightdress. "She covets my rings and my laces more than she covets my husband."

At this moment the thought of her sister's rapacity seemed to cast a dark shadow between her and the helpless figure of her little girl. "Arthur," she said, "you must take off my rings. I shall not be buried in them. One of these days my daughter shall wear them—my rings and my laces and silks. I had them all brought out and shown me to-day. It's a great wardrobe—there's not such another in the Province; I can say it without vanity, now that I have done with it. It will be a great inheritance for my daughter when she grows into a young woman. There are things there that a man never buys twice, and if they are lost you will never again see the like. So you will watch them well. Some dozen things I have left to Rosalind; I have named them to my mother. I have given her that blue and silver; it was meant for her; I wore it only once, I looked ill in it. But the rest are to be sacredly kept for this little innocent. It's such a providence that she should be my colour; she can wear my gowns; she has her mother's eyes. You know the same fashions come back every twenty years. She can wear my gowns as they are. They will lie there quietly waiting till she grows into them—wrapped in camphor and rose-leaves, and keeping their colours in the sweet-scented darkness. She shall have black hair, she shall wear my carnation satin. Do you promise me, Arthur?"

"Promise you what, dearest?"

"Promise me to keep your poor little wife's old gowns."

"Are you afraid I shall sell them?"

"No, but that they may get scattered. My mother will have them properly wrapped up, and you shall lay them away under a double-lock. Do you know the great chest in the attic, with the iron bands? There is no end to what it will hold. You can put them all there. My mother and the housekeeper will do it, and give you the key. And you will keep the key in your secretary, and never give it to anyone but your child. Do you promise me?"

"Ah, yes, I promise you," said Lloyd, puzzled at the intensity with which his wife appeared to cling to this idea.

"Will you swear?" repeated Perdita.

"Yes, I swear."

"Well—I trust you—I trust you," said the poor lady, looking into his eyes with eyes in which, if he had suspected her vague apprehensions, he might have read an appeal quite as much as an assurance.

Lloyd bore his bereavement rationally and manfully. A month after his wife's death, in the course of business, circumstances arose which offered him an opportunity of going to England. He took advantage of it, to change the current of his thoughts. He was absent nearly a year, during which his little girl was tenderly nursed and guarded by her grandmother. On his return he had his house again thrown open, and announced his intention of keeping the same state as during his wife's lifetime. It very soon came to be predicted that he would marry again, and there were at least a dozen young women of whom one may say that it was by no fault of theirs that, for six months after his return, the prediction did not come true. During this interval he still left his little daughter in Mrs. Wingrave's hands, the latter assuring him that a change of residence at so tender an age would be full of danger for her health. Finally, however, he declared that his heart longed for his daughter's presence and that she must be brought up to town. He sent his coach and his housekeeper to fetch her home. Mrs. Wingrave was in terror lest something should befall her on the road; and, in accordance with this feeling, Rosalind offered to accompany her. She could return the next day. So she went up to town with her little niece, and Mr. Lloyd met her on the threshold of his house, overcome with her kindness and with paternal joy. Instead of returning the next day Rosalind stayed out the week; and when at last she reappeared, she had only come for her clothes. Arthur would not hear of her coming home, nor would the baby. That little person cried and choked if Rosalind left her; and at the sight of her grief Arthur lost his wits, and swore that she was going to die. In fine, nothing would suit them but that the aunt should remain until the little niece had grown used to strange faces.

It took two months to bring this consummation about; for it was not until this period had elapsed that Rosalind took leave of her brother-in-law. Mrs. Wingrave had shaken her head over her daughter's absence; she had declared that it was not becoming, that it was the talk of the whole country. She had reconciled herself to it only because, during the girl's visit, the household enjoyed an unwonted term of peace. Bernard Wingrave had brought his wife home to live, between whom and her sister-in-law there was as little love as you please. Rosalind was perhaps no angel; but in the daily practice of life she was a sufficiently good-natured girl, and if she quarrelled with Mrs. Bernard, it was not without provocation. Quarrel, however, she did, to the great annoyance not only of her antagonist, but of the two spectators of these constant altercations. Her stay in the household of her brother-in-law, therefore, would have been delightful, if only because it removed her from contact with the object of her antipathy at home. It was doubly—it was ten times—delightful, in that it kept her near the object of her early passion. Mrs. Lloyd's sharp suspicions had fallen very far short of the truth. Rosalind's sentiment had been a passion at first, and a passion it remained—a passion of whose radiant heat, tempered to the delicate state of his feelings, Mr. Lloyd very soon felt the influence. Lloyd, as I have hinted, was not a modern Petrarch; it was not in his nature to practise an ideal constancy. He had not been many days in the house with his sister-in-law before he began to assure himself that she was, in the language of that day, a devilish fine woman. Whether Rosalind really practised those insidious arts that her sister had been tempted to impute to her it is needless to inquire. It is enough to say that she found means to appear to the very best advantage. She used to seat herself every morning before the big fireplace in the dining-room, at work upon a piece of tapestry, with her little niece disporting herself on the carpet at her feet, or on the train of her dress, and playing with her woollen balls. Lloyd would have been a very stupid fellow if he had remained insensible to the rich suggestions of this charming picture. He was exceedingly fond of his little girl, and was never weary of taking her in his arms and tossing her up and down, and making her crow with delight. Very often, however, he would venture upon greater liberties than the young lady was yet prepared to allow, and then she would suddenly vociferate her displeasure. Rosalind, at this, would drop her tapestry, and put out her handsome hands with the serious smile of the young girl whose virgin fancy has revealed to her all a mother's healing arts. Lloyd would give up the child, their eyes would meet, their hands would touch, and Rosalind would extinguish the little girl's sobs upon the snowy folds of the kerchief that crossed her bosom. Her dignity was perfect, and nothing could be more discreet than the manner in which she accepted her brother-in-law's hospitality. It may almost be said, perhaps, that there was something harsh in her reserve. Lloyd had a provoking feeling that she was in the house and yet was unapproachable. Half-an-hour after supper, at the very outset of the long winter evenings, she would light her candle, make the young man a most respectful curtsey, and march off to bed. If these were arts, Rosalind was a great artist. But their effect was so gentle, so gradual, they were calculated to work upon the young widower's fancy with a *crescendo* so finely shaded, that, as the reader has seen, several weeks elapsed before Rosalind began to feel sure that her returns would cover her outlay. When this became morally certain she packed up her trunk and returned to her mother's house. For three days she waited: on the fourth Mr. Lloyd made his appearance—a respectful but pressing suitor. Rosalind heard him to the end, with great humility, and accepted him with infinite modesty. It is hard to imagine that Mrs. Lloyd would have forgiven her husband; but if anything might have disarmed her resentment it would have been the ceremonious continence of this interview. Rosalind imposed upon her lover but a short probation. They were married, as was becoming, with great privacy—almost with secrecy—in the hope perhaps, as was waggishly remarked at the time, that the late Mrs. Lloyd wouldn't hear of it.

The marriage was to all appearance a happy one, and each party obtained what each had desired—Lloyd "a devilish fine woman," and Rosalind—but Rosalind's desires, as the reader will have observed, had remained a good deal of a mystery. There were, indeed, two blots upon their felicity, but time would perhaps efface them. During the first three years of her marriage Mrs. Lloyd failed to become a mother, and her husband on his side suffered heavy losses of money. This latter circumstance compelled a material retrenchment in his expenditure, and Rosalind was perforce less of a fine lady than her sister had been. She contrived, however, to carry it like a woman of considerable fashion. She had long since ascertained that her sister's copious wardrobe had been sequestrated for the benefit of her daughter, and that it lay languishing in thankless gloom in the dusty attic. It was a revolting thought that these exquisite fabrics should await the good pleasure of a little girl who sat in a high chair and ate bread-and-milk with a wooden spoon. Rosalind had the good taste, however, to say nothing about the matter until several months had expired. Then, at last, she timidly broached it to her husband. Was it not a pity that so much finery should be lost?—for lost it would be, what with colours fading, and moths eating it up, and the change of fashions. But Lloyd gave her so abrupt and peremptory a refusal, that she saw, for the present, her attempt was vain. Six months went by, however, and brought with them new needs and new visions. Rosalind's thoughts hovered lovingly about her sister's relics. She went up and looked at the chest in which they lay imprisoned. There was a sullen defiance in its three great padlocks and its iron bands which only quickened her cupidity. There was something exasperating in its incorruptible immobility. It was like a grim and grizzled old household servant, who locks his jaws over a family secret. And then there was a look of capacity in its vast extent, and a sound as of dense fulness, when Rosalind knocked its side with the toe of her little shoe, which caused her to flush with baffled longing. "It's absurd," she cried; "it's improper, it's wicked"; and she forthwith resolved upon another attack upon her husband. On the following day, after dinner, when he had had his wine, she boldly began it. But he cut her short with great sternness.

"Once for all, Rosalind," said he, "it's out of the question. I shall be gravely displeased if you return to the matter."

"Very good," said Rosalind. "I am glad to learn the esteem in which I am held. Gracious heaven," she cried, "I am a very happy woman! It's an agreeable thing to feel one's self sacrificed to a caprice!" And her eyes filled with tears of anger and disappointment.

Lloyd had a good-natured man's horror of a woman's sobs, and he attempted—I may say he condescended—to explain. "It's not a caprice, dear, it's a promise," he said—"an oath."

"An oath? It's a pretty matter for oaths! and to whom, pray?"

"To Perdita," said the young man, raising his eyes for an instant, and immediately dropping them.

"Perdita—ah, Perdita!" and Rosalind's tears broke forth. Her bosom heaved with stormy sobs—sobs which were the long-deferred sequel of the violent fit of weeping in which she had indulged herself on the night when she discovered her sister's betrothal. She had hoped, in her better moments, that she had done with her jealousy; but her temper, on that occasion, had taken an ineffaceable hold. "And pray, what right had Perdita to dispose of my future?" she cried. "What right had she to bind you to meanness and cruelty? Ah, I occupy a dignified place, and I make a very fine figure! I am welcome to what Perdita has left! And what has she left? I never knew till now how little! Nothing, nothing, nothing."

This was very poor logic, but it was very good as a "scene." Lloyd put his arm around his wife's waist and tried to kiss her, but she shook him off with magnificent scorn. Poor fellow! he had coveted a "devilish fine woman," and he had got one. Her scorn was intolerable. He walked away with his ears tingling—irresolute, distracted. Before him was his secretary, and in it the sacred key which with his own hand he had turned in the triple lock. He marched up and opened it, and took the key from a secret drawer, wrapped in a little packet which he had sealed with his own honest bit of glazonry. *Je garde,* said the motto—"I keep." But he was ashamed to put it back. He flung it upon the table beside his wife.

"Put it back!" she cried. "I want it not. I hate it!"

"I wash my hands of it," cried her husband. "God forgive me!"

Mrs. Lloyd gave an indignant shrug of her shoulders, and swept out of the room, while the young man retreated by another door. Ten minutes later Mrs. Lloyd returned, and found the room occupied by her little step-daughter and the nursery-maid. The key was not on the table. She glanced at the child. Her little niece was perched on a chair, with the packet in her hands. She had broken the seal with her own small fingers. Mrs. Lloyd hastily took possession of the key.

At the habitual supper-hour Arthur Lloyd came back from his counting-room. It was the month of June, and supper was served by daylight. The meal was placed on the table, but Mrs. Lloyd failed to make her appearance. The servant whom his master sent to call her came back with the assurance that her room was empty, and that the women informed him that she had not been seen since dinner. They had, in truth, observed her to have been in tears, and, supposing her to be shut up in her chamber, had not disturbed her. Her husband called her name in various parts of the house, but without response. At last it occurred to him that he might find her by taking the way to the attic. The thought gave him a strange feeling of discomfort, and he bade his servants remain behind, wishing no witness in his quest. He reached the foot of the staircase leading to the topmost flat, and stood with his hand on the banisters, pronouncing his wife's name. His voice trembled. He called again louder and more firmly. The only sound which disturbed the absolute silence was a faint echo of his own tones, repeating his question under the great eaves. He nevertheless felt irresistibly moved to ascend the staircase. It opened upon a wide hall, lined with wooden closets, and terminating in a window which looked westward, and admitted the last rays of the sun. Before the window stood the great chest. Before the chest, on her knees, the young man saw with amazement and horror the figure of his wife. In an instant he crossed the interval between them, bereft of utterance. The lid of the chest stood open, exposing, amid their perfumed napkins, its treasure of stuffs and jewels. Rosalind had fallen backward from a kneeling posture, with one hand supporting her on the floor and the other pressed to her heart. On her limbs was the stiffness of death, and on her face, in the fading light of the sun, the terror of something more than death. Her lips were parted in entreaty, in dismay, in agony; and on her blanched brow and cheeks there glowed the marks of ten hideous wounds from two vengeful ghostly hands.

POISON

Roald Dahl

It must have been around midnight when I drove home, and as I approached the gates of the bungalow I switched off the headlamps of the car so the beam wouldn't swing in through the window of the side bedroom and wake Harry Pope. But I needn't have bothered. Coming up the drive I noticed his light was still on, so he was awake anyway—unless perhaps he'd dropped off while reading.

I parked the car and went up the five steps to the balcony, counting each step carefully in the dark so I wouldn't take an extra one which wasn't there when I got to the top. I crossed the balcony, pushed through the screen doors into the house itself and switched on the light in the hall. I went across to the door of Harry's room, opened it quietly, and looked in.

He was lying on the bed and I could see he was awake. But he didn't move. He didn't even turn his head towards me, but I heard him say, " Timber, Timber, come here."

He spoke slowly, whispering each word carefully, separately, and I pushed the door right open and started to go quickly across the room.

" Stop. Wait a moment, Timber." I could hardly hear what he was saying. He seemed to be straining enormously to get the words out.

" What's the matter, Harry?"

" Sshhh!" he whispered. " Sshhh! For God's sake don't make a noise. Take your shoes off before you come nearer. *Please* do as I say, Timber."

The way he was speaking reminded me of George Barling after he got shot in the stomach when he stood leaning against a crate containing a spare aeroplane engine, holding both hands on his stomach and saying things about the German pilot in just the same hoarse straining half whisper Harry was using now.

" Quickly, Timber, but take your shoes off first."

I couldn't understand about taking off the shoes but I figured that if he was as ill as he sounded I'd better humour him, so I bent down and removed the shoes and left them in the middle of the floor. Then I went over to his bed.

" Don't touch the bed! For God's sake don't touch the bed!" He was still speaking like he'd been shot in the stomach and I could see him lying there on his back with a single sheet covering three-quarters of his body. He was wearing a pair of pyjamas with blue, brown, and white stripes, and he was sweating terribly. It was a hot night and I was sweating a little myself, but not like Harry. His whole face was wet and the pillow around his head was sodden with moisture. It looked like a bad go of malaria to me.

" What is it, Harry?"

" A krait," he said.

" A *krait*! Oh, my God! Where'd it bite you? How long ago?"

" Shut up," he whispered.

" Listen, Harry," I said, and I leaned forward and touched his shoulder. " We've got to be quick. Come on now, quickly, tell me where it bit you." He was lying there very still and tense as though he was holding on to himself hard because of sharp pain.

" I haven't been bitten," he whispered. " Not yet. It's on my stomach. Lying there asleep."

I took a quick pace backwards. I couldn't help it, and I stared at his stomach or rather at the sheet that covered it. The sheet was rumpled in several places and it was impossible to tell if there was anything underneath.

" You don't really mean there's a krait lying on your stomach now?"

" I swear it."

" How did it get there?" I shouldn't have asked the question because it was easy to see he wasn't fooling. I should have told him to keep quiet.

" I was reading," Harry said, and he spoke very slowly, taking each word in turn and speaking it carefully so as not to move the muscles of his stomach. " Lying on my back reading and I felt something on my chest, behind the book. Sort of tickling. Then out of the corner of my eye saw this little krait sliding over my pyjamas. Small, about ten inches. Knew I mustn't move. Couldn't have anyway. Lay there watching it. Thought it would go over top of the sheet." Harry paused and was silent for a few moments. His eyes looked down along his body towards the place where the sheet covered his stomach, and I could see he was watching to make sure his whispering wasn't disturbing the thing that lay there.

"There was a fold in the sheet," he said, speaking more slowly than ever now and so softly I had to lean close to hear him. "See it, it's still there. It went under that. I could feel it through my pyjamas, moving on my stomach. Then it stopped moving and now it's lying there in the warmth. Probably asleep. I've been waiting for you." He raised his eyes and looked at me.

"How long ago?"

"Hours," he whispered. "Hours and bloody hours and hours. I can't keep still much longer. I've been wanting to cough."

There was not much doubt about the truth of Harry's story. As a matter of fact it wasn't a surprising thing for a krait to do. They hang around people's houses and they go for the warm places. The surprising thing was that Harry hadn't been bitten. The bite is quite deadly except sometimes when you catch it at once and they kill a fair number of people each year in Bengal, mostly in the villages.

"All right, Harry," I said, and now I was whispering too. "Don't move and don't talk any more unless you have to. You know it won't bite unless it's frightened. We'll fix it in no time."

I went softly out of the room in my stocking feet and fetched a small sharp knife from the kitchen. I put it in my trouser pocket ready to use instantly in case something went wrong while we were still thinking out a plan. If Harry coughed or moved or did something to frighten the krait and got bitten, I was going to be ready to cut the bitten place and try to suck the venom out. I came back to the bedroom and Harry was still lying there very quiet and sweating all over his face. His eyes followed me as I moved across the room to his bed and I could see he was wondering what I'd been up to. I stood beside him, trying to think of the best thing to do.

"Harry," I said, and now when I spoke I put my mouth

almost on his ear so I wouldn't have to raise my voice above the softest whisper, "I think the best thing to do is for me to draw the sheet back very, very gently. Then we could have a look first. I think I could do that without disturbing it."

"Don't be a damn' fool." There was no expression in his voice. He spoke each word too slowly, too carefully, and too softly for that. The expression was in the eyes and around the corners of the mouth.

"Why not?"

"The light would frighten him. It's dark under there now.

"Then how about whipping the sheet back quick and brushing it off before it has time to strike?"

"Why don't you get a doctor?" Harry said. The way he looked at me told me I should have thought of that myself in the first place.

"A doctor. Of course. That's it. I'll get Ganderbai."

I tiptoed out to the hall, looked up Ganderbai's number in the book, lifted the phone and told the operator to hurry.

"Dr. Ganderbai," I said. "This is Timber Woods."

"Hello, Mr. Woods. You not in bed yet?"

"Look, could you come round at once? And bring serum—for a krait bite."

"Who's been bitten?" The question came so sharply it was like a small explosion in my ear.

"No one. No one yet. But Harry Pope's in bed and he's got one lying on his stomach—asleep under the sheet on his stomach."

For about three seconds there was silence on the line. Then speaking slowly, not like an explosion now but slowly, precisely, Ganderbai said, "Tell him to keep quite still. He is not to move or to talk. Do you understand?"

"Of course."

"I'll come at once!" He rang off and I went back to the bedroom. Harry's eyes watched me as I walked across to his bed.

"Ganderbai's coming. He said for you to lie still."

"What in God's name does he think I'm doing!"

"Look, Harry, he said no talking. Absolutely no talking. Either of us."

"Why don't you shut up then?" When he said this, one side

of his mouth started twitching with rapid little downward movements that continued for a while after he finished speaking. I took out my handkerchief and very gently I wiped the sweat off his face and neck, and I could feel the slightest twitching of the muscle—the one he used for smiling—as my fingers passed over it with the handkerchief.

I slipped out to the kitchen, got some ice from the ice-box, rolled it up in a napkin, and began to crush it small. That business of the mouth, I didn't like that. Or the way he talked, either. I carried the ice pack back to the bedroom and laid it across Harry's forehead.

"Keep you cool."

He screwed up his eyes and drew breath sharply through his teeth. "Take it away," he whispered. "Make me cough." His smiling-muscle began to twitch again.

The beam of a headlamp shone through the window as Ganderbai's car swung around to the front of the bungalow. I went out to meet him, holding the ice pack with both hands.

"How is it?" Ganderbai asked, but he didn't stop to talk; he walked on past me across the balcony and through the screen doors into the hall. "Where is he? Which room?"

He put his bag down on a chair in the hall and followed me into Harry's room. He was wearing soft-soled bedroom slippers and he walked across the floor noiselessly, delicately, like a careful cat. Harry watched him out of the sides of his eyes. When Ganderbai reached the bed he looked down at Harry and smiled, confident and reassuring, nodding his head to tell Harry it was a simple matter and he was not to worry but just to leave it to Dr. Ganderbai. Then he turned and went back to the hall and I followed him.

"First thing is to try and get some serum into him," he said, and he opened his bag and started to make preparations. "Intravenously. But I must do it neatly. Don't want to make him flinch."

We went into the kitchen and he sterilized a needle. He had a hypodermic syringe in one hand and a small bottle in the other and he stuck the needle through the rubber top of the bottle and began drawing a pale yellow liquid up into the syringe by pulling out the plunger. Then he handed the syringe to me.

"Hold that till I ask for it."

He picked up the bag and together we returned to the room. Harry's eyes were bright now and wide open. Ganderbai bent over Harry and very cautiously, like a man handling sixteenth-century lace, he rolled up the pyjama sleeve to the elbow without moving the arm. I noticed he stood well away from the bed.

He whispered, "I'm going to give you an injection. Serum. Just a prick but try not to move. Don't tighten your stomach muscles. Let them go limp."

Harry looked at the syringe.

Ganderbai took a piece of red rubber tubing from his bag and slid one end under and up and around Harry's biceps; then he tied the tubing tight with a knot. He sponged a small area of the bare forearm with alcohol, handed the swab to me and took the syringe from my hand. He held it up to the light, squinting at the calibrations, spurting out some of the yellow fluid. I stood still beside him, watching. Harry was watching too and sweating all over his face so it shone like it was smeared thick with face cream melting on his skin and running down on to the pillow.

I could see the blue vein on the inside of Harry's forearm, swollen now because of the tourniquet, and then I saw the needle above the vein, Ganderbai holding the syringe almost flat against the arm, sliding the needle in sideways through the skin into the blue vein, sliding it slowly but so firmly it went in smooth as into cheese. Harry looked at the ceiling and closed his eyes and opened them again, but he didn't move.

When it was finished Ganderbai leaned forward putting his mouth close to Harry's ear. "Now you'll be all right even if you *are* bitten. But don't move. Please don't move. I'll be back in a moment."

He picked up his bag and went out to the hall and I followed.

"Is he safe now?" I asked.

"No."

"How safe is he?"

The little Indian doctor stood there in the hall rubbing his lower lip.

"It must give some protection, mustn't it?" I asked.

He turned away and walked to the screen doors that led on to the veranda. I thought he was going through them, but he stopped this side of the doors and stood looking out into the night.

"Isn't the serum very good?" I asked.

"Unfortunately not," he answered without turning round. "It might save him. It might not. I am trying to think of something else to do."

"Shall we draw the sheet back quick and brush it off before it has time to strike?"

"Never! We are not entitled to take a risk." He spoke sharply and his voice was pitched a little higher than usual.

"We can't very well leave him lying there," I said. "He's getting nervous."

"Please! Please!" he said, turning round, holding both hands up in the air. "Not so fast, please. This is not a matter to rush into baldheaded." He wiped his forehead with his handkerchief and stood there, frowning, nibbling his lip.

"You see," he said at last. "There is a way to do this. You know what we must do—we must administer an anæsthetic to the creature where it lies."

It was a splendid idea.

"It is not safe," he continued, "because a snake is cold-blooded and anæsthetic does not work so well or so quick with such animals, but it is better than any other thing to do. We could use ether . . . chloroform . . ." He was speaking slowly and trying to think the thing out while he talked.

"Which shall we use?"

"Chloroform," he said suddenly. "Ordinary chloroform. That is best. Now quick!" He took my arm and pulled me towards the balcony. "Drive to my house! By the time you get there I will have waked up my boy on the telephone and he will show you my poisons cupboard. Here is the key of the cupboard. Take a bottle of chloroform. It has an orange label and the name is printed on it. I stay here in case anything happens. Be quick now, hurry! No, no, you don't need your shoes!"

I drove fast and in about fifteen minutes I was back with the bottle of chloroform. Ganderbai came out of Harry's room and met me in the hall. "You got it?" he said. "Good, good.

I just been telling him what we are going to do. But now we must hurry. It is not easy for him in there like that all this time. I am afraid he might move."

He went back to the bedroom and I followed, carrying the bottle carefully with both hands. Harry was lying on the bed in precisely the same position as before with the sweat pouring down his cheeks. His face was white and wet. He turned his eyes towards me and I smiled at him and nodded confidently. He continued to look at me. I raised my thumb, giving him the okay signal. He closed his eyes. Ganderbai was squatting down by the bed, and on the floor beside him was the hollow rubber tube that he had previously used as a tourniquet, and he'd got a small paper funnel fitted into one end of the tube.

He began to pull a little piece of the sheet out from under the mattress. He was working directly in line with Harry's stomach, about eighteen inches from it, and I watched his fingers as they tugged gently at the edge of the sheet. He worked so slowly it was almost impossible to discern any movement either in his fingers or in the sheet that was being pulled.

Finally he succeeded in making an opening under the sheet and he took the rubber tube and inserted one end of it in the opening so that it would slide under the sheet along the mattress towards Harry's body. I do not know how long it took him to slide that tube in a few inches. It may have been twenty minutes, it may have been forty. I never once saw the tube move. I knew it was going in because the visible part of it grew gradually shorter, but I doubted that the krait could have felt even the faintest vibration. Ganderbai himself was sweating now, large pearls of sweat standing out all over his forehead and along his upper lip. But his hands were steady and I noticed that his eyes were watching, not the tube in his hands, but the area of crumpled sheet above Harry's stomach.

Without looking up, he held out a hand to me for the chloroform. I twisted out the ground-glass stopper and put the bottle right into his hand, not letting go till I was sure he had a good hold on it. Then he jerked his head for me to come closer and he whispered, "Tell him I'm going to soak the mattress and that it will be very cold under his body. He must be ready for that and he must not move. Tell him now."

I bent over Harry and passed on the message.

"Why doesn't he get on with it?" Harry said.

"He's going to now, Harry. But it'll feel very cold, so be ready for it."

"Oh, God Almighty, get on, get on!" For the first time he raised his voice, and Ganderbai glanced up sharply, watched him for a few seconds, then went back to his business.

Ganderbai poured a few drops of chloroform into the paper funnel and waited while it ran down the tube. Then he poured some more. Then he waited again, and the heavy sickening smell of chloroform spread out over the room bringing with it faint unpleasant memories of white-coated nurses and white surgeons standing in a white room around a long white table. Ganderbai was pouring steadily now and I could see the heavy vapour of the chloroform swirling slowly like smoke above the paper funnel. He paused, held the bottle up to the light, poured one more funnelful and handed the bottle back to me. Slowly he drew out the rubber tube from under the sheet; then he stood up.

The strain of inserting the tube and pouring the chloroform must have been great, and I recollect that when Ganderbai turned and whispered to me, his voice was small and tired. "We'll give it fifteen minutes. Just to be safe."

I leaned over to tell Harry. "We're going to give it fifteen minutes, just to be safe. But it's probably done for already."

"Then why for God's sake don't you look and see!" Again he spoke loudly and Ganderbai sprang round, his small brown face suddenly very angry. He had almost pure black eyes and he stared at Harry and Harry's smiling-muscle started to twitch. I took my handkerchief and wiped his wet face, trying to stroke his forehead a little for comfort as I did so.

Then we stood and waited beside the bed, Ganderbai watching Harry's face all the time in a curious intense manner. The little Indian was concentrating all his will power on keeping Harry quiet. He never once took his eyes from the patient and although he made no sound, he seemed somehow to be shouting at him all the time, saying: Now listen, you've got to listen, you're not going to go spoiling this now, d'you hear me; and Harry lay there twitching his mouth, sweating, closing his eyes, opening them, looking at me, at the sheet, at the ceiling, at me again, but never at Ganderbai. Yet somehow Ganderbai was holding him. The smell of chloroform was oppressive and it made me feel sick, but I couldn't leave the room now. I had the feeling someone was blowing up a huge balloon and I could see it was going to burst, but I couldn't look away.

At length Ganderbai turned and nodded and I knew he was ready to proceed. "You go over to the other side of the bed," he said. "We will each take one side of the sheet and draw it back together, but very slowly, please, and very quietly."

"Keep still now, Harry," I said and I went around to the other side of the bed and took hold of the sheet. Ganderbai stood opposite me, and together we began to draw back the sheet, lifting it up clear of Harry's body, taking it back very slowly, both of us standing well away but at the same time bending forward, trying to peer underneath it. The smell of chloroform was awful. I remember trying to hold my breath and when I couldn't do that any longer I tried to breathe shallow so the stuff wouldn't get into my lungs.

The whole of Harry's chest was visible now, or rather the striped pyjama top which covered it, and then I saw the white cord of his pyjama trousers, neatly tied in a bow. A little farther and I saw a button, a mother-of-pearl button, and that was something I had never had on my pyjamas, a fly button, let alone a mother-of-pearl one. This Harry, I thought, he is very refined. It is odd how one sometimes has frivolous thoughts at exciting moments, and I distinctly remember thinking about Harry being very refined when I saw that button.

Apart from the button there was nothing on his stomach.

We pulled the sheet back faster then, and when we had uncovered his legs and feet we let the sheep drop over the end of the bed on to the floor.

"Don't move," Ganderbai said, "don't move, Mr. Pope"; and he began to peer around along the side of Harry's body and under his legs.

"We must be careful," he said. "It may be anywhere. It could be up the leg of his pyjamas."

When Ganderbai said this, Harry quickly raised his head

from the pillow and looked down at his legs. It was the first time he had moved. Then suddenly he jumped up, stood on his bed and shook his legs one after the other violently in the air. At that moment we both thought he had been bitten and Ganderbai was already reaching down into his bag for a scalpel and a tourniquet when Harry ceased his caperings and stood still and looked at the mattress he was standing on and shouted, "It's not there!"

Ganderbai straightened up and for a moment he too looked at the mattress; then he looked up at Harry. Harry was all right. He hadn't been bitten and now he wasn't going to get bitten and he wasn't going to be killed and everything was fine. But that didn't seem to make anyone feel any better.

"Mr. Pope, you are of course *quite* sure you saw it in the first place?" There was a note of sarcasm in Ganderbai's voice that he would never have employed in ordinary circumstances. "You don't think you might possibly have been dreaming, do you, Mr. Pope?" The way Ganderbai was looking at Harry, I realized that the sarcasm was not seriously intended. He was only easing up a bit after the strain.

Harry stood on his bed in his striped pyjamas, glaring at Ganderbai, and the colour began to spread out over his cheeks.

"Are you telling me I'm a liar?" he shouted.

Ganderbai remained absolutely still, watching Harry. Harry took a pace forward on the bed and there was a shining look in his eyes.

"Why, you dirty little Hindu sewer rat!"

"Shut up, Harry!" I said.

"You dirty black——"

"Harry!" I called. "Shut up, Harry!" It was terrible, the things he was saying.

Ganderbai went out of the room as though neither of us was there and I followed him and put my arm around his shoulder as he walked across the hall and out on to the balcony.

"Don't you listen to Harry," I said. "This thing's made him so he doesn't know what he's saying."

We went down the steps from the balcony to the drive and across the drive in the darkness to where his old Morris car was parked. He opened the door and got in.

"You did a wonderful job," I said. "Thank you so very much for coming."

"All he needs is a good holiday," he said quietly, without looking at me, then he started the engine and drove off.

LUCKY'S GROVE

Herbert Russell Wakefield

And Loki begat Hel, Goddess of the Grave, Fenris, the Great Wolf, and the Serpent, Nidnogg, who lives beneath The Tree.

Mr. Braxton strolled with his land-agent, Curtis, into the Great Barn.

"There you are," said Curtis, in a satisfied tone, "the finest little larch I ever saw, and the kiddies will never set eyes on a lovelier Christmas tree."

Mr. Braxton examined it; it stood twenty feet from huge green pot to crisp, straight peak, and was exquisitely sturdy, fresh and symmetrical.

"Yes, it's a beauty," he agreed. "Where did you find it?"

"In that odd little spinney they call Lucky's Grove in the long meadow near the river boundary."

"Oh!" remarked Mr. Braxton uncertainly. To himself he was saying vaguely, "He shouldn't have got it from there, of course he wouldn't realise it, but he shouldn't have got it from there."

"Of course we'll replant it," said Curtis, noticing his employer's diminished enthusiasm. "It's a curious thing, but it isn't a young tree; it's apparently full-grown. Must be a dwarf variety, but I don't know as much about trees as I should like."

Mr. Braxton was surprised to find there was one branch of country lore on which Curtis was not an expert; for he was about the best-known man at his job in the British Isles. Pigs, bees, chickens, cattle, crops, running a shoot, he had mastered them one and all. He paid him two thousand a year with house and car. He was worth treble.

"I expect it's all right," said Mr. Braxton; "it's just that Lucky's Grove is—is—well, 'sacred' is perhaps too strong a word. Maybe I should have told you, but I expect it's all right."

"That accounts for it then," laughed Curtis. "I thought there seemed some reluctance on the part of the men while we were yanking it up and getting it on the lorry. They handled it a bit gingerly; on the part of the older men, I mean; the youngsters didn't worry."

"Yes, there would be," said Mr. Braxton. "But never mind, it'll be back in a few days and it's a superb little tree. I'll bring Mrs. Braxton along to see it after lunch," and he strolled back into Abingdale Hall.

Fifty-five years ago Mr. Braxton's father had been a labourer on this very estate, and in that year young Percy, aged eight, had got an errand boy's job in Oxford. Twenty years later he'd owned one small shop. Twenty-five years after that fifty big shops. Now, though he had finally retired, he owned two hundred and eighty vast shops and was a millionaire whichever way you added it up. How had this happened? No one can quite answer such questions. Certainly he'd worked like a brigade of Trojans, but midnight oil has to burn in Aladdin's Lamp before it can transform ninepence into one million pounds. It was just that he asked no quarter from the unforgiving minute, but squeezed from it the fruit of others' many hours. Those like Mr. Braxton seem to have their own time-scale; they just say the word and up springs a fine castle of commerce, but the knowledge of that word cannot be imparted; it is as mysterious as the Logos. But all through his great labours he had been moved by one fixed resolve—to avenge his father—that fettered spirit—for he had been an able, intelligent man who had had no earthly chance of revealing the fact to the world. Always the categorical determination had blazed in his son's brain, "I will own Abingdale Hall, and, where my father sweated, I will rule and be lord." And of course it happened. Fate accepts the dictates of such men as Mr. Braxton, shrugs its shoulders, and leaves its revenge to Death. The Hall had come on the market just when he was about to retire, and with an odd delight, an obscure sense of home-coming, the native returned, and his riding boots, shooting boots, golf shoes, and all the many glittering guineas' worth, stamped in and obliterated the prints of his father's hob-nails.

That was the picture he often re-visualised, the way it amused him to "put it to himself," as he roamed his broad acres and surveyed the many glowing triumphs of his model husbandry.

Some credit was due to buxom, blithe and debonair Mrs. Braxton, kindly, competent and innately adaptable. She was awaiting him in the morning-room and they went in solitary state, to luncheon. But it was the last peaceful lunch they would have for a spell—" the Families " were pouring in on the morrow.

As a footman was helping them to Sole Meunière Mr. Braxton said, " Curtis has found a very fine Christmas tree. It's in the barn. You must come and look at it after lunch."

" That *is* good," replied his wife. " Where did he get it from?"

Mr. Braxton hesitated for a moment.

" From Lucky's Grove."

Mrs. Braxton looked up sharply.

" From the grove!" she said, surprised.

" Yes, of course he didn't realise—anyway it'll be all right, it's all rather ridiculous, and it'll be replanted before the New Year."

" Oh, yes," agreed Mrs. Braxton. " After all it's only just a clump of trees."

" Quite. And it's just the right height for the ballroom. It'll be taken in there to-morrow morning and the electricians will work on it in the afternoon."

" I heard from Lady Pounser just now," said Mrs. Braxton. " She's bringing six over, that'll make seventy-four; only two refusals. The presents are arriving this afternoon."

They discussed the party discursively over the cutlets and Peach Melba and soon after lunch walked across to the barn. Mr. Braxton waved to Curtis, who was examining a new tractor in the garage fifty yards away, and he came over.

Mrs. Braxton looked the tree over and was graciously delighted with it, but remarked that the pot could have done with another coat of paint. She pointed to several streaks, rust-coloured, running through the green. " Of course it won't show when it's wrapped, but they didn't do a very good job."

Curtis leant down. " They certainly didn't," he answered irritably. " I'll see to it. I think it's spilled over from the soil; that copse is on a curious patch of red sand—there are some at Frilford too. When we pulled it up I noticed the roots were stained a dark crimson." He put his hand down and scraped at the stains with his thumb. He seemed a shade puzzled.

"It shall have another coat at once," he said. "What did you think of Lampson and Colletts' scheme for the barn?"

"Quite good," replied Mrs. Braxton, "but the sketches for the chains are too fancy."

"I agree," said Curtis, who usually did so in the case of unessentials; reserving his tactful vetoes for the others.

The Great Barn was by far the most æsthetically satisfying, as it was the oldest feature of the Hall buildings; it was vast, exquisitely proportioned, and mellow. That could hardly be said of the house itself, which the 4th Baron of Abingdale had rebuilt on the cinders of its predecessors in 1752.

This nobleman had travelled abroad extensively and returned with most enthusiastic, grandiose and indigestible ideas of architecture. The result was a gargantuan piece of rococo-jocoso which only an entirely humourless pedant could condemn. It contained forty-two bedrooms and eighteen reception rooms—so Mrs. Braxton had made it at the last recount. But Mr. Braxton had not repeated with the interiors the errors of the 4th Baron. He'd briefed the greatest expert in Europe, with the result that the interior was quite tasteful and sublimely comfortable.

"Ugh!" he exclaimed, as they stepped out into the air, "it *is* getting nippy!"

"Yes," said Curtis, "there's a nor'-easter blowing up—may be snow for Christmas."

On getting back to the house Mrs. Braxton went into a huddle with butler and housekeeper and Mr. Braxton retired to his study for a doze. But instead his mind settled on Lucky's Grove. When he'd first seen it again after buying the estate, it seemed as if fifty years had rolled away, and he realised that Abingdale was far more summed up to him in the little copse than in the gigantic barracks two miles away. At once he felt at home again. Yet, just as when he'd been a small boy, the emotion the Grove had aroused in him had been sharply tinged with awe, so it had been now, half a century later. He still had a sneaking dread of it. How precisely he could see it, glowing darkly in the womb of the fire before him, standing starkly there in the centre of the big, fallow field, a perfect circle ; and first, a ring of holm-oaks and, facing east, a breach therein to the larches and past them on the west a gap to the yews. It had always required a tug at his courage—not always forthcoming—to pass through them and face the mighty Scotch fir, rearing up its great bole from the grass mound. And when he stood before it, he'd always known an odd longing to fling himself down and—well, worship—it was the only word—the towering tree. His father had told him his forebears had done that very thing, but always when alone and at certain seasons of the year ; and that no bird or beast was ever seen there. A lot of traditional nonsense, no doubt, but he himself had absorbed the spirit of the place and knew it would be always so.

One afternoon in late November, a few weeks after they had moved in, he'd gone off alone in the drowsing misty dusk ; and when he'd reached the holm-oak bastion and seen the great tree surrounded by its sentinels, he'd known again that quick turmoil of confused emotions. As he'd walked slowly toward it, it had seemed to quicken and be aware of his coming. As he passed the shallow grassy fosse and entered the oak ring he felt there was something he ought to say, some greeting, password or prayer. It was the most aloof, silent little place under the sun, and oh, so old. He'd tiptoed past the larches and faced the barrier of yews. He'd stood there for a long musing minute, tingling with the sensation that he was being watched and regarded. At length he stepped forward and stood before the God—that mighty word came abruptly and unforeseen—and he felt a wild desire to fling himself down on the mound and do obeisance. And then he'd hurried home. As he recalled all this most vividly and minutely, he was seized with a sudden gust of uncontrollable anger at the thought of the desecration of the grove. He knew now that if he'd had the slightest idea of Curtis's purpose he'd have resisted and opposed it. It was too late now. He realised he'd " worked himself up " rather absurdly. What could it matter! He was still a superstitious bumpkin at heart. Anyway it was no fault of Curtis. It was the finest Christmas tree anyone could hope for, and the whole thing was too nonsensical for words. The general tone of these cadentic conclusions did not quite accurately represent his thoughts—a very rare failing with Mr. Braxton.

About dinner-time the blizzard set furiously in, and the snow was lying.

"Chains on the cars to-morrow," Mrs. Braxton told the head chauffeur.

"Boar's Hill'll be a beggar," thought that person.

Mr. and Mrs. Braxton dined early, casually examined the presents, and went to bed. Mr. Braxton was asleep at once as usual, but was awakened by the beating of a blind which had slipped its moorings. Reluctantly he got out of bed and went to fix it. As he was doing so he became conscious of the frenzied hysterical barking of a dog. The sound, muffled by the gale, came, he judged, from the barn. He believed the underkeeper kept his whippet there. Scared by the storm, he supposed, and returned to bed.

The morning was brilliantly fine and cold, but the snowfall had been heavy.

"I heard a dog howling in the night, Perkins," said Mr. Braxton to the butler at breakfast; "Drake's, I imagine. What's the matter with it?"

"I will ascertain, sir," replied Perkins.

"It *was* Drake's dog," he announced a little later. "Apparently something alarmed the animal, for when Drake went to let it out this morning, it appeared to be extremely frightened. When the barn door was opened, it took to its heels and, although Drake pursued it, it jumped into the river and Drake fears it was drowned."

"Um," said Mr. Braxton, "must have been the storm; whippets are nervous dogs."

"So I understand, sir."

"Drake was so fond of it," said Mrs. Braxton, "though it always looked so naked and shivering to me."

"Yes, madam," agreed Perkins, "it had that appearance."

Soon after, Mr. Braxton sauntered out into the blinding glitter. Curtis came over from the garage. He was heavily muffled up.

"They've got chains on all the cars," he said. "Very seasonable and all that, but farmers have another word for it." His voice was thick and hoarse.

"Yes," said Mr. Braxton. "You're not looking very fit."

"Not feeling it. Had to get up in the night. Thought I heard someone trying to break into the house; thought I saw him, too."

"Indeed," said Mr. Braxton. "Did you see what he was like?"

"No," replied Curtis uncertainly. "It was snowing like the devil. Anyway, I got properly chilled to the marrow, skipping around in my nightie."

"You'd better get to bed," said Mr. Braxton solicitously. He had affection and a great respect for Curtis.

"I'll stick it out to-day and see how I feel to-morrow. We're going to get the tree across in a few minutes. Can I borrow the two footmen? I want another couple of pullers and haulers."

Mr. Braxton consented, and went off on his favourite little stroll across the sparkling meadows to the river and the pool where the big trout set their cunning noses to the stream.

Half an hour later Curtis had mobilised his scratch team of sleeve-rolled assistants and, with Perkins steering and himself braking, they got to grips with the tree and bore it like a camouflaged battering ram towards the ballroom, which occupied the left centre of the frenetic frontage on the ground floor. There was a good deal of bumping and boring and genial blasphemy before the tree was manœuvred into the middle of the room and levered by rope and muscle into position. As it came up its pinnacle just cleared the ceiling. Sam, a cow-man, whose ginger mop had been buried in the foliage for some time, exclaimed tartly as he slapped the trunk, "There ye are, ye old sod! Thanks for the scratches on me mug, ye old——"

The next moment he was lying on his back, a livid weal across his right cheek.

This caused general merriment, and even Perkins permitted himself a spectral smile. There was more astonishment than pain on the face of Sam. He stared at the tree in a humble way for a moment, like a chastised and guilty dog, and then slunk from the room. The merriment of the others died away.

"More spring in these branches than you'd think," said Curtis to Perkins.

"No doubt, sir, that is due to the abrupt release of the tension," replied Perkins scientifically.

"The "Families" met at Paddington and travelled down together, so at five o'clock three car-loads drew up at the Hall. There were Jack and Mary with Paddy aged eight, Walter and Pamela with Jane and Peter, seven and five respectively, and George and Gloria with Gregory and Phyllis, ten and eight.

Jack and Walter were sons of the house. They were much of a muchness, burly, handsome and as dominating as their sire; a fine pair of commercial kings, entirely capable rulers, but just lacking that something which founds dynasties. Their wives conformed equally to the social type to which they belonged, good-lookers, smart dressers, excellent wives and mothers; but rather coolly colourless, spiritually. Their offspring were "charming children", flawless products of the English matrix, though Paddy showed signs of some obstreperous originality. "George" was the Honourable George, Calvin, Roderick, etcetera Penables, and Gloria was Mr. and Mrs. Braxton's only daughter. George had inherited half a million and had started off at twenty-four to be something big in the City. In a sense he achieved his ambition, for two years later he was generally reckoned the biggest "Something" in the City, from which he then withdrew, desperately clutching his last hundred thousand and vowing lachrymose repentance. He had kept his word and his wad, hunted and shot six days a week in the winter, and spent most of the summer wrestling with the two dozen devils in his golf bag. According to current jargon he was the complete extrovert, but what a relief are such, in spite of the pitying shrugs of those who for ever are peering into the septic recesses of their souls.

Gloria had inherited some of her father's force. She was rather overwhelmingly primed with energy and pep for her opportunities of releasing it. So she was always rather pent up and explosive, though maternity had kept the pressure down. She was dispassionately fond of George who had presented her with a nice little title and aristocratic background and two "charming children." Phyllis gave promise of such extreme beauty that, beyond being the cynosure of every press-camera's eye, and making a resounding match, no more was to be expeected of her. Gregory, however, on the strength of some artistic precocity and a violent temper was already somewhat prematurely marked down as a genius to be.

Such were the " Families."

During the afternoon four engineers arrived from one of the Braxton factories to fix up the lighting of the tree. The fairy lamps for this had been specially designed and executed for the occasion. Disney figures had been grafted upon them and made to revolve by an ingenious mechanism; the effect being to give the tree, when illuminated, an aspect of whirling life meant to be very cheerful and pleasing.

Mr. Braxton happened to see these electricians departing in their lorry and noticed one of them had a bandaged arm and a rather white face. He asked Perkins what had happened.

" A slight accident, sir. A bulb burst and burnt him in some manner. But the injury is, I understand, not of a very serious nature."

" He looked a bit white."

" Apparently, sir, he got a fright, a shock of some kind, when the bulb exploded."

After dinner the grown-ups went to the ballroom. Mr. Braxton switched on the mechanism and great enthusiasm was shown. " Won't the kiddies love it," said George, grinning at the kaleidoscope. " Look at the Big Bad Wolf. He looks so darn realistic I'm not sure I'd give him a ' U ' certificate."

" It's almost frightening," said Pamela, " they look incredibly real. Daddie, you really are rather bright, darling."

It was arranged that the work of decoration should be tackled on the morrow and finished on Christmas Eve.

" All the presents have arrived," said Mrs. Braxton, " and are being unpacked. But I'll explain about them to-morrow."

They went back to the drawing-room. Presently Gloria puffed and remarked: " Papa, aren't you keeping the house rather too hot?"

" I noticed the same thing," said Mrs. Braxton.

Mr. Braxton walked over to a thermometer on the wall. " You're right," he remarked, " seventy." He rang the bell.

" Perkins," he asked, " who's on the furnace?"

"Churchill, sir."

"Well, he's overdoing it. It's seventy. Tell him to get it back to fifty-seven."

Perkins departed and returned shortly after.

"Churchill informs me he has damped down and cannot account for the increasing warmth, sir."

"Tell him to get it back to fifty-seven at once," rapped Mr. Braxton.

"Very good, sir."

"Open a window," said Mrs. Braxton.

"It's snowing again, madam."

"Never mind."

"My God" exclaimed Mary, when she and Jack went up to bed. "That furnace man is certainly stepping on it. Open all the windows."

A wild flurry of snow beat against the curtains.

Mr. Braxton did what he very seldom did, woke up in the early hours. He awoke sweating from a furtive and demoralising dream. It had seemed to him that he had been crouching down in the fosse round Lucky's Grove and peering beneath the holm-oaks, and that there had been activity of a sort vaguely to be discerned therein, some quick, shadowy business. He knew a very tight terror at the thought of being detected at this spying, but he could not wrench himself away. That was all, and he awoke still trembling and troubled. No wonder he'd had such a nightmare, the room seemed like a stokehold. He went to the windows and flung another open, and as he did so glanced out. His room looked over the rock garden and down the path to the maze. Something moving just outside it caught his eye. He thought he knew what it was, that big Alsatian which had been sheep-worrying in the neighbourhood. What an enormous brute! Or was it just because it was outlined against the snow? It vanished suddenly, apparently into the maze. He'd organise a hunt for it after Christmas; if the snow lay, it should be easy to track.

The first thing he did after breakfast was to send for Churchill, severely reprimand him and threaten him with dismissal from his ship. That person was almost tearfully insistent that he had obeyed orders and kept his jets low. "I can't make it out, sir. It's got no right to be as 'ot as what it is."

"That's nonsense!" said Mr. Braxton. "The system has been perfected and cannot take charge, as you suggest. See to it. You don't want me to get an engineer down, do you?"

"No, sir."

"That's enough. Get it to fifty-seven and keep it there."

Shortly after, Mrs. Curtis rang up to say her husband was quite ill with a temperature and that the doctor was coming. Mr. Braxton asked her to ring him again after he'd been.

During the morning the children played in the snow. After a pitched battle in which the girls lost their tempers, Gregory organised the erection of a snow-man. He designed, the others fetched the material. He knew he had a reputation for brilliance to maintain, and he produced something Epsteinish, huge and squat. The other children regarded it with little enthusiasm, but, being Gregory, they supposed it must be admired. When it was finished Gregory wandered off by himself while the others went in to dry. He came in a little late for lunch, during which he was silent and preoccupied. Afterwards the grown-ups sallied forth.

"Let's see your snow-man, Greg," said Gloria, in a mother-of-genius tone.

"It isn't all his, we helped," said Phyllis, voicing a point of view which was to have many echoes in the coming years.

"Why, he's changed it!" exclaimed a chorus two minutes later.

"What an ugly thing!" exclaimed Mary, rather pleased at being able to say so with conviction.

Gregory had certainly given his imagination its head, for now the squat, inert trunk was topped by a big wolf's head with open jaw and ears snarlingly laid back, surprisingly well modelled. Trailing behind it was a coiled, serpentine tail.

"Whatever gave you the idea for that?" asked Jack.

Usually Gregory was facile and eloquent in explaining his inspiration, but this time he refused to be drawn, bit his lip and turned away.

There was a moment's silence and then Gloria said with convincing emphasis, "I think it's wonderful, Greg!"

And then they all strolled off to examine the pigs and the poultry and the Suffolk punches.

They had just got back for tea when the telephone rang in Mr. Braxton's study. It was Mrs. Curtis. The patient was no better and Doctor Knowles had seemed rather worried, and so on. So Mr. Braxton rang up the doctor.

"I haven't diagnosed his trouble yet," he said. "And I'm going to watch him carefully and take a blood-test if he's not better to-morrow. He has a temperature of a hundred and two, but no other superficial symptoms, which is rather peculiar. By the way, one of your cow-men, Sam Colley, got a nasty wound on the face yesterday and shows signs of blood poisoning. I'm considering sending him to hospital. Some of your other men have been in to see me—quite a little outbreak of illness since Tuesday. However, I hope we'll have a clean bill again soon. I'll keep you informed about Curtis."

Mr. Braxton was one of those incredible people who never have a day's illness—till their first and last. Consequently his conception of disease was unimaginative and mechanical. If one of his more essential human machines was running unsatisfactorily, there was a machine-mender called a doctor whose business it was to ensure that all the plug leads were attached firmly and that the manifold drainpipe was not blocked. But he found himself beginning to worry about Curtis, and this little epidemic amongst his henchmen affected him disagreeably—there was something disturbing to his spirit about it. But just what and why, he couldn't analyse and decide.

After dinner, with the children out of the way, the business of decorating the tree was begun. The general scheme had been sketched out and coloured by one of the Braxton display experts and the company consulted this as they worked, which they did rather silently; possibly Mr. Braxton's palpable anxiety somewhat affected them.

Pamela stayed behind after the others had left the ballroom to put some finishing touches to her section of the tree. When she rejoined the others she was looking rather white and tight-lipped. She said good-night a shade abruptly and went to her room. Walter, a very, very good husband, quickly joined her.

"Anything the matter, old girl?" he asked anxiously.

"Yes," replied Pamela. "I'm frightened."

"Frightened! What d'you mean?"

"You'll think it's all rot, but I'll tell you. When you'd all left the ballroom, I suddenly felt very uneasy—you know the sort of feeling when one keeps on looking round and can't concentrate. However, I stuck at it. I was a little way up the steps when I heard a sharp hiss from above me in the tree. I jumped back to the floor and looked up; now, of course, you won't believe me, but the trunk of the tree was moving—it was like the coils of a snake writhing upward, and there was something at the top of the tree, horrid-looking, peering at me. I know you won't believe me."

Walter didn't, but he also didn't know what to make of it. "I know what happened!" he improvised lightly. "You'd been staring in at that trunk for nearly two hours and you got dizzy—like staring at the sun on the sea; and that snow dazzle this afternoon helped it. You've heard of snow-blindness—something like that, it still echoes from the retina or whatever . . ."

"You think it might have been that?"

"I'm sure of it."

"And that horrible head?"

"Well, as George put it rather brightly, I don't think some of those figures on the lamps should get a 'U' certificate. There's the wolf to which he referred, and the witch."

"Which witch?" laughed Pamela a little hysterically. "I didn't notice one."

"I did. I was working just near it, at least, I suppose it's meant to be a witch. A figure in black squinting round from behind a tree. As a matter of fact fairies never seemed all fun and frolic to me, there's often something diabolical about them—or rather casually cruel. Disney knows that."

"Yes, there is," agreed Pamela. "So you think that's all there was to it?"

"I'm certain. One's eyes can play tricks on one."

"Yes," said Pamela, "I know what you mean, as if they saw what one knew wasn't there or was different. Though who would 'one' be then?"

"Oh, don't ask me that sort of question!" laughed Walter. "Probably Master Gregory will be able to tell you in a year or two."

"He's a nice little boy, really," protested Pamela. "Gloria just spoils him and it's natural."

"I know he is, it's not his fault, but they will *force* him. Look at that snow-man—and staying behind to do it. A foul-looking thing!"

"Perhaps his eyes played funny tricks with him," said Pamela.

"What d'you mean by that?"

"I don't know why I said it," said Pamela, frowning. "Sort of echo, I suppose. Let's go to bed."

Walter kissed her gently but fervently, as he loved her. He was a one-lady's-man and had felt a bit nervous about her for a moment or two.

Was the house a little cooler? wondered Mr. Braxton, as he was undressing, or was it that he was getting more used to it? He was now convinced there was something wrong with the installation; he'd get an expert down. Meanwhile they must stick it. He yawned, wondered how Curtis was, and switched off the light.

Soon all the occupants were at rest and the great house swinging silently against the stars. Should have been at rest, rather, for one and all recalled that night with reluctance and dread. Their dreams were harsh and unhallowed, yet oddly enough related, being concerned with dim, uncertain and yet somehow urgent happenings in and around the house, as though some thing or things were stirring while they slept and communicated their motions to their dreaming consciousness. They awoke tired with a sense of unaccountable malaise.

Mrs. Curtis rang up during breakfast and her voice revealed her distress. Timothy was delirious and much worse. The doctor was coming at 10.30.

Mr. and Mrs. Braxton decided to go over there, and sent for the car. Knowles was waiting just outside the house when they arrived.

"He's very bad," he said quietly. "I've sent for two nurses and Sir Arthur Galley; I want another opinion. Has he had some trouble with a tree?"

"Trouble with a tree!" said Mr. Braxton, his nerves giving a flick.

"Yes, it's probably just a haphazard, irrational idea of delirium, but he continually fusses about some tree."

"How bad is he?" asked Mrs. Braxton.

The doctor frowned. "I wish I knew. I'm fairly out of my

depth. He's keeping up his strength fairly well, but he can't go on like this."

"As bad as that!" exclaimed Mr. Braxton.

"I'm very much afraid so. I'm anxiously awaiting Sir Arthur's verdict. By the way, that cow-man is very ill indeed; I'm sending him into hospital."

"What happened to him?" asked Mr. Braxton, absently, his mind on Curtis.

"Apparently a branch of your Christmas tree snapped back at him and struck his face. Blood-poisoning set in almost at once."

Mr. Braxton felt that tremor again, but merely nodded.

"I was just wondering if there might be some connection between the two, that Curtis is blaming himself for the accident. Seems an absurd idea, but judging from his ravings he appears to think he is lashed to some tree and that the great heat he feels comes from it."

They went into the house and did their best to comfort and reassure Mrs. Curtis, instructed Knowles to ring up as soon as Sir Arthur's verdict was known, and then drove home.

The children had just come in from playing in the snow.

"Grandpa, the snow-man's melted," said Paddy, "did it thaw in the night?"

"Must have done," replied Mr. Braxton, forcing a smile.

"Come and look, Grandpa," persisted Paddy, "there's nothing left of it."

"Grandpa doesn't want to be bothered," said Mary, noticing his troubled face.

"I'll come," said Mr. Braxton. When he reached the site of the snow-man his thoughts were still elsewhere, but his mind quickly refocused itself, for he was faced with something a little strange. Not a vestige of the statue remained, though the snow was frozen crisp and crunched hard beneath their feet; and yet that snow-man was completely obliterated and where it had stood was a circle of bare, brown grass.

"It must have thawed in the night and then frozen again," he said uncertainly.

"Then why——" began Paddy.

"Don't bother Grandpa," said Mary sharply. "He's told you what happened."

They wandered off towards the heavy, hurrying river.

"Are those dog-paw marks?" asked Phyllis.

That reminded Mr. Braxton. He peered down. "Yes," he replied. "And I bet they're those of that brute of an Alsation; it must be a colossal beast."

"And it must have paws like a young bear," laughed Mary. "They're funny dogs, sort of Jekyll-and-Hydes. I rather adore them."

"You wouldn't adore this devil. He's all Hyde." (I'm in the wrong mood for these festivities, he thought irritably.)

During the afternoon George and Walter took the kids to a cinema in Oxford; the others finished the decoration of the tree.

The presents, labelled with the names of their recipients, were arranged on tables round the room and the huge cracker, ten feet long and forty inches in circumference, was placed on its gaily decorated trestle near the tree. Just as the job was finished, Mary did a three-quarters faint, but was quickly revived with brandy.

"It's the simply ghastly heat in the house!" exclaimed Gloria, who was not looking too grand herself. "The installation must be completely diseased. Ours always works perfectly." Mary had her dinner in bed and Jack came up to her immediately he had finished his.

"How are you feeling, darling?" he asked.

"Oh, I'm all right."

"It *was* the heat, of course?"

"Oh, yes," replied Mary with rather forced emphasis.

"Scared you a bit, going off like that?" suggested Jack, regarding her rather sharply.

"I'm quite all right, thank you," said Mary in the tone she always adopted when she'd had enough of a subject. "I'd like to rest. Switch off the light."

But when Jack had gone, she didn't close her eyes, but lay on her back staring up at the faint outline of the ceiling. She frowned and lightly chewed the little finger of her left hand, a habit of hers when unpleasantly puzzled. Mary, like most people of strong character and limited imagination, hated to be puzzled. Everything, she considered, ought to have a simple explanation if one tried hard enough to find it. But how could one explain this odd thing that had happened to her? Besides the grandiose gifts on the tables which bore a number, as well as the recipient's name, a small present for everyone was hung on the tree. This also bore a number, the same one as the lordly gift, so easing the Braxtons' task of handing these out to the right people. Mary had just fixed Curtis's label to a cigarette lighter and tied it on the tree when it swung on its silk thread, so that the back of the card was visible; and on it was this inscription: "Died, December 25th, 1938." It spun away again and back and the inscription was no longer there.

Now Mary came of a family which rather prided itself on being unimaginative. Her father had confined his flights of fancy to the Annual Meeting of his Shareholders, while, to her mother, imagination and mendacity were at least first cousins. So Mary could hardly credit the explanation that, being remotely worried about Mr. Curtis, she had subconsciously concocted that sinister sentence. On the other hand she knew poor Mr. Curtis was very ill and, therefore, perhaps, if her brain had played that malign little trick on her, it might have done so in "tombstone writing."

This was a considerable logical exercise for Mary, the effort tired her, the impression began to fade and she started wondering how much longer Jack was going to sit up. She dozed off and there, as if flashed on the screen "inside her head," was "Died, December 25th, 1938." This, oddly enough, completely reassured her. There was "nothing there" this time. There had been nothing that other time. She'd been very weak and imaginative even to think otherwise.

While she was deciding this, Dr. Knowles rang up. "Sir Arthur has just been," he said. "And I'm sorry to say he's pessimistic. He says Curtis is very weak."

"But what's the matter with him?" asked Mr. Braxton urgently.

"He doesn't know. He calls it P.U.O., which really means nothing."

"But what's it stand for?"

"Pyrexia unknown origin. There are some fevers which cannot be described more precisely."

"How ill is he really?"

"All I can say is, we must hope for the best."

"My God!" exclaimed Mr. Braxton. "When's Sir Arthur coming again?"

"At eleven to-morrow. I'll ring you up after he's been."

Mr. Braxton excused himself and went to his room. Like many men of his dominating, sometimes ruthless type, he was capable of an intensity of feeling, anger, resolution, desire for revenge, but also affection and sympathy, unknown to more superficially Christian and kindly souls. He was genuinely attached to Curtis and his wife and very harshly and poignantly moved by this news which, he realised, could hardly have been worse. He would have to exercise all his will power if he was to sleep.

If on the preceding night the rest of the sleepers had been broken by influences which had insinuated themselves into their dreams, that which caused the night of that Christmas Eve to be unforgettable was the demoniacal violence of the elements. The north-easter had been waxing steadily all the evening and by midnight reached hurricane force, driving before it an almost impenetrable wall of snow. Not only so, but continually all through the night the wall was enflamed, and the roar of the hurricane silenced, by fearful flashes of lightning and raffales of thunder. The combination was almost intolerably menacing. As the great house shook from the gale and trembled at the blasts and the windows blazed with strange polychromatic balls of flame, all were tense and troubled. The children fought or succumbed to their terror according to their natures; their parents soothed and reassured them.

Mr. Braxton was convinced the lightning conductors were struck three times within ten minutes, and he could imagine them recoiling from the mighty impacts and seething from the terrific charges. Not till a dilatory, chaotic dawn staggered up the sky did the storm temporarily lull. For a time the sky cleared and the frost came hard. It was a yawning and haggard company which assembled at breakfast. But determined efforts were made to engender a communal cheerfulness. Mr. Braxton did his best to contribute his quota of seasonable bonhomie, but his mind was plagued by thoughts of Curtis. Before the meal was finished the vicar rang up to say the church tower had been struck and almost demolished, so there could be no services. It rang again to say that Brent's farmhouse had been burnt to the ground.

While the others went off to inspect the church Mr. Braxton remained in the study. Presently Knowles rang to say Sir Arthur had been and pronounced Curtis weaker, but his condition was not quite hopeless. One of the most ominous symptoms was the violence of the delirium. Curtis appeared to be in great terror and sedatives had no effect.

"How's that cow-man?" asked Mr. Braxton.

"He died in the night, I'm sorry to say."

Whereupon Mr. Braxton broke one of his strictest rules by drinking a very stiff whisky with very little soda.

Christmas dinner was tolerably hilarious, and after it, the children, bulging and incipiently bilious, slept some of it off, while their elders put the final touches to the preparations for the party.

In spite of the weather, not a single "cry-off" was telephoned. There was a good reason for this; Mr. Braxton's entertainments were justly famous.

So from four-thirty onwards the "Cream of North Berkshire Society" came ploughing through the snow to the Hall; Lady Pounser and party bringing up the rear in her heirloom Rolls which was dribbling steam from its ancient and aristocratic beak. A tea of teas, not merely a high-tea, an Everest tea, towering, sky-scraping, was then attacked by the already stuffed juveniles who, by the end of it, were almost livid with repletion, finding even the efforts of cracker-pulling almost beyond them.

They were then propelled into the library where rows of chairs had been provided for them. There was a screen at one end of the room, a projector at the other. Mr. Braxton had provided one of his famous surprises! The room was darkened and on the screen was flashed the sentence: "*The North Berks News Reel.*"

During the last few weeks Mr. Braxton had had a sharp-witted and discreetly furtive camera-man at work shooting some of the guests while busy about their more or less lawful occasions.

For example, there was a sentence from a speech by Lord Gallen, the Socialist Peer: "It is a damnable and calculated lie for our opponents to suggest we aim at a preposterous and essentially *inequitable* equalisation on income——" And then there was His Lordship just entering his limousine, and an obsequious footman, rug in hand, holding the door open for him.

His Lordship's laughter was raucous and vehement, though he *would* have liked to have said a few words in rebuttal.

And there was Lady Pounser's Rolls, locally known as " the hippogriffe," stuck in a snow-drift and enveloped in steam, with the caption, " Oh, Mr. Mercury, *do* give me a start!" And other kindly, slightly sardonic japes at the expense of the North Berks Cream.

The last scene was meant as an appropriate prelude to the climax of the festivities. It showed Curtis and his crew digging up the tree from Lucky's Grove. Out they came from the holm-oaks straining under their load, but close observers noticed there was one who remained behind, standing menacing and motionless, a very tall, dark, brooding figure. There came a blinding lightning flash which seemed to blaze sparking round the room, and a fearsome metallic bang. The storm had returned with rasping and imperious salute.

The lights immediately came on and the children were marshalled to the ballroom. As they entered and saw the high tree shining there and the little people so lively upon its branches a prolonged " O—h!" of astonishment was extorted from the blasé brats. But there was another wave of flame against the windows which rattled wildly at the ensuing roar, and the cries of delight were tinged with terror. And, indeed, the hard, blue glare flung a sinister glow on the tree and its whirling throng.

The grown-ups hastened to restore equanimity and, forming rings of children, circled round the tree.

Presently Mrs. Braxton exclaimed: " Now then, look for your names on the cards and see what Father Christmas has brought you."

Though hardly one of the disillusioned infants retained any belief in that superannuated Deliverer of Goods, the response was immediate. For they had sharp ears which had eagerly absorbed the tales of Braxton munificence. At the same time it was noticeable that some approached the tree with diffidence, almost reluctance, and started back as a livid flare broke against the window-blinds and the dread peals shook the streaming snow from the eaves.

Mary had just picked up little Angela Rayner so that she could reach her card, when the child screamed and pulled away her hand.

"The worm!" she cried, and a thick, black-grey squirming maggot fell from her fingers to the floor and writhed away. George, who was near, put his shoe on it with a squish.

One of the Pounser tribe, whose card was just below the Big Bad Wolf, refused to approach it. No wonder, thought Walter, for it looked horribly hunting and alive. There were other mischances too. The witch behind the sombre tree seemed to pounce out at Clarissa Balder, so she tearfully complained, and Gloria had to pull off her card for her. Of course Gregory was temperamental, seeming to stare at a spot just below the taut peak of the tree, as if mazed and entranced. But the presents were wonderful and more than worth the small ordeal of finding one's card and pretending not to be frightened when the whole room seemed full of fiery hands and the thunder cracked against one's ear-drums and shook one's teeth. Easy to be afraid!

At length the last present had been bestowed and it was time for the *pièce de résistance*, the pulling of the great cracker. Long, silken cords streamed from each end with room among them for fifty chubby fists, and a great surprise inside, for sure. The languid, uneasy troops were lined up at each end and took a grip on the silken cords.

At that moment a footman came in and told Mr. Braxton he was wanted on the telephone.

Filled with foreboding he went to his study. He heard the voice of Knowles——

"I'm afraid I have very bad news for you. . . ."

The chubby fists gripped the silken cords.

"Now pull!" cried Mrs. Braxton.

The opposing teams took the strain.

A leaping flash and a blasting roar. The children were hurled, writhing and screaming over each other.

Up from the middle of the cracker leapt a rosy shaft of flame which, as it reached the ceiling, seemed to flatten its peak so that it resembled a great snake of fire which turned and hurled itself against the tree in a blinding embrace. There was a fierce sustained "Hiss," the tree flamed like a torch, and all the fairy globes upon it burst and splintered. And then the roaring torch cast itself down amongst the screaming chaos. For a moment the great pot, swathed in green, was a carmine cauldron and its paint streamed like blood upon the floor. Then the big room was a dream of fire and those within it driven wildly from its heat.

Phil Tangler, whose farmhouse, on the early slopes of Missen Rise, overlooked both Lucky's Grove and the Hall, solemnly declared that at 7.30 on Christmas Day, 1938, he was watching from a window and marvelling at the dense and boiling race of snow, the bitter gale, and the wicked flame and fury of the storm, when he saw a huge fist of fire form a rift in the cloud-rack, a fist with two huge blazing fingers, one of which speared down on the Hall, another touched and kindled the towering fir in Lucky's Grove, as though saluting it. Five minutes later he was racing through the hurricane to join in a vain night-long fight to save the Hall, already blazing from stem to stern.

HOUSEBOUND

R. Chetwynd-Hayes

He, if indeed that which remained of Charlie Wheatland could be designated as he, was most happy when he was in the woodwork. The wainscoting, the picture rails, the large wardrobe, the dressing-table, and sometimes the floorboards; the coarse grained pine, the tough oak, enabled him to spread out, to become as water on blotting paper, to dim down his never sleeping consciousness to a gentle twilight. The walls were not so kind, the bricks and plaster did not absorb him so easily, and the thoughts of the room's occupants clung to the faded wallpaper like flies on a hot day. A certain measure of peace was to be found during the daylight hours when the bedroom was empty, and he could roll out across the woodwork in soft invisible waves and not be disturbed by the mental vibrations of living people. The man did not disturb him much, although his harsh passions sometimes seared Charlie's consciousness like a white hot knife, but the woman was a magnet that drew him towards her and some form of grotesque life. Charlie hated and feared her; the powerful raw power reached out tentacles that found him no matter where he might hide. Like a mouse chased by a cat he fled before them, sometimes drawing himself up into a tight ball, at others, spreading himself over every square inch of room and furniture, quelling the urge to submit and allow the power to make of him what it would. "I want to be nothing," the sobbing cry sometimes made itself heard in the form of a deep sigh, and the woman would pause in the midst of bed-making and look fearfully over one shoulder, "I want to forget, to sleep—to sleep."

"Surely you know," said Mrs. Hardcastle sipping her tea in a most ladylike fashion, "I mean the estate agent should have told you before actually selling you the house."

"Not a word," Celia Cooper breathed deeply and wondered

when the woman would leave. She knew that her visitor's bright little eyes were valuing the furniture to the exact penny, and mentally noting her personal defects as to dress and hair style. "You see we were so pleased to get finally settled, you know what it's like trying to find a decent house at a reasonable price?"

"Do I not, dear," Mrs. Hardcastle waved her free hand and with practised skill balanced the tea cup with the other. "The trouble Arthur and I had before we found 'Quiet Haven,' but all said and done, the man should have told you."

"What is the story?" Celia did her best to sound interested, but she could imagine what was coming. A previous tenant who had loved well but unwisely; an outwardly respectable clerk who had absconded with the contents of his employer's safe; or perhaps something more sordid. She had long since discovered that the sins and misfortunes of the few give much joy to the many.

"My dear," Mrs. Hardcastle's eyes shone with pleasurable horror, "a man was shot dead in this house, in your front bedroom."

Celia Cooper did not move, refused to allow a single muscle to betray her, but the naked fear was now out in the open. She said calmly:

"How terrible, was it—murder?"

"Not exactly. It all happened ten years ago, just after this estate was built, I'm surprised you don't remember the details, they were in all the newspapers."

"You forget," Celia managed to smile, "until last month Harold and I had not set foot in England for fifteen years."

"Of course," Mrs. Hardcastle tittered behind her hand, "how silly of me. Well, he was a little crook, the man that was shot, I mean, called Charlie Wheatland, and he held up the bank in the High Street. He shot a clerk who managed to push the alarm button or whatever it is they do push, and made his getaway chased by a police car. They finally got him pinned down in this road, and he took cover in this very house which was empty as the builders had only moved out the previous day. There was a terrific gun battle which lasted for hours, until a police marksman got a bead on him from the house opposite. They found him in your front bedroom with a hole in his head. My dear, you've gone quite pale, I shouldn't have told you, but really, I did think you ought to know."

"Please don't mind me," Celia smiled again, "but it is rather a shock to find out your house was once the scene of a violent death. I gather this notoriety did not stop the house being sold, I mean it hasn't stood empty these past ten years?"

"Good heavens, no," Mrs. Hardcastle put down her cup and started to pull on a pair of black lace gloves, "Mr. and Mrs. Dowsett lived here until Mr. Dowsett was killed in a motor accident. Mind you, Jane did say to me on one occasion she never really felt happy in that front bedroom. But that's to be expected, I mean when one knows what happened there. . . . Oh, how tactless of me, I do hope you won't. . . ."

"I won't give it another thought," lied Celia, "I have no time to spare to worry about ghosts. Must you leave so soon, it has been nice meeting you. . . ."

"Harold," Celia looked at her husband seated on the other side of the dining-room table, "did you know a man had been shot dead in this house?"

Harold Cooper put down his soup spoon and watched his wife with an appreciative eye as she took the plates of roast lamb from the heated food trolley. "Yes, I knew. The chap at the estate agents told me when I bought the place. I didn't see any point in telling you, it might have put you off, and I believe that what the ear doesn't hear, the mind doesn't worry over. Who told you?"

"A neighbour, a Mrs. Hardcastle. She paid me a visit this afternoon, superficially to make my acquaintance, but in reality I suspect to see what we had, and estimate its cost."

"Big mouthed old hussy," Harold grunted. "Well, now you know. I shouldn't let it worry you. Someone was bound to die in the house sooner or later; we shall probably die here ourselves one day. The manner of dying isn't all that important, the main thing is the little rat did die. It's a pity a lot more of his kind don't come to the same end. Shoot the lot, I say, there's too much moddle-coddling of these young thugs."

Celia said: "Yes, dear, you have mentioned the matter on various occasions," and then steered the conversation into more mundane channels until the time came for her to clear the table and wash up in the stainless steel and Formica panelled kitchen. When she had finished her work and hung the wiping up towel on the telescopic towel rail, she returned to the living-room and found Harold watching television, but not she noted with any great interest, for his head was already drooping and it would not be long before he was prone in his seat with fast closed eyes and gaping mouth. Celia turned off the set and took up a book, and every once in a while glanced at her sleeping husband. After twenty-five years of married life together she knew him as well as any one human being knows another; if she were attacked by a gang of thugs he would fight to defend her, even to the sacrifice of his life; if she were in some sort of trouble, no matter how dreadful, he would help her, for Harold was above all a husband, and she was his wife. But supposing she were threatened by a danger inconceivable to his practical turn of mind; if she were now to wake him and cry: "There is a—something in our bedroom, something horrible, wicked and pathetic, that torments me, floods my mind with unspeakable horror, fascinates me, please let us move away from here." He would, after the initial surprise, talk of tonics, rundown, pop along and see the old quack, and if she persisted, his thin lips would set in a straight obstinate line, and he would point out this was a good house in a nice neighbourhood, it suited him, he had done a lot of work on it, and be damned if he was going to move because of her hysteria and imagination. His unimaginative logic would become an iron wall, and if she continued to fight him, something vital in their marriage would die, to be replaced by fear, mistrust and finally hatred. This was one battle she must fight by herself, try to decide what was fact and how much of this terror was due to imagination. Of late Celia had come to believe that there was no such thing as imagination, only fact viewed from different angles; what was life but a series of coloured lights reflected on a white screen.

"Harold," she called softly, "wake up."

"What's the matter?" he started and blinked foolishly, looking like a grey-haired schoolboy, "must have dozed off."

"You'll never sleep to-night," she smiled indulgently, "would you like a hot drink?"

"If you like," he yawned as she rose and went into the kitchen.

She lay beside Harold in the large double bed and listened to the even tempo of his breathing. He slept so deeply, encased in a cocoon of unconsciousness from which it would take five minutes of shaking to rouse him. She tried to keep her thoughts under control and not to let them wander round the darkened room, seeking, prodding, even as a mischievous child might goad a sleeping snake, aware of the danger, but drawn to that danger, like a moth who must fly into a lighted candle.

He had spread himself out, along the wainscoting, over the wardrobe, into the dressing-table; a thin layer of whimpering, hate-streaked fear. Without being aware that she had exerted any effort, Celia found she had driven him out of the dressing-table, made him retreat from the wardrobe; now he flowed up the walls; she knew he hated the walls and pursued him relentlessly, and all the while her body shook with sickening horror. Now came the climax; she must change her tactics, draw him towards the bed and make him become a ball of pulsating life. He came, fighting every inch of the way; but he came, the walls and the woodwork were free, and he was there, on the floor at the foot of the bed. Celia shivered with intense cold as the power drained out of her, but there was no going back; whatever it was that crouched on the floor mingled with the life force that flowed from her body and grew into something tangible, rising slowly into view. The window curtains were drawn back and the top sash was open, for Harold insisted that fresh air was essential in a bedroom, allowing the street lamp to light the room with a soft radiance. He was a black shadow that bore a rough resemblance to a masculine shape; the shoulders appeared to be bowed, a kind of oafish slouch, and Celia thought she could define the pale outlines of a face, but that may have been due to imagination. A whisper came to her, or so she at the time believed, although afterwards it seemed more likely that she translated some mental communication into sound.

"What do you want of me?"

It was then that Celia Cooper came face to face with truth; it came hand in hand with knowledge and stood beside the black shadow, and of the two truth was the more fearful. "*What do you want of me?*" She knew why she had summoned this thing from the woodwork, why week after week she had developed the power, which until they had moved into this house she did not suspect she possessed. Celia Cooper, the placid, commonplace housewife of fifty was akin to Charlie Wheatland who had died in this room ten years ago. At that moment she could only think of the man who slept by her side; could only remember the dreadful boring years, his selfishness, his lack of imagination, his exasperating commonsense; the fact that she had never consciously realised the extent of these shortcomings before, or knew how much she despised, even hated him for them, made this moment all the more terrifying—truth was relentless, more exciting. It was as though she had been blind from birth and now saw for the first time. The fear dropped away like a dark heavy mantle, and a great sense of power flooded her being. Sitting up in bed she pointed to the sleeping form of her husband and cried in a loud voice:

"Kill him, make him as you are—kill him."

The figure moved slowly round the bed, grew more tangible until Celia could have sworn a living man was preparing to obey her command; then she saw the white little face, the blazing black eyes, and screamed with renewed terror:

"No, I didn't mean it."

The figure stopped, turned his face to her, then disintegrated. Celia collapsed back onto her pillow and knew no more until the alarm roused her in the morning.

No one can say he or she is good or virtuous until they have been made to face temptation and found the strength to resist. Celia Cooper had never been tempted before; she never felt the urge to commit adultery; having always been blessed with sufficient money for her simple needs, there was no temptation to steal, and murder was a crime committed by depraved creatures who were beyond a middle class housewife's comprehension. This was still true; Celia could no more have physically murdered her husband than she could have set fire to her own house. But this was different, murder by necromancy was not by the laws of the realm murder at all. Celia fought her temptation; it was a battle that raged minute by minute, hour by hour, day by day, and worst of all night by night. As she lay beside the sleep drunk Harold the urge to summon that vile creature in the woodwork was nigh irresistible. The knowledge that it would obey her will overcame the loathing and terror, and made her realise in full her hatred for Harold, which once it had revealed itself grew rather than diminished as time passed. Celia could feel her character changing in the same way a man who has contracted a fatal disease can watch his body disintegrating, she could do nothing to slow down the process, let alone kill it. She toyed with the idea of running away; but where would she go, what could she do at her time of life? She had neither the ability nor the urge to earn her own living, whereas if Harold were to suddenly die she would find herself in very easy circumstances. His life was insured for a considerable sum, and despite their simple mode of living he had a respectable fortune in gilt edged securities; there was also the widow's pension that the oil company for whom he had worked for over thirty years would pay her. Once this unwanted spouse was safely in the grave she could move far away and live under a golden umbrella.

Perhaps she might have successfully fought her battle, if not for ever, at least for a long time, had she not one afternoon walked into the bedroom and found Charlie Wheatland fully materialised and standing by the window. So accustomed had she grown to living with this horror, she felt no fear, only surprise as to how he came to be there. She had not consciously summoned him, and could only suppose that having once been called up he had waxed strong on his own account, or fed surreptitiously on her power, possibly while she slept. He turned slowly, his white face a mask of fear and hate, then whispered:

"When?"

Celia stood perfectly still and tried to absorb the knowledge that her eyes witnessed, and at the same time come to terms with the warning bells that were ringing in her brain. Would she be able to control this creature? If he were capable of murdering Harold, what of her? The apparition answered her unspoken question.

"You give me strength, without you I have no substance."

"But," Celia's thoughts were cold as steel, "suppose Harold were to . . . linger?"

Charlie Wheatland's lips did not move but the words came in a low, distinctive whisper.

"Only bad men are housebound."

"But what of me," Celia asked the all-important question, "when my time comes . . .?"

There was a suggestion of a smile on the white face. "Can you not repent—afterwards?"

The last barrier collapsed and Celia breathed a deep sigh of relief, she surrendered completely to the great temptation that had dominated her for weeks, now she could face truth without flinching. Murder could be committed without fear of detection; she wondered how Harold's death would appear; heart failure possibly, and there need be no price to pay. As the phantom said, she could always repent afterwards.

"To-night," she thought the answer to his first question, "must I be present?"

"No." The black eyes glittered with a joyful light. "But you must order me to it."

"I order you to kill my husband."

"No, I cannot kill, only free your husband from his body. Order me to free your husband from his body."

"I order you to free my husband from his body."

Something essential went out of Celia as her mind formed these last words, she would have retained it if that had been possible, but it was too late, the fatal step had been taken, and now she stood face to face with her familiar, and knew that repentance was but a word; she must accept this new world where evil reigned supreme. There was pride in her voice when she said aloud:

"I will send him to you this evening."

She went out closing the bedroom door behind her.

The evening passed much the same as twenty-five years of evenings had passed, only this was the last one. Celia watched Harold eat his steak and kidney pie, served him the college pudding he liked so much, then washed up and put the dishes away neatly in the built-in dresser, and all the time she could feel the presence of the thing that lurked in the bedroom.

Was it still standing by the window, the very window where its body had been destroyed ten years ago? Or was it resting in the woodwork, waiting for her summons; waiting for Harold to walk into the room?

Harold was sleeping in front of the television, his usual evening prelude to the nightly feast of sleeping; soon he would wallow in sleep; not the snorting, gasping sleep that had so often disturbed her rest, but a dignified cold repose that all the alarm clocks in the world would never break.

The hands of the clock slowly made their endless journey round the white dial; the television relayed its canned trivial entertainment, until Celia turned it off. Her hand was gentle as it shook Harold's shoulder, and her voice was that of a kind, indulgent mother.

"Harold, it's time for bed, wake up or you'll never sleep to-night."

"Wassat!" He opened his eyes, blinked and looked at the clock. "Ten o'clock, must have dozed off."

She made the cocoa and sat opposite as he sipped from his cup, talking of what he must do to-morrow, but his words made little impression upon her. She could feel the thing stirring in the room above.

"Time for bed-de-byes," he rose, stretched, then yawned, "coming, old girl?"

"In a moment, you go up, I'll be with you in a moment."

"Right," he walked heavily from the room, "don't be long, must be up bright and early to-morrow."

As he left the room she wanted to cry out, to take him by the hand and run from this house never to return, but even as her mouth opened she felt the power drain out of her. She sank into a chair unable to speak or move a muscle; the thing upstairs was building himself up, gathering strength for the supreme effort. She heard Harold climbing the stairs; he went into the bathroom and after a lapse of time pulled the lavatory chain, there was a roar of cascading water, then he crossed the landing, and opened the bedroom door.

"Forgive me, God, forgive me," Celia was praying in a loud whisper, tears streaming down her face, "forgive me, don't let it happen. . . ."

A loud scream pinned her back against the chair; a cry of

indescribable terror followed by a crash that made the ceiling lamp swing gently from side to side, and light danced with shadows in a mad frenzy of horror. The power flowed back into her limbs, and Celia knew Charlie Wheatland no longer needed her strength, perhaps, this one terrible deed performed, he was now free to descend into the hell from which he had so long been detained, or possibly he was now in some limbo where time and human values were without meaning. Whatever the reason, she could not feel his presence either in the room above or in any part of the house. She sat motionless, trying to accept the fact that Harold lay dead on the bedroom floor, killed by terror and his wife's mad, unsuspected hatred. She could not move, had not the strength or courage to ascend the stairs, only sit and realise that from now onwards she belonged to the damned.

The clock in the hall broke the silence by striking two, and as though this were a signal, Celia heard a sound from the bedroom above. The creak of a loose floorboard, the slightly louder sound of a heavy body climbing to its feet, then a slow tread crossing the carpeted room; slippered feet moving out onto the landing; a banister groaning its protest when a hand pressed upon it, a loose stair rod rattling; a terrible harsh breathing growing louder by the second; Celia knew Harold was coming down. At first she experienced a sense of great relief, he was not dead, she was not a murderess; then she realised the foot treads were not Harold's; the harsh breathing was that of a man who has not breathed for a long time; whatever, whoever was coming down the stairs, it was not Harold.

She could not tear her eyes away from the closed door, for surely approaching it from the other side was a horror that rightfully belonged to some dark valley in Hades, and it was coming in to her. She tried to scream when the door handle turned, for to scream would let out some of the icy fear, but the vocal cords froze and no sound came; she clawed at the chair arms as the door swung slowly open, then became still as a corpse, only her eyes and ears continued to function. The body was Harold's, his face dead white, his arms hanging loosely; but the eyes burned with blazing hate, and the laboured breathing turned into rasping speech as he approached the armchair.

"Why couldn't you leave me alone—there was peace in the woodwork—peace. . . ."

She found her voice and screamed once as the thing moved in, its arms outstretched.

THE SHUTTERED ROOM

H. P. Lovecraft and August Derleth

1

At dusk, the wild, lonely country guarding the approaches to the village of Dunwich in north central Massachusetts seems more desolate and forbidding than it ever does by day. Twilight lends the barren fields and domed hills a strangeness that sets them apart from the country around that area ; it brings to everything a kind of sentient, watchful animosity—to the ancient trees, to the brier-bordered stone walls pressing closely upon the dusty road, to the low marshes with their myriads of fireflies and their incessantly calling whippoorwills vying with the muttering of frogs and the shrill songs of toads, to the sinuous windings of the upper reaches of the Miskatonic flowing among the dark hills seaward, all of which seem to close in upon the traveller as if intent upon holding him fast, beyond all escape.

On his way to Dunwich, Abner Whateley felt all this again, as once in childhood he had felt and run screaming in terror to beg his mother to take him away from Dunwich and Grandfather Luther Whateley. So many years ago! He had lost count of them. It was curious that the country should affect him so, pushing through all the years he had lived since then—the years at the Sorbonne, in Cairo, in London—pushing through all the learning he had assimilated since those early visits to grim old Grandfather Whateley in his ancient house attached to the mill along the Miskatonic, the country of his childhood, coming back now out of the mists of time as were it but yesterday that he had visited his kinfolk.

They were all gone now—Mother, Grandfather Whateley, Aunt Sarey, whom he had never seen but only knew to be living somewhere in that old house—the loathsome cousin Wilbur and his terrible twin brother few had ever known before his frightful death on top of Sentinel Hill. But

Dunwich, he saw as he drove through the cavernous covered bridge, had not changed; its main street lay under the looming mound of Round Mountain, its gambrel roofs as rotting as ever, its houses deserted, the only store still in the broken-steepled church, over everything the unmistakable aura of decay.

He turned off the main street and followed a rutted road up along the river, until he came within sight of the great old house with the mill wheel on the river-side. It was his property now, by the will of Grandfather Whateley, who had stipulated that he must settle the estate and "take such steps as may be necessary to bring about that dissolution I myself was not able to take." A curious proviso, Abner thought. But then, everything about Grandfather Whateley had been strange, as if the decadence of Dunwich had infected him irrevocably.

And nothing was stranger than that Abner Whateley should come back from his cosmopolitan way of life to heed his grandfather's adjurations for property which was scarcely worth the time and trouble it would take to dispose of it. He reflected ruefully that such relatives as still lived in or near Dunwich might well resent his return in their curious inward growing and isolated rustication which had kept most of the Whateleys in this immediate region, particularly since the shocking events which had overtaken the country branch of the family on Sentinel Hill.

The house appeared to be unchanged. The river-side of the house was given over to the mill, which had long ago ceased to function, as more and more of the fields around Dunwich had grown barren; except for one room above the mill wheel —Aunt Sarey's room—the entire side of the structure bordering the Miskatonic had been abandoned even in the time of his boyhood, when Abner Whateley had last visited his grandfather, then living alone in the house except for the never seen Aunt Sarey who abode in her shuttered room with her door locked, never to move about the house under prohibition of such movement by her father, from whose domination only death at last had freed her.

A verandah, fallen in at the corner of the house, circled that part of the structure used as a dwelling; from the lattice-work under the eaves great cobwebs hung, undisturbed by anything save the wind for years. And dust lay over everything, inside as well as out, as Abner discovered when he had found the right key among the lot the lawyer had sent him. He found a lamp and lit it, for Grandfather Whateley had scorned electricity. In the yellow glow of light, the familiarity of the old kitchen with its nineteenth century appointments smote him like a blow. Its spareness, the hand-hewn table and chairs, the century-old clock on the mantel, the worn broom—all were tangible reminders of his fear-haunted childhood visits to this formidable house and its even more formidable occupant, his mother's aged father.

The lamplight disclosed something more. On the kitchen table lay an envelope addressed to him in handwriting so crabbed that it could only be that of a very old or infirm man—his grandfather. Without troubling to bring the rest of the things from the car, Abner sat down to the table, blowing the dust off the chair and sufficiently from the table to allow him a resting place for his elbows, and opened the envelope.

The spidery script leapt out at him. The words were as severe as he remembered his grandfather to have been. And abrupt, with no term of endearment, not even the prosaic form of greeting.

"Grandson:

"When you read this, I will be some months dead. Perhaps more, unless they find you sooner than I believe they will. I have left you a sum of money—all I have and die possessed of—which is in the bank at Arkham under your name now. I do this not alone because you are my own and only grandson but because among all the Whateleys—we are an accursed clan, my boy—you have gone forth into the world and gathered to yourself learning sufficient to permit you to look upon all things with an inquiring mind ridden neither by the superstition of ignorance nor the superstition of science. You will understand my meaning.

"It is my wish that at least the mill section of this house be destroyed. Let it be taken apart, board by board. *If anything in it lives, I adjure you solemnly to kill it. No matter how small it may be. No matter what form it may have, for if it seem to you human it will beguile you and endanger your life and God knows how many others.*

"Heed me in this.

"If I seem to have the sound of madness, pray recall that worse than madness has spawned among the Whateleys. I have stood free of it. It has not been so of all that is mine. There is more stubborn madness in those who are unwilling to believe in what they know not of and deny that such exists, than in those of our blood who have been guilty of terrible practices, and blasphemy against God, and worse.

Your Grandfather, Luther S. Whateley."

How like Grandfather! thought Abner. He remembered, spurred into memory by this enigmatic, self-righteous communication, how on one occasion when his mother had mentioned her sister Sarah, and clapped her fingers across her mouth in dismay, he had run to his grandfather to ask,

"Grandpa, where's Aunt Sarey?"

The old man had looked at him out of eyes that were basilisk and answered, "Boy, we do not speak of Sarah here."

Aunt Sarey had offended the old man in some dreadful way—dreadful, at least, to that firm disciplinarian—for from that time beyond even Abner Whateley's memory, his aunt had been only the name of a woman, who was his mother's older sister, and who was locked in the big room over the mill and kept forever invisible within those walls, behind the shutters nailed to her windows. It had been forbidden both Abner and his mother even to linger before the door of that shuttered room, though on one occasion Abner had crept up to the door and put his ear against it to listen to the snuffling and whimpering sounds that went on inside, as from some large person, and Aunt Sarey, he had decided, must be as large as a circus fat lady, for she devoured so much, judging by the great platters of food—chiefly meat, which she must have prepared herself, since so much of it was raw—carried to the room twice daily by old Luther Whateley himself, for there were no servants in that house, and had not been since the time Abner's mother had married, after Aunt Sarey had come back, strange and mazed, from a visit to distant kin in Innsmouth.

He refolded the letter and put it back into the envelope. He would think of its contents another day. His first need now was to make sure of a place to sleep. He went out and got his two remaining bags from the car and brought them to the kitchen. Then he picked up the lamp and went into the interior of the house. The old-fashioned parlour, which was always kept closed against that day when visitors came—and none save Whateleys called upon Whateleys in Dunwich—he ignored. He made his way instead to his grandfather's bedroom; it was fitting that he should occupy the old man's bed now that he, and not Luther Whateley, was master here.

The large, double bed was covered with faded copies of the *Arkham Advertiser*, carefully arranged to protect the fine cloth of the spread, which had been embossed with an armigerous design, doubtless a legitimate Whateley heritage. He set down the lamp and cleared away the newspapers. When he turned down the bed, he saw that it was clean and fresh, ready for occupation; some cousin of his grandfather's had doubtless seen to this, against his arrival, after the obsequies.

Then he got his bags and transferred them to the bedroom, which was in that corner of the house away from the village; its windows looked along the river, though they were more than the width of the mill from the bank of the stream. He opened the only one of them which had a screen across its lower half, then sat down on the edge of the bed, bemused, pondering the circumstances which had brought him back to Dunwich after all these years.

He was tired now. The heavy traffic around Boston had tired him. The contrast between the Boston region and this desolate Dunwich country depressed and troubled him. Moreover, he was conscious of an intangible uneasiness. If he had not had need of his legacy to continue his research into the ancient civilisations of the South Pacific, he would not have come here. Yet family ties existed, for all that he would deny them. Grim and forbidding as old Luther Whateley had always been, he was his mother's father, and to him his grandson owed the allegiance of common blood.

Round Mountain loomed close outside the bedroom; he felt its presence as he had when a boy, sleeping in the room above. Trees, for long untended, pressed upon the house, and from one of them at this hour of deep dusk, a screech owl's bell-like notes dropped into the still summer air. He lay back for a moment, strangely lulled by the owl's pleasant song. A thousand thoughts crowded upon him, a myriad memories. He saw himself again as the little boy he was, always half-fearful of enjoying himself in these foreboding surroundings, always happy to come and happier to leave.

But he could not lie here, however relaxing it was. There was so much to be done before he could hope to take his departure that he could ill afford to indulge himself in rest and make a poor beginning of his nebulous obligation. He swung himself off the bed, picked up the lamp again, and began a tour of the house.

He went from the bedroom to the dining-room which was situated between it and the kitchen—a room of stiff, uncomfortable furniture, also handmade,—and from there across to the parlour, the door of which opened upon a world far closer in its furniture and decorations to the eighteenth century than to the nineteenth, and far removed from the twentieth. The absence of dust testified to the tightness of the doors closing the room off from the rest of the house. He went up the open stairs to the floor above, from bedroom to bedroom—all dusty, with faded curtains, and showing every sign of having remained unoccupied for many years even before old Luther Whateley died.

Then he came to the passage which led to the shuttered room—Aunt Sarey's hideaway—or prison—he could now never learn what it might have been, and, on impulse, he went down and stood before that forbidden door. No snuffling, no whimpering greeted him now—nothing at all, as he stood before it, remembering, still caught in the spell of the prohibition laid upon him by his grandfather.

But there was no longer any reason to remain under that adjuration. He pulled out the ring of keys, and patiently tried one after another in the lock, until he found the right one. He unlocked the door and pushed; it swung protestingly open. He held the lamp high.

He had expected to find a lady's boudoir, but the shuttered room was startling in its condition—bedding scattered about, pillows on the floor, the remains of food dried on a huge platter hidden behind a bureau. An odd, ichthyic smell pervaded the room, rushing at him with such musty strength that he could hardly repress a gasp of disgust. The room was in shambles; moreover, it wore the aspect of having been in such wild disorder for a long, long time.

Abner put the lamp on a bureau drawn away from the wall, crossed to the window above the mill wheel, unlocked it, and raised it. He strove to open the shutters before he remembered that they had been nailed shut. Then he stood back, raised his foot, and kicked the shutters out to let a welcome blast of fresh, damp air into the room.

He went around to the adjoining outer wall and broke away the shutters from the single window in that wall, as well. It was not until he stood back to survey his work that he noticed he had broken a small corner out of the pane of the window above the mill wheel. His quick regret was as quickly repressed in the memory of his grandfather's insistence that the mill and this room above it be torn down or otherwise destroyed. What mattered a broken pane!

He returned to take up the lamp again. As he did so, he gave the bureau a shove to push it back against the wall once more. At the same moment he heard a small, rustling sound along the baseboard, and, looking down, caught sight of a long-legged frog or toad—he could not make out which—vanishing under the bureau. He was tempted to rout the creature out, but he reflected that its presence could not matter—if it had existed in these locked quarters for so long on such cockroaches and other insects as it had managed to uncover, it merited being left alone.

He went out of the room, locked the door again, and returned to the master bedroom downstairs. He felt, obscurely, that he had made a beginning, however trivial; he had scouted the ground, so to speak. And he was twice as tired for his brief look around as he had been before. Though the hour was not late, he decided to go to bed and get an early start in the morning. There was the old mill yet to be gone through—perhaps some of the machinery could be sold, if any remained—and the mill wheel was now a curiosity, having continued to exist beyond its time.

He stood for a few minutes on the verandah, marking with surprise the welling stridulation of the crickets and katydids, and the almost overwhelming choir of whippoorwills and frogs, which rose on all sides to assault him with a deafening insistence of such proportion as to drown out all other sounds, even such as might have risen from Dunwich. He stood there until he could tolerate the voices of the night no longer; then he retreated, locking the door, and made his way to the bedroom.

He undressed and got into bed, but he did not sleep for almost an hour, bedevilled by the chorus of natural sounds outside the house and from within himself by a rising confusion about what his grandfather had meant by the "dissolution" he himself had not been able to make. But at last he drifted into a troubled sleep.

2

He woke with the dawn, little rested. All night he had dreamed of strange places and beings that filled him with beauty and wonder and dread—of swimming in the ocean's depths and up the Miskatonic among fish and amphibia and strange men, half batrachian in aspect—of monstrous entities that lay sleeping in an eerie stone city at the bottom of the sea—of utterly outré music as of flutes accompanied by weird ululations from throats far, far from human—of Grandfather Luther Whateley standing accusingly before him and thundering forth his wrath at him for having dared to enter Aunt Sarey's shuttered room.

He was troubled, but he shrugged his unease away before the necessity of walking into Dunwich for the provisions he had neglected to bring with him in his haste. The morning was bright and sunny; pewees and thrushes sang, and dew pearled on leaf and blade reflected the sunlight in a thousand jewels along the winding path that led to the main street of the village. As he went along, his spirits rose; he whistled happily, and contemplated the early fulfilment of his obligation, upon which his escape from this desolate, forgotten pocket of ingrown humanity was predicated.

But the main street of Dunwich was no more reassuring under the light of the sun than it had been in the dusk of the past evening. The village huddled between the Miskatonic and the almost vertical slope of Round Mountain, a dark and brooding settlement which seemed somehow never to have passed 1900, as if time had ground to a stop before the turn of the last century. His gay whistle faltered and died away; he averted his eyes from the buildings falling into ruin; he avoided the curiously expressionless faces of passersby, and went directly to the old church with its general store, which he knew he would find slovenly and ill-kept, in keeping with the village itself.

A gaunt-faced storekeeper watched his advance down the aisle, searching his features for any familiar lineament.

Abner strode up to him and asked for bacon, coffee, eggs and milk.

The storekeeper peered at him. He made no move. "Ye'll be a Whateley," he said at last. "I dun't expeck ye know me. I'm yer cousin Tobias. Which one uv 'em are ye?"

"I'm Abner—Luther's grandson." He spoke reluctantly.

Tobias Whateley's face froze. "Libby's boy—Libby, that married cousin Jeremiah. Yew folks ain't back—back at Luther's? Yew folks ain't a-goin' to start things again?"

"There's no one but me," said Abner shortly. "What things are you talking about?"

"If ye dun't know, 'tain't fer me to say."

Nor would Tobias Whateley speak again. He put together what Abner wanted, took his money sullenly, and watched him out of the store with ill-concealed animosity.

Abner was disagreeably affected. The brightness of the morning had dimmed for him, though the sun shone from the same unclouded heaven. He hastened away from the store and main street, and hurried along the lane toward the house he had but recently quitted.

He was even more disturbed to discover, standing before the house, an ancient rig drawn by an old work-horse. Beside it stood a boy, and inside it sat an old, white-bearded man, who, at sight of Abner's approach, signalled to the boy for assistance, and by the lad's aid, laboriously descended to the ground and stood to await Abner.

As Abner came up, the boy spoke, unsmiling. "Great-grampa'll talk to yew."

"Abner," said the old man quaveringly, and Abner saw for the first time how very old he was.

"This here's Great-grampa Zebulon Whateley," said the boy.

Grandfather Luther Whateley's brother—the only living

Whateley of his generation. "Come in, sir," said Abner, offering the old man his arm.

Zebulon Whateley took it.

The three of them made slow progress towards the verandah, where the old man halted at the foot of the steps, turning his dark eyes upon Abner from under their bushy white brows, and shaking his head gently.

"Naow, if ye'll fetch me a cheer, I'll set."

"Bring a chair from the kitchen, boy," said Abner.

The boy sped up the steps and into the house. He was out as fast with a chair for the old man, and helped to lower him to it, and stood beside him while Zebulon Whateley caught his breath.

Presently he turned his eyes full upon Abner and contemplated him, taking in every detail of his clothes, which, unlike his own, were not made by hand.

"Why have ye come, Abner?" he asked, his voice firmer now.

Abner told him, as simply and directly as he could.

Zebulon Whateley shook his head. "Ye know no more'n the rest, and less'n some," he said. "What Luther was abaout, only God knowed. Naow Luther's gone, and ye'll have it to dew. I kin tell ye, Abner, I vaow afur God, I dun't know why Luther took on so and locked hisself up and Sarey that time she come back Innsmouth—but I kin say it was suthin' turrible, turrible—and the things what happened was turrible. Ain't nobody left to say Luther was to blame, nor poor Sarey—but take care, take care, Abner."

"I expect to follow my grandfather's wishes," said Abner.

The old man nodded. But his eyes were troubled, and it was plain that he had little faith in Abner.

"How'd you find out I was here, Uncle Zebulon?" Abner asked.

"I had the word ye'd come. It was my bounden duty to talk to ye, the Whateleys has a curse on 'em. Thar's been them naow gone to graoun' has had to dew with the devil, and thar's some that whistled turrible things aout o' the air, and thar's some what had to dew with things that wasn't all human nor all fish but lived in the water and swum aout—way aout—to sea, and thar's some what growed in on themselves and got all mazed and queer—and thar's what thappened on

Sentinel Hill that time—Lavinny's Wilbur—and that other one by the Sentinel Stone—Gawd, I shake when I think on it. . . ."

"Now, Grampa—don't ye git yer dander up," chided the boy.

"I wun't, I wun't," said the old man tremulously. "It's all died away naow. It's forgot—by all but me and them what took the signs daown—the signs that pointed to Dunwich, sayin', it was too turrible a place to know abaout. . . ." He shook his head and was silent.

"Uncle Zebulon," said Abner. "I never saw my Aunt Sarah."

"No, no, boy—she was locked up that time. Afore you was borned, I think it was."

"Why?"

"Only Luther knowed—and Gawd. Now Luther's gone, and Gawd dun't seem like He knowed Dunwich was still here."

"What was Aunt Sarah doing in Innsmouth?"

"Visitin' kin."

"Are there Whateleys there, too?"

"Not Whateleys. Marshes. Old Obed Marsh that was Pa's cousin. Him and his wife that he faound in the trade—at Ponape, if ye know whar that is."

"I do."

"Ye dew? I never knowed. They say Sarey was visitin' Marsh kin—Obed's son or grandson—I never knowed which. Never heered. Dun't care. She was thar quite a spell. They say when she come back she was different. Flighty. Unsettled. Sassed her pa. And then, not long after, he locked her up in that room till she died."

"How long after?"

"Three, four months. And Luther never said what fer. Nobody saw her again after that till the day she wuz laid aout in her coffin. Two year, might be three year ago. Thar was that time nigh onto a year after she come back from Innsmouth thar was sech goin's-on here at this house—a-fightin' and a-screamin' and a-screechin'—most everyone in Dunwich heerd it, but no one went to see whut it was, and next day Luther he said it was only Sarey took with a spell. Might be it was. Might be it was suthin' else. . . ."

"What else, Uncle Zebulon?"

"Devil's work," said the old man instantly. "But I fergit —ye're the eddicated one. Ain't many Whateleys ever bin eddicated. Thar was Lavinny—she read them turrible books what was no good for her. And Sarey—she read some. Them as has only a little learnin' might's well have none—they ain't fit to handle life with only a little learnin', they're fitter with none a-tall."

Abner smiled.

"Dun't ye laugh, boy!"

"I'm not laughing, Uncle Zebulon. I agree with you."

"Then ef ye come face to face with it, ye'll know what to dew. Ye wun't stop and think—ye'll just dew."

"With what?"

"I wisht I knowed, Abner. I dun't. Gawd knows. Luther knowed. Luther's dead. It comes on me Sarey knowed, too. Sarey's dead. Now nobody knows whut turrible thing it was. Ef I was a prayin' man, I'd pray you dun't find aout—but ef ye dew, dun't stop to figger it aout by eddication, just dew whut ye have to dew. Yer Grandpa kep' a record—look fer it. Ye might learn whut kind a people the Marshes was— they wasn't like us—suthin' turrible happened to 'em—and might be it reached aout and tetched Sarey. . . ."

Something between the old man and Abner Whateley— some thing unvoiced, perhaps unknown; but it was something that cast a chill about Abner for all his conscious attempt to belittle what he felt.

"I'll learn what I can, Uncle Zebulon," he promised.

The old man nodded and beckoned to the boy. He signified that he wished to rise, to return to the buggy. The boy came running.

"Ef ye need me, Abner, send word to Tobias," said Zebulon Whateley. "I'll come—ef I can."

"Thank you."

Abner and the boy helped the old man back into the buggy. Zebulon Whateley raised his forearm in a gesture of farewell, the boy whipped up the horse, and the buggy drew away.

Abner stood for a moment looking after the departing vehicle. He was both troubled and irritated—troubled at the suggestion of something dreadful which lurked beneath Zebulon Whateley's words of warning, irritated because his grandfather, despite all his adjurations, had left him so little to act upon. Yet this must have been because his grandfather evidently believed there might be nothing untoward to greet his grandson when at last Abner Whateley arrived at the old house. It could be nothing other by way of explanation.

Yet Abner was not entirely convinced. Was the matter one of such horror that Abner should not know of it unless he had to? Or had Luther Whateley laid down a key to the riddle elsewhere in the house? He doubted it. It would not be grandfather's way to seek the devious when he had always been so blunt and direct.

He went into the house with his groceries, put them away, and sat down to map out a plan of action. The very first thing to be accomplished was a survey of the mill part of the structure, to determine whether any machinery could be salvaged. Next he must find someone who would undertake to tear down the mill and the room above it. Thereafter he must dispose of the house and adjoining property, though he had a sinking feeling of futility at the conviction that he would never find anyone who would want to settle in so forlorn a corner of Massachusetts as Dunwich.

He began at once to carry out his obligations.

His search of the mill, however, disclosed that the machinery which had been in it—save for such pieces as were fixed to the running of the wheel—had been removed, and presumably sold. Perhaps the increment from the sale was part of that very legacy Luther Whateley had deposited in the bank at Arkham for his grandson. Abner was thus spared the necessity of removing the machinery before beginning the planned demolition. The dust in the old mill almost suffocated him; it lay an inch thick over everything, and it rose in great gusts to cloud about him when he walked through the empty, cobwebbed rooms. Dust muffled his footsteps and he was glad to leave the mill to go around and look at the wheel.

He worked his way around the wooden ledge to the frame of the wheel, somewhat uncertain, lest the wood give way and plunge him into the water beneath; but the construction was firm, the wood did not give, and he was soon at the wheel. It appeared to be a splendid example of middle nineteenth century work. It would be a shame to tear it apart, thought Abner. Perhaps the wheel could be removed, and a place could be found for it either in some museum or in some one of those buildings which were forever being reconstructed by wealthy persons interested in the preservation of the American heritage.

He was about to turn away from the wheel, when his eye was caught by a series of small wet prints on the paddles. He bent closer to examine them, but, apart from ascertaining that they were already in part dried, he could not see in them more than marks left by some small animal, probably batrachian—a frog or a toad—which had apparently mounted the wheel in the early hours before the rising of the sun. His eyes, raising, followed the line of the wheel to the broken out shutters of the room above.

He stood for a moment, thinking. He recalled the batrachian creature he had glimpsed along the baseboard of the shuttered room. Perhaps it had escaped through the broken pane? Or, more likely, perhaps another of its kind had discovered its presence and gone up to it. A faint apprehension stirred in him, but he brushed it away in irritation that a man of his intelligence should have been sufficiently stirred by the aura of ignorant, superstitious mystery clinging to his grandfather's memory to respond to it.

Nevertheless, he went around and mounted the stairs to the shuttered room. He half expected, when he unlocked the door, to find some significant change in the aspect of the room as he remembered it from last night, but, apart from the unaccustomed daylight streaming into the room, there was no alteration.

He crossed to the window.

There were prints on the sill. There were two sets of them. One appeared to be leading out, the other entering. They were not the same size. The prints leading outward were tiny, only half an inch across. Those leading in were double that size. Abner bent closer and stared at them in fixed fascination.

He was not a zoologist, but he was by no means ignorant of zoology. The prints on the sill were like nothing he had ever seen before, not even in dream. Save from being or seeming to be webbed, they were the perfect prints in miniature of human hands and feet.

Though he made a cursory search for the creature, he saw no sign of it, and finally, somewhat shaken, he retreated from the room and locked the door behind him, already regretting the impulse which had led him to it in the first place and which had caused him to burst open the shutters which for so long had walled the room away from the outer world.

3

He was not entirely surprised to learn that no one in Dunwich could be found to undertake the demolition of the mill. Even such carpenters as those who had not worked for a long time were reluctant to undertake the task, pleading a variety of excuses, which Abner easily recognised as a disguise for the superstitious fear of the place under which one and all laboured. He found it necessary to drive into Aylesbury, but, though he encountered no difficulty in engaging a trio of husky young men who had formed a partnership to tear down the mill, he was forced to wait upon their previous commitments and had to return to Dunwich with the promise that they would come "in a week or ten days."

Thereupon he set about at once to examine into all the effects of Luther Whateley which still remained in the house. There were stacks of newspapers—chiefly the *Arkham Advertiser* and the *Aylesbury Transcript*—now yellowing with age and mouldering with dust, which he set aside for burning. There were books which he determined to go over individually in order that he might not destroy anything of value. And there were letters which he would have burned at once had he not happened to glance into one of them and caught sight of the name "Marsh," at which he read on.

"Luther, what happened to cousin Obed is a singular thing. I do not know how to tell it to you. I do not know how to make it credible. I am not sure I have all the facts in this matter. I cannot believe but that it is a rigmarole deliberately invented to conceal something of a scandalous nature, for you know the Marshes have always been given to exaggeration and had a pronounced flair for deception. Their ways are devious. They have always been.

"But the story, as I have it from cousin Alizah, is that when he was a young man Obed and some others from Innsmouth, sailing their trading ships into the Polynesian Islands, encountered there a strange people who called themselves the 'Deep Ones' and who had the ability to live either in the water or on the earth. Amphibians, they would then be. Does this sound credible to you? It does not to me. What is most astonishing is that Obed and some others married women of these people and brought them home to live with them.

"Now that is the *legend*. Here are the *facts*. Ever since that time, the Marshes have prospered mightily in the trade. Mrs. Marsh is never seen abroad, save on such occasions as she goes to certain closed affairs of the Order of Dagon Hall. 'Dagon' is said to be a sea god. I know nothing of these pagan religions, and wish to know nothing. The Marsh children have *a very strange* look. I do not exaggerate, Luther, when I tell you that they have such wide mouths and such chinless faces and such large staring eyes that I swear they sometimes look more like frogs than human beings! They are not, at least, so far as I can see, *gilled*. The 'Deep Ones' are said to be possessed of gills, and to belong to Dagan or to some other deity of the sea whose name I cannot even pronounce, far less set down. No matter. It is such a rigmarole as the Marshes might well invent to serve their purposes, but by God, Luther, judging by the way the ships Captain Marsh has in the East India trade keep afloat without a smitchin of damage done to them by storm or wear—the brigantine *Columbia*, the barque *Sumatra Queen*, the brig *Hetty* and some others—it might almost seem that he has made some sort of bargain with Neptune himself!

"Then there are all the doings off the coast where the Marshes live. Night swimming. They swim way out off Devil Reef, which, as you know, is a mile and a half out from the harbour here at Innsmouth. People keep away from the Marshes—except the Martins and some such others among them who were also in the East India trade. Now that Obed is gone—and I suppose Mrs. Marsh may be also, since she is no longer seen anywhere—the children and the grandchildren of old Captain Obed follow in his strange ways."

The letter dwindled down to commonplaces about prices—ridiculously low figures seen from this vantage of over half a century later, for Luther Whateley must have been a young man, unmarried, at the time this letter had been written to him by Ariah, a cousin of whom Abner had never heard. What it had to say of the Marshes was nothing—or all, perhaps, if Abner had had the key to the puzzle of which, he began to believe with mounting irritation, he held only certain disassociated parts.

But if Luther Whateley had believed this rigmarole, would he, years later, have permitted his daughter to visit the Marsh cousins? Abner doubted it.

He went through other letters—bills, receipts, trivial accounts of journeys made to Boston, Newburyport, Kingsport—postcards, and came at last to another letter from Cousin Ariah, written, if a comparison of dates was sufficient evidence, immediately after the one Abner had just read. They were ten days apart, and Luther would have had time to reply to that first.

Abner opened it eagerly.

The first page was an account of certain small family matters pertinent to the marriage of another cousin, evidently a sister of Ariah's; the second a speculation about the future of the East India trade, with a paragraph about a new book by Whitman—evidently Walt; but the third was manifestly in answer to something Grandfather Whateley had evidently written concerning the Marsh branch of the family.

"Well, Luther, you may be right in this matter of race prejudice as responsible for the feeling against the Marshes. I know how people here feel about other races. It is unfortunate, perhaps, but such is their lack of education that they find much room for such prejudices. But I am not convinced that it is *all* due to race prejudice. I don't know what kind of race it is that would give the Marshes after Obed that strange *look*. The East India people—such as I have seen and recall from my early days in the trade—have features much like our own, and only a different colour to the skin—copper, I would call it. Once I did see a native who had a similar appearance, but he was evidently not typical, for he was shunned by all the workers around the ships in the harbour where I saw him. I've forgotten now where it was, but I think Ponape.

"To give them their due, the Marshes keep pretty much to

themselves—or to those families living here under the same cloud. And they more or less run the town. It may be significant—it may have been accident—that one selectman who spoke out against them was found drowned soon after. I am the first to admit that coincidences more startling than this frequently occur, but you may be sure that people who disliked the Marshes made the most of this.

" But I know how your analytical mind is cold to such talk; I will spare you more of it."

Thereafter not a word. Abner went through bundles of letters in vain. What Ariah wrote in subsequent letters dealt scrupulously with family matters of the utmost triviality. Luther Whateley had evidently made his displeasure with mere gossip clear; even as a young man, Luther must have been strictly self-disciplined. Abner found but one further reference to any mystery at Innsmouth—that was a newspaper clipping dealing in very vague terms, suggesting that the reporter who sent in the story did not really know what had taken place, with certain Federal activity in and near Innsmouth in 1928—the attempted destruction of Devil Reef, and the blowing up of large sections of the waterfront, together with wholesale arrests of Marshes and Martins and some others. But this event was decades removed from Ariah's early letters.

Abner put the letters dealing with the Marshes into his pocket, and summarily burned the rest, taking the mass of material he had gone through out along the riverbank and setting fire to it. He stood guarding it, lest a chance wind carry a spark to surrounding grass, which was unseasonably dry. He welcomed the smell of the smoke, however, for a certain dead odour lingered along the riverbank, rising from the remains of fish upon which some animal had feasted—an otter, he thought.

As he stood beside the fire, his eyes roved over the old Whateley building, and he saw, with a rueful reflection that it was high time the mill were coming down, that several panes of the window he had broken in the room that had been Aunt Sarey's, together with a portion of the frame, had fallen out. Fragments of the window were scattered on the paddles of the mill wheel.

By the time the fire was sufficiently low to permit his leaving it, the day was drawing to a close. He ate a meagre supper, and, having had his fill of reading for the day, decided against attempting to turn up his grandfather's "record" of which Uncle Zebulon Whateley had spoken, and went out to watch the dusk and the night in from the verandah, hearing again the rising chorus of the frogs and whippoorwills.

He retired early, unwontedly weary.

Sleep, however, would not come. For one thing, the summer night was warm; hardly a breath of air stirred. For another, even above the ululation of the frogs and the demoniac insistence of the whippoorwills, sounds from within the house invaded his consciousness—the creaks and groans of a many-timbered house settling in for the night; a peculiar scuffling or shuffling sound, half-drop, half-hop, which Abner laid to rats, which must abound in the mill section of the structure—and indeed, the noises were muffled, and seemed to reach him as from some distance; and, at one time, the cracking of wood and the tinkle of glass, which, Abner guessed, very probably came from the window above the mill wheel. The house was virtually falling to pieces about him; it was as if he served as a catalytic agent to bring about the final dissolution of the old structure.

This concept amused him because it struck him that, willy-nilly, he was carrying out his grandfather's adjuration. And, so bemused, he fell asleep.

He was awakened early in the morning by the ringing of the telephone, which he had had the foresight to have connected for the duration of his visit in Dunwich. He had already taken down the receiver from the ancient instrument attached to the wall before he realised that the call was on a party line and not intended for him. Nevertheless, the woman's voice that leapt out at him, burst upon his ear with such screaming insistence that he remained frozen to the telephone.

"I tell ye, Mis' Corey, I heard things las' night—the graoun' was a-talkin' agen, and along abaout midnight I heerd that scream—I never figgered a caow'd scream that way—jest like a rabbit, only deeper. That was Lutey Sawyer's caow—they faoun' her this morning—more'n haff et by animals. . . ."

"Mis' Bishop, you dun't s'pose . . . it's come back?"

"I dun't know. I hope t' Gawd it ain't. But it's the same as the las' time."

"Was it jest that one caow took?"

"Jest the one. I ain't heerd abaout no more. But that's how it begun the las' time, Mis' Corey."

Quietly, Abner replaced the receiver. He smiled grimly at this evidence of the rampant superstitions of the Dunwich natives. He had never really known the depths of ignorance and superstition in which dwellers in such out-of-the-way places at Dunwich lived, and this manifestation of it was, he was convinced, but a mild sample.

He had little time, however, to dwell upon the subject, for he had to go into town for fresh milk, and he strode forth into the morning of sun and clouds with a certain feeling of relief at such brief escape from the house.

Tobias Whateley was uncommonly sullen and silent at Abner's entrance. Abner sensed not only resentment, but a certain tangible fear. He was astonished. To all Abner's comments Tobias replied in muttered monosyllables. Thinking to make conversation, he began to tell Tobias what he had overheard on the party line.

"I know it," said Tobias, curtly, for the first time gazing at Abner's face with naked terror.

Abner was stunned into silence. Terror vied with animosity in Tobias's eyes. His feelings were plain to Abner before he dropped his gaze and took the money Abner offered in payment.

"Yew seen Zebulon?" he asked in a low voice.

"He was at the house," said Abner.

"Yew talk to him?"

"We talked."

It seemed as if Tobias expected that certain matters had passed between them, but there was that in his attitude that suggested he was puzzled by subsequent events, which seemed to indicate that Zebulon had not told him what Tobias had expected the old man to tell him, or else that Abner had disregarded some of his Uncle's advice. Abner began to feel completely mystified; added to the superstitious talk of the natives on the telephone, to the strange hints Uncle Zebulon had dropped, this attitude of his cousin Tobias filled him with utter perplexity. Tobias, no more than Zebulon, seemed inclined to come out frankly and put into words what lay behind his sullen features—each acted as if Abner, as a matter of course, should know.

In his bafflement, he left the store, and walked back to the Whateley house determined to hasten his tasks as much as he could so that he might get away from this forgotten hamlet with its queer, superstition-ridden people, for all that many of them were his relatives.

To that end, he returned to the task of sorting his grandfather's things as soon as he had had his breakfast, of which he ate very little, for his disagreeable visit to the store had dulled the appetite which he had felt when he had set out for the store earlier.

It was not until late afternoon that he found the record he sought—an old ledger, in which Luther Whateley had made certain entries in his crabbed hand.

4

By the light of the lamp, Abner sat down to the kitchen table after he had had a small repast, and opened Luther Whateley's ledger. The opening pages had been torn out, but, from an examination of the fragments of sheets still attached to the threads of the sewing, Abner concluded that these pages were purely of accounts, as if his grandfather had taken up an old, not completely used account book for a purpose other than keeping accounts, and had removed such sheets as had been more prosaically utilised.

From the beginning, the entries were cryptic. They were undated, except for the day of the week.

"This Saturday Ariah answered my inquiry. S. was seen sev times with Ralsa Marsh. Obed's great-grandson. *Swam* together by night."

Such was the first entry, clearly pertaining to Aunt Sarey's visit to Innsmouth, about which Grandfather had plainly inquired of Ariah. Something had impelled Luther to make such inquiry. From what he knew of his grandfather's character, Abner concluded that the inquiry had been made after Sarey had returned to Dunwich.

Why?

The next entry was pasted in, and was clearly part of a typewritten letter received by Luther Whateley.

"Ralsa Marsh is probably the most repellent of all the family. He is almost *degenerate* in his looks. I know you have said that it was Libby of your daughters who was the fairest; even so, we cannot imagine how Sarah came to take up with someone who is so repulsive as Ralsa, in whom all those recessive characteristics which have been seen in the Marsh family after Obed's strange marriage to that Polynesian woman—(the Marshes have denied that Obed's wife was Polynesian, but of course, he was trading there at that time, and I don't credit those stories about that uncharted island where he was supposed to have dallied)—seem to have come to fullest fruit.

"As far as I can now ascertain—after all, it is over two months—close to four, I think—since her return to Dunwich—they were constantly together. I am surprised that Ariah did not inform you of this. None of us here had any mandate to halt Sarah's seeing Ralsa, and, after all, they are cousins and she was visiting at Marshes—not here."

Abner judged that this letter had been written by a woman, also a cousin, who bore Luther some resentment for Sarah's not having been sent to stay with her branch of the family. Luther had evidently made inquiry of her regarding Ralsa.

The third entry was once again in Luther's hand, summarising a letter from Ariah.

"Saturday. Ariah maintains Deep Ones a sect or quasi-religious group. Sub-human. Said to live in the sea and worship Dagon. Another God named Cthulhu. Gilled people. Resembling frogs or toads more than fish, but eyes ichthyic. Claims Obed's late wife was one. Holds that Obed's children all bore the marks. Marshes gilled? How else could they swim a mile and a half to Devil Reef, and back? Marshes eat sparingly, can go without food and drink a long time, diminish or expand in size rapidly." (To this Luther had appended four scornful exclamation marks.)

"Zadok Allen swears he saw Sarah swimming out to Devil Reef. Marshes carrying her along. All *naked*. Swears he saw Marshes with tough, warty skin. Some with *scales*, like fish! Swears he saw them chase and eat fish! Tear them apart like animals."

The next entry was again a portion of a letter, patently a reply to one from Grandfather Whateley.

"You ask who is responsible for those *ridiculous* tales about the Marshes. Well, Luther, it would be impossible to single out any one of a dozen people over several generations. I agree that old Zadok Allen talks too much, drinks, and may be romancing. But he is only one. The fact is this legendry—or *rigmarole*, as you call it—has grown up from one generation to the next. Through three generations. You have only to look at some of the descendants of Captain Obed to understand why this could have come about. There are some Marsh off-spring said to have been too horrible to look upon. Old wives' tales? Well, Dr. Rowley Marsh was too ill to attend one of the Marsh women one time; so they had to call Dr. Gilman, and Gilman always said that what he delivered was less than human. And nobody ever saw that particular Marsh, though there were people later who claimed to have seen *things moving on two legs that weren't human*."

Following this there was but a brief but revealing entry in two words: "Punished Sarah."

This must then mark the date of Sarah Whateley's confinement to the room above the mill. For some time after this entry, there was no mention of his daughter in Luther's script. Instead, his jottings were not dated in any way, and, judging by the difference in the colour of the ink, were made at different times, though run together.

"Many frogs. Seem to bear in on the mill. Seem to be more than in the marshes across the Miskatonic. Sleeping difficult. Are whippoorwills on the increase, too, or is this imagination? . . . Counted thirty-seven frogs at the porch steps to-night."

There were more entries of this nature. Abner read them all, but there was no clue in them to what the old man had been getting at. Luther Whateley had thereafter kept book on frogs, fog, fish and their movements in the Miskatonic—when they rose and leaped from the water, and so on. This seemed to be unrelated data, and was not in any way connected to the problem of Sarah.

There was another hiatus after this series of notes, and then came a single, underscored entry.

"*Ariah was right!*"

But about what had Ariah been right? Abner wondered. And how had Luther Whateley learned that Ariah had been right? There was no evidence that Ariah and Luther had continued their correspondence, or even that Ariah desired to write to the crochety Luther without a letter of direct inquiry from Luther.

There followed a section of the record to which newspaper clippings had been pasted. These were clearly unrelated, but they did establish for Abner the fact that somewhat better than a year had passed before Luther's next entry, one of the most puzzling Abner found. Indeed, the time hiatus seemed to be closer to two years.

"R. out again."

If Luther and Sarah were the only people in the house, who was "R."? Could it have been Ralsa Marsh come to visit? Abner doubted it, for there was nothing to show that Ralsa Marsh harboured any affection for his distant cousin, or certainly he would have pursued her before this.

The next notation seemed to be unrelated.

"Two turtles, one dog, remains of woodchuck. Bishop's—two cows, found on the Miskatonic end of the pasture."

A little further along, Luther had set down further such data.

"After one month a total of 17 cattle, 6 sheep. Hideous alterations; size commensurate with amt. of food. Z. over. Anxious about talk going around."

Could Z. stand for Zebulon? Abner thought it did. Evidently then Zebulon had come in vain, for he had left him, Abner, with only vague and uncertain hints about the situation at the house when Aunt Sarey was confined to the shuttered room. Zebulon, on the evidence of such conversation as he had shared with Abner, knew less than Abner himself did after reading his grandfather's record. But he did know of Luther's record; so Luther must have told him he had set down certain facts.

These notations, however, were more in the nature of notes for something to be completed later; they were unaccountably cryptic, unless one had the key of basic knowledge which belonged to Luther Whateley. But a growing sense of urgency was clearly manifest in the old man's further entries.

"Ada Wilkerson gone. Trace of scuffle. Strong feeling in

Dunwich. John Sawyer shook his fist at me—safely across the street, where I couldn't reach him."

"Monday. Howard Willie this time. They found one shoe, with the foot still in it!"

The record was now near its end. Many pages, unfortunately, had been detached from it—some with violence—but no clue remained as to why this violence had been done to Grandfather Whateley's account. It could not have been done by anyone but Luther himself; perhaps, thought Abner, Luther felt he had told too much, and intended to destroy anything which might put a later reader on the track of the true facts regarding Aunt Sarey's confinement for the rest of her life. He had certainly succeeded.

The next entry once again referred to the elusive "R."

"R. back at last."

Then, "Nailed the shutters to the windows of Sarah's room."

And at last: "Once he has lost weight, he must be kept on a careful diet and to a controllable size."

In a way, this was the most enigmatic entry of them all. Was "he" also "R."? If so, why must he be kept on a careful diet, and what did Luther Whateley mean by controlling his size? There was no ready answer to these questions in such material as Abner had read thus far, either in this record—or the fragmentary account still left in the record—or in letters previously perused.

He pushed away the record-book, resisting an impulse to burn it. He was exasperated, all the more so because he was uneasily aware of an urgent need to learn the secret embalmed within this old building.

The hour was now late; darkness had fallen some time ago, and the ever-present clamour of the frogs and the whippoorwills had begun once more, rising all around the house. Pushing from his thoughts briefly the apparently unconnected jottings he had been reading, he called from his memory the superstitions of the family, representing those prevalent in the countryside—associating frogs and the calling of whippoorwills and owls with death, and from this meditation progressed readily to the amphibian link which presented itself—the presence of the frogs brought before his mind's eye a grotesque caricature of one of the Marsh clan of Innsmouth, as described in the letters Luther Whateley had saved for so many years.

Oddly, this very thought, for all that it was so casual, startled him. The insistence of frogs and toads on singing and calling in the vicinity was truly remarkable. Yet, batrachia had always been plentiful in the Dunwich vicinity, and he had no way of knowing for how long a period before his arrival they had been calling about the old Whateley house. He discounted the suggestion that his arrival had anything at all to do with it; more than likely, the proximity of the Miskatonic and a low, swampy area immediately across the river on the edge of Dunwich, accounted for the presence of so many frogs.

His exasperation faded away; his concern about the frogs did likewise. He was weary. He got up and put the record left by Luther Whateley carefully into one of his bags, intending to carry it away with him, and to puzzle over it until some sort of meaning came out of it. Somewhere there must exist a clue. If certain horrible events had taken place in the vicinity, something more in the way of a record must exist than Luther Whateley's spare notes. It would do no good to inquire of Dunwich people; Abner knew they would maintain a close-mouthed silence before an "outsider" like himself, for all that he was related to many of them.

It was then that he thought of the stacks of newspapers, still set aside to be burned. Despite his weariness, he began to go through packs of the *Aylesbury Transcript*, which carried, from time to time, a Dunwich department.

After an hour's hasty search, he found three vague articles, none of them in the regular Dunwich columns, which corroborated entries in Luther Whateley's ledger. The first appeared under the heading: *Wild Animal Slays Stock Near Dunwich*——

"Several cows and sheep have been slain on farms just outside Dunwich by what appears to be a wild animal of some kind. Traces left at the scenes of the slaughter suggest some large beast, but Professor Bethnall of Miskatonic University's anthropology department points out that it is not inconceivable that packs of wolves could lurk in the wild hill country around Dunwich. No beast of the size suggested by the traces reported was ever known to inhabit the eastern seaboard within the memory of man. County officials are investigating."

Search as he might, Abner could find no follow-up story. He did, however, come upon the story of Ada Wilkerson.

"A widow-lady, Ada Wilkerson, 57, living along the Miskatonic out of Dunwich, may have been the victim of foul play three nights ago. When she failed to visit a friend by appointment in Dunwich, her home was visited. No trace of her was found. However, the door of her house had been broken in, and the furniture had been wildly thrown about, as if a violent struggle had taken place. A very strong musk is said to have pervaded the entire area. Up to press time to-day, Mrs. Wilkerson has not been heard from."

Two subsequent paragraphs reported briefly that authorities had not found any clue to Mrs. Wilkerson's disappearance. The account of a "large animal" was resurrected, lamely, and Professor Bethnall's beliefs on the possible existence of a wolf-pack, but nothing further, for investigation had disclosed that the missing lady had neither money nor enemies, and no one would have had any motive for killing her.

Finally, there was the account of Howard Willie's death, headed, *Shocking Crime at Dunwich.*

"Some time during the night of the twenty-first Howard Willie, 37, a native of Dunwich, was brutally slain as he was on his way home from a fishing trip along the upper reaches of the Miskatonic. Mr. Willie was attacked about half a mile past the Luther Whateley property, as he walked through an arboured lane. He evidently put up a fierce fight, for the ground is badly torn up in all directions. The poor fellow was overcome, and must have been literally torn limb from limb, for the only physical remains of the victim consisted of his right foot, still encased in its shoe. It had evidently been cruelly torn from his leg by great force.

"Our correspondent in Dunwich advises us that people there are very sullen and in a great rage of anger and fear. They suspect many of their number of being at least partly to blame, though they stoutly deny that anyone in Dunwich murdered either Willie or Mrs. Wilkerson, who disappeared a fortnight ago, and of whom no word has since been heard."

The account concluded with some data about Willie's family connections. Thereafter, subsequent editions of the

Transcript were distinguished only for the lack of information about the events which had taken place in Dunwich, where authorities and reporters alike apparently ran up against blank walls in the stolid refusal of the natives to talk or even speculate about what had happened. There was, however, one insistent note which recurred in the comments of investigators, relayed to the press, and that was that such trail or track as could be seen appeared to have disappeared into the waters of the Miskatonic, suggesting that if an animal were responsible for the orgy of slaughter which had occurred at Dunwich, it may have come from and returned to the river.

Though it was now close to midnight, Abner massed the discarded newspapers together and took them out to the river-bank, where he set them on fire, having saved only torn pages relative to the occurrences at Dunwich. The air being still, he did not feel obliged to watch the fire, since he had already burned a considerable area, and the grass was not likely to catch on fire. As he started away, he heard suddenly above the ululation of the whippoorwills and frogs, now at a frenzied crescendo, the tearing and breaking sound of wood. He thought at once of the window of the shuttered room, and retraced his steps.

In the very dim light flickering toward the house from the burning newspapers, it seemed to Abner that the window gaped wider than before. Could it be that the entire mill part of the house was about to collapse? Then, out of the corner of his eye, he caught sight of a singularly formless moving shadow just beyond the mill wheel, and a moment later heard a churning sound in the water. The voices of the frogs had now risen to such a volume that he could hear nothing more.

He was inclined to dismiss the shadow as the creation of the wild flames leaping upward from the fire. The sound in the water might well have been that of the movement made by a school of fish, darting forward in concert. Nevertheless, he thought, it would do no harm to have another look at Aunt Sarey's room.

He returned to the kitchen, took the lamp, and mounted the stairs. He unlocked the door of the shuttered room, threw open the door, and was almost felled by the powerful musk which pushed hallward. The smell of the Miskatonic, of the marshes, the odour of that slimy deposit left on the stones and sunken débris when the Miskatonic receded to its low water stage, the cloying pungence of some animal lairs—all these were combined in the shuttered room.

Abner stood for a moment, wavering on the threshold. True, the odour in the room could have come in through the open window. He raised the lamp so that more of its light fell upon the wall above the mill wheel. Even from where he stood, it was possible to see that not only was all the window itself now gone, but so was the frame. Even at this distance it was manifest that the frame had been broken out *from inside*!

He fell back, slammed the door shut, locked it, and fled downstairs with the shell of his rationalisations tumbling about him.

5

Downstairs, he fought for self control. What he had seen was but one more detail added to the proliferating accumulation of seemingly unrelated data upon which he had stumbled ever since his coming to his grandfather's home. He was convinced now that however unlikely it had at first seemed to him, all these data must be related. What he needed to learn was the one basic fact or element which bound them together.

He was badly shaken, particularly because he had the uneasy conviction that he did indeed have all the facts he needed to know, that it was his scientific training which made it impossible for him to make the primary assumption, to state the premise which the facts before him would inevitably prove. The evidence of his senses told him that something laired in that room—some bestial creature; it was folly to assume that odours from outside could so permeate Aunt Sarey's old room and not be noticeable outside the kitchen and at the windows of his own bedroom.

The habit of rational thinking was strong in him. He took out Luther Whateley's final letter to him once more and read it again. That was what his grandfather had meant when he had written " you have gone forth into the world and gathered to yourself learning sufficient to permit you to look upon all things with an inquiring mind ridden neither by the superstition of ignorance nor the superstition of science." Was this puzzle, with all its horrible connotations, beyond rationalisation?

The wild ringing of the telephone broke in upon his confused thoughts. Slipping the letter back into his pocket, he strode rapidly to the wall and took the receiver off the hook.

A man's voice screamed over the wire, amid a chaos of inquiring voices as everyone on the line picked up his receiver as if they waited, like Abner Whateley himself, for word of another tragedy. One of the voices—all were disembodied and unidentifiable for Abner—identified the caller.

"It's Luke Lang!"

"Git a posse up an' come quick," Luke shouted hoarsely over the wire. "It's jest aoutside my door. Snufflin' araoun' Tryin' the door. Feelin' at the winders."

"Luke, what is it?" asked a woman's voice.

"Oh, Gawd! It's some unairthly thing. It's a-hoppin' raoun' like it was too big to move right—like jelly. Oh, hurry, hurry, afore it's too late. It got my dog . . ."

"Git off the wire so's we can call fer help," interrupted another subscriber.

But Luke never heard in his extremity. "It's a-pushin' at the door—it's a-bowin' the door in . . ."

"Luke! Luke! Git off'n the wire!"

"It's a-tryin' the winder naow." Luke Lang's voice rose in a scream of terror. "There goes the glass. Gawd! Gawd! Hain't yew comin'? Oh, that hand! That turr'ble arm! Gawd! That face . . .!"

Luke's voice died away in a frightful screech. There was the sound of breaking glass and rending wood—then all was still at Luke Lang's, and for a moment all was still along the wire. Then the voices burst forth again in a fury of excitement and fear.

"Git help!"

"We'll meet at Bishops' place."

And someone put in, "It's Abner Whateley done it!"

Sick with shock and half-paralysed with a growing awareness, Abner struggled to tear the receiver from his ear, to shut off the half-crazed bedlam on the party line. He managed it with an effort. Confused, upset, frightened himself, he stood for a moment with his head leaning against the wall. His thoughts seethed around but one central point—the fact that the Dunwich rustics considered him somehow responsible for what was happening. And their conviction, he knew intuitively, was based on more than the countryman's conventional distrust of the stranger.

He did not want to think of what had happened to Luke Lang—and to those others. Luke's frightened, agonised voice still rang in his ears. He pulled himself away from the wall, almost stumbling over one of the kitchen chairs. He stood for a moment beside the table, not knowing what to do, but as his mind cleared a little, he thought only of escape. Yet he was caught between the desire to get away, and the obligation to Luther Whateley he had not yet fulfilled.

But he had come, he had gone through the old man's things—all save the books—he had made arrangements to tear down the mill part of the house—he could manage its sale through some agency; there was no need for him to be present. Impulsively, he hastened to the bedroom, threw such things as he had unpacked, together with Luther Whateley's note-filled ledger, into his bags and carried them out to his car.

Having done this, however, he had second thoughts. Why should he take flight? He had done nothing. No guilt of any kind rested upon him. He returned to the house. All was still, save for the unending chorus of frogs and whippoorwills. He stood briefly undecided; then he sat down at the table and took out Grandfather Whateley's final letter to read it once more.

He read it over carefully, thoughtfully. What had the old man meant when, in referring to the madness that had spawned among the Whateleys, he had said "It has not been so of all that is mine" though he himself had kept free of that madness? Grandmother Whateley had died long before Abner's birth; his Aunt Julia had died as a young girl; his mother had led a blameless life. There remained Aunt Sarey. What had been her madness then? Luther Whateley could have meant none other. Only Sarey remained. What had she done to bring about her imprisonment unto death?

And what had he intended to hint at when he adjured

Abner to kill anything in the mill section of the house, anything that lived? *No matter how small it may be. No matter what form it may have. . . .* Even something so small as an inoffensive toad? A spider? A fly? Luther Whateley wrote in riddles, which in itself was an affront to an intelligent man. Or did his grandfather think Abner a victim to the superstition of science? Ants, spiders, flies, various kinds of bugs, millers, centipedes, daddy long-legs—all occupied the old mill; and doubtless in its walls were mice as well. Did Luther Whateley expect his grandson to go about exterminating all these?

Behind him suddenly something struck the window. Glass fragmented to the floor, together with something heavy. Abner sprang to his feet and whirled around. From outside came the sound of running footsteps.

A rock lay on the floor amid the shattered glass. There was a piece of " store paper " tied to it by common store string. Abner picked it up, broke the strings, and unfolded the paper.

Crude lettering stared up at him. " Git out before ye get kilt!" Store paper and string. It was not meant so much as a threat as a well-intentioned warning. And it was clearly the work of Tobias Whateley, thought Abner. He tossed it contemptuously to the table.

His thoughts were still in turmoil, but he had decided that precipitate flight was not necessary. He would stay, not only to learn if his suspicions about Luke Lang were true—as if the evidence of the telephone left room for doubt—but also to make a final attempt to fathom the riddle Luther Whateley had left behind.

He put out the light and went in darkness to the bedroom where he stretched out, fully clothed, upon the bed.

Sleep, however, would not come. He lay probing the maze of his thoughts, trying to make sense out of the mass of data he had accumulated, seeking always that basic fact which was the key to all the others. He felt sure it existed ; worse, he was positive that it lay before his eyes—he had but failed to interpret it or to recognise it.

He had been lying there scarcely half an hour, when he heard, rising above the pulsating choir of the frogs and whippoorwills, a splashing from the direction of the Miskatonic—an approaching sound, as if a large wave were washing up the banks on its seaward way. He sat up, listening. But even as he did so, the sound stopped and another took its place—one he was loath to identify, and yet could define as no other than that of someone trying to climb the mill wheel.

He slid off the bed and went out of the room.

From the direction of the shuttered room came a muffled, heavy falling sound—then a curious, choking whimpering that sounded, horribly, like a child at a great distance trying to call out—then all was still, and it seemed that even the noise and clamour of the frogs diminished and fell away.

He returned to the kitchen and lit the lamp.

Pooled in the yellow glow of light, Abner made his way slowly up the stairs toward the shuttered room. He walked softly, careful to make no sound.

Arriving at the door, he listened. At first he heard nothing—then a susurration smote his ears.

Something in that room—*breathed*!

Fighting back his fear, Abner put the key in the lock and turned it. He flung open the door and held the lamp high.

Shock and horror paralysed him.

There, squatting in the midst of the tumbled bedding from that long-abandoned bed, sat a monstrous, leathery-skinned creature that was neither frog nor man, one gorged with food, with blood still slavering from its batrachian jaws and upon its webbed fingers—a monstrous entity that had strong, powerfully long arms, grown from its bestial body like those of a frog, and tapering off into a man's hands, save for the webbing between the fingers . . .

The tableau held for only a moment.

Then, with a frenzied grawling sound—" *Eh-ya-ya-ya-yayaa-haah—ngh'aaa—h'yuh, h'yuh*—" it rose up, towering, and launched itself at Abner.

His reaction was instantaneous, born of terrible, shattering knowledge. He flung the kerosene-filled lamp with all his might straight at the thing reaching toward him.

Fire enveloped the thing. It halted and began to tear frantically at its burning body, unmindful of the flames rising from the bedding behind it and the floor of the room, and at the same instant the calibre of its voice changed from a deep growling to a shrill, high wailing—*Mamamama—ma-aa-ma-aa-ma-aah*!"

Abner pulled the door shut and fled.

Down the stairs, half falling, through the rooms below, with his heart pounding madly, and out of the house. He tumbled into the car, almost bereft of his senses, half-blinded by the perspiration of his fear, turned the key in the ignition, and roared away from the accursed place from which the smoke already poured, while spreading flames in that tinder-dry building began to cast a red glow into the sky.

He drove like one possessed—through Dunwich—through the covered bridge—his eyes half-closed, as if to shut out forever the sight of that which he had seen, while the dark, brooding hills seemed to reach for him and the chanting whippoorwills and frogs mocked him.

But nothing could erase that final, cataclysmic knowledge seared into his mind—the key to which he had had all along and not known it—the knowledge implicit in his own memories as well as in the notes Luther Whateley had left—the chunks of raw meat he had childishly supposed were going to be prepared in Aunt Sarey's room instead of to *be eaten raw*, the reference to " R." who had come " back at last " after having escaped, back to the only home " R." knew—the seemingly unrelated references also in his grandfather's hand to missing cows, sheep, and the remains of other animals—the hideous suggestion clearly defined now in those entries of Luther Whateley's about R.'s " size commensurate with amt. of food," and " he must be kept on a careful diet and to a controllable size "—like the Innsmouth people!—controlled to nothingness after Sarah's death, with Luther hoping that foodless confinement might shrivel the thing in the shuttered room and kill it beyond revival, despite the doubt that had led him to adjure Abner to kill " anything in it that lives,"—*the thing Abner had unwittingly liberated when he broke the pane and kicked out the shutters, liberated to seek its own food and its hellish growth again, at first with fish from the Miskatonic, then with small animals, then cattle, and at last human beings—the thing that was half-batrachian, half human, but human enough to come back to the only home it had ever known and to cry out in terror for its Mother in the face of the fatal holocaust —the thing that had been born to the unblessed union of Sarah Whateley and Ralsa Marsh, spawn of tainted and degenerate blood, the monster that would loom forever on the perimeter of Abner Whateley's awareness—his cousin Ralsa, doomed by his grandfather's iron will, instead of being released long ago into the sea to join the Deep Ones among the minions of Dagon and great Cthulhu!*

AT THE END OF THE PASSAGE

Rudyard Kipling

The sky is lead and our faces are red,
  And the gates of Hell are opened and riven,
  And the winds of Hell are loosened and driven,
And the dust flies up in the face of Heaven,
  And the clouds come down in a fiery sheet,
Heavy to raise and hard to be borne,
  And the soul of man is turned from his meat,
Turned from the trifles for which he has striven,
  Sick in his body, and heavy-hearted,
  And his soul flies up like the dust in the street,
  Breaks from his flesh and is gone and departed,
As the blasts they blow on the cholera-horn.

Himalayan

Four men, each entitled to "life, liberty, and the pursuit of happiness," sat at a table playing whist. The thermometer marked—for them—one hundred and one degrees of heat. The room was darkened till it was only just possible to distinguish the pips of the cards and the very white faces of the players. A tattered, rotten punkah of whitewashed calico was puddling the hot air and whining dolefully at each stroke. Outside lay gloom of a November day in London. There was neither sky, sun, nor horizon—nothing but a brown purple haze of heat. It was as though the earth were dying of apoplexy.

From time to time clouds of tawny dust rose from the ground without wind or warning, flung themselves tablecloth-wise among the tops of the parched trees, and came down again. Then a whirling dust-devil would scutter across the plain for a couple of miles, break, and fall outward, though there was nothing to check its flight save a long low line of piled railway-sleepers white with the dust, a cluster of huts made of mud, condemned rails, and canvas, and the one squat four-roomed bungalow that belonged to the assistant engineer in charge of the section of a Gaudhari State line then under construction.

The four, stripped to the thinnest of sleeping-suits, played whist crossly, with wranglings as to leads and returns. It was not the best kind of whist, but they had taken some trouble to arrive at it. Mottram of the Indian Survey had ridden thirty and railed one hundred miles from his lonely post in the desert since the night before; Lowndes of the Civil Service, on special duty in the political department, had come as far to escape for an instant the miserable intrigues of an impoverished native State whose king alternately fawned and blustered for more money from the pitiful revenues contributed by hard-wrung peasants and despairing camel-breeders; Spurstow, the doctor of the line, had left a cholera-stricken camp of coolies to look after itself for forty-eight hours while he associated with white men once more. Hummil, the assistant engineer, was the host. He stood fast and received his friends thus every Sunday if they could come in. When one of them failed to appear, he would send a telegram to his last address, in order that he might know whether the defaulter were dead or alive. There are very many places in the East where it is not good or kind to let your acquaintances drop out of sight even for one short week.

The players were not conscious of any special regard for each other. They squabbled whenever they met; but they ardently desired to meet, as men without water desire to drink. They were lonely folk who understood the dread meaning of loneliness. They were all under thirty years of age—which is too soon for any man to possess that knowledge.

"Pilsener?" said Spurstow, after the second rubber, mopping his forehead.

"Beer's out, I'm sorry to say, and there's hardly enough soda-water for to-night," said Hummil.

"What filthy bad management!" Spurstow snarled.

"Can't help it. I've written and wired; but the trains don't come through regularly yet. Last week the ice ran out—as Lowndes knows."

"Glad I didn't come. I could ha' sent you some if I had known, though. Phew! it's too hot to go on playing bumble-puppy." This with a savage scowl at Lowndes, who only laughed. He was a hardened offender.

Mottram rose from the table and looked out of a chink in the shutters.

"What a sweet day!" said he.

The company yawned all together and betook themselves to an aimless investigation of all Hummil's possessions—guns, tattered novels, saddlery, spurs, and the like. They had fingered them a score of times before, but there was really nothing else to do.

"Got anything fresh?" said Lowndes.

"Last week's *Gazette of India*, and a cutting from a Home paper. My father sent it out. It's rather amusing."

"One of those vestrymen that call 'emselves M.P.'s again, is it?" said Spurstow, who read his newspapers when he could get them.

"Yes. Listen to this. It's to your address, Lowndes. The man was making a speech to his constituents, and he piled it on. Here's a sample, "And I assert unhesitatingly that the Civil Service in India is the preserve—the pet preserve—of the aristocracy of England. What does the democracy—what do the masses—get from that country, which we have step by step fraudulently annexed? I answer, nothing whatever. It is farmed with a single eye to their own interests by the scions of the aristocracy. They take good care to maintain their lavish scale of incomes, to avoid or stifle any inquiries into the nature and conduct of their administration, while they themselves force the unhappy peasant to pay with the sweat of his brow for all the luxuries in which they are lapped." Hummil waved the cutting above his head. "'Ear! 'ear!" said his audience.

Then Lowndes, meditatively, "I'd give—I'd give three months' pay to have that gentleman spend one month with me and see how the free and independent native prince works things. Old Timbersides"—this was his flippant title for an honoured and decorated feudatory prince—"has been wearing my life out this week past for money. By Jove, his latest performance was to send me one of his women as a bribe!"

"Good for you! Did you accept it?" said Mottram.

"No. I rather wish I had, now. She was a pretty little person, and she yarned away to me about the horrible destitution among the king's women-folk. The darlings haven't had any new clothes for nearly a month, and the old man wants to buy a new drag from Calcutta—solid silver railings and silver lamps, and trifles of that kind. I've tried to make him understand that he has played the deuce with the revenues for the last twenty years and must go slow. He can't see it."

"But he has the ancestral treasure-vaults to draw on. There must be three millions at least in jewels and coin under his palace," said Hummil.

"Catch a native king disturbing the family treasure! The priests forbid it except as the last resort. Old Timbersides has added something like a quarter of a million to the deposit in his reign."

"Where the mischief does it all come from?" said Mottram.

"The country. The state of the people is enough to make you sick. I've known the taxmen wait by a milch-camel till the foal was born and then hurry off the mother for arrears. And what can I do? I can't get the court clerks to give me any accounts; I can't raise anything more than a fat smile from the commander-in-chief when I find out the troops are three months in arrears; and old Timbersides begins to weep when I speak to him. He has taken to the King's Peg heavily—liqueur brandy for whisky, and Heidsieck for soda-water."

"That's what the Rao of Jubela took to. Even a native can't last long at that," said Spurstow. "He'll go out."

"And a good thing, too. Then I suppose we'll have a council of regency, and a tutor for the young prince, and hand him back his kingdom with ten years' accumulations."

"Whereupon that young prince, having been taught all the vices of the English, will play ducks and drakes with the money and undo ten years' work in eighteen months. I've seen that business before," said Spurstow. "I should tackle the king with a light hand if I were you, Lowndes. They'll hate you quite enough under any circumstances."

"That's all very well. The man who looks on can talk about the light hand; but you can't clean a pig-sty with a pen dipped in rose-water. I know my risks; but nothing has happened yet. My servant's an old Pathan, and he cooks for me. They are hardly likely to bribe him, and I don't accept food from my true friends, as they call themselves. Oh, but it's weary work! I'd sooner be with you, Spurstow. There's shooting near your camp."

"Would you? I don't think it. About fifteen deaths a day

don't incite a man to shoot anything but himself. And the worst of it is that the poor devils look at you as though you ought to save them. Lord knows, I've tried everything. My last attempt was empirical, but it pulled an old man through. He was brought to me apparently past hope, and I gave him gin and Worcester sauce with cayenne. It cured him; but I don't recommend it."

"How do the cases run generally?" said Hummil.

"Very simply indeed. Chlorodyne, opium pill, chlorodyne, collapse, nitre, bricks to the feet, and then—the burning ghaut. The last seems to be the only thing that stops the trouble. It's black cholera, you know. Poor devils! But, I will say, little Bunsee Lal, my apothecary, works like a demon. I've recommended him for promotion if he comes through it all alive."

"And what are your chances, old man?" said Mottram.

"Don't know; don't care much; but I've sent the letter in. What are you doing with yourself generally?"

"Sitting under a table in the tent and spitting on the sextant to keep it cool," said the man of the Survey. "Washing my eyes to avoid ophthalmia, which I shall certainly get, and trying to make a sub-surveyor understand that an error of five degrees in an angle isn't quite so small as it looks. I'm altogether alone, y' know, and shall be till the end of the hot weather."

"Hummil's the lucky man," said Lowndes, flinging himself into a long chair. "He has an actual roof—torn as to the ceiling-cloth, but still a roof—over his head. He sees one train daily. He can get beer and soda-water and ice 'em when God is good. He has books, pictures"—they were torn from the *Graphic*—"and the society of the excellent sub-contractor Jevins, besides the pleasure of receiving us weekly."

Hummil smiled grimly. "Yes, I'm the lucky man, I suppose. Jevins is luckier."

"How? Not——"

"Yes. Went out. Last Monday."

"By his own hand?" said Spurstow quickly, hinting the suspicion that was in everybody's mind. There was no cholera near Hummil's section. Even fever gives a man at least a week's grace, and sudden death generally implied self-slaughter.

"I judge no man this weather," said Hummil. "He had a touch of the sun, I fancy; for last week, after you fellows had left, he came into the verandah and told me that he was going home to see his wife, in Market Street, Liverpool, that evening.

"I got the apothecary in to look at him, and we tried to make him lie down. After an hour or two he rubbed his eyes and said he believed he had had a fit—hoped he hadn't said anything rude. Jevins had a great idea of bettering himself socially. He was very like Chucks in his language."

"Well?"

"Then he went to his own bungalow and began cleaning a rifle. He told the servant that he was going to shoot buck in the morning. Naturally he fumbled with the trigger, and shot himself through the head—accidentally. The apothecary sent in a report to my chief, and Jevins is buried somewhere out there. I'd have wired to you, Spurstow, if you could have done anything."

"You're a queer chap," said Mottram. "If you'd killed the man yourself you couldn't have been more quiet about the business."

"Good lord! what does it matter?" said Hummil calmly. "I've got to do a lot of his overseeing work in addition to my own. I'm the only person that suffers. Jevins is out of it—by pure accident, of course, but out of it. The apothecary was going to write a long screed on suicide. Trust a babu to drivel when he gets the chance."

"Why didn't you let it go in as suicide?" said Lowndes.

"No direct proof. A man hasn't many privileges in this country, but he might at least be allowed to mishandle his own rifle. Besides, some day I may need a man to smother up an accident to myself. Live and let live. Die and let die."

"You take a pill," said Spurstow, who had been watching Hummil's white face narrowly. "Take a pill, and don't be an ass. That sort of talk is skittles. Anyhow, suicide is shirking your work. If I were Job ten times over, I should be so interested in what was going to happen next that I'd stay on and watch."

"Ah! I've lost that curiosity," said Hummil.

"Liver out of order?" said Lowndes feelingly.

"No. Can't sleep. That's worse."

"By jove, it is!" said Mottram. "I'm that way every now and then, and the fit has to wear itself out. What do you take for it?"

"Nothing. What's the use? I haven't had ten minutes' sleep since Friday morning."

"Poor chap! Spurstow, you ought to attend to this," said Mottram. "Now you mention it, your eyes are rather gummy and swollen."

Spurstow, still watching Hummil, laughed lightly. "I'll patch him up, later on. Is it too hot, do you think, to go for a ride?"

"Where to?" said Lowndes wearily. "We shall have to go away at eight, and there'll be riding enough for us then. I hate a horse when I have to use him as a necessity. Oh, heavens! what it there to do?"

"Begin whist again, at chick points [a "chick" is supposed to be eight shillings] and a gold mohur on the rub," said Spurstow promptly.

"Poker. A month's pay all round for the pool—no limit—and fifty-rupee raises. Somebody would be broken before we got up," said Lowndes.

"Can't say that it would give me any pleasure to break any man in this company," said Mottram. "There isn't enough excitement in it, and it's foolish." He crossed over to the worn and battered little camp-piano—wreckage of a married household that had once held the bungalow—and opened the case.

"It's used up long ago," said Hummil. "The servants have picked it to pieces."

The piano was indeed hopelessly out of order, but Mottram managed to bring the rebellious notes into a sort of agreement, and there rose from the ragged keyboard something that might once have been the ghost of a popular music-hall song. The men in the long chairs turned with evident interest as Mottram banged the more lustily.

"That's good" said Lowndes. "By Jove! the last time I heard that song was in '79, or thereabouts, just before I came out."

"Ah!" said Spurstow with pride, "I was home in '80." And he mentioned a song of the streets popular at that date.

Mottram executed it roughly. Lowndes criticised and volunteered emendations. Mottram dashed into another ditty, not of the music-hall character, and made as if to rise.

"Sit down," said Hummil. "I didn't know that you had any music in your composition. Go on playing until you can't think of anything more. I'll have that piano tuned up before you come again. Play something festive."

Very simple indeed were the tunes to which Mottram's art and the limitations of the piano could give effect, but the men listened with pleasure, and in the pauses talked all together of what they had seen or heard when they were last at home. A dense dust-storm sprang up outside, and swept roaring over the house, enveloping it in the choking darkness of midnight, but Mottram continued unheeding, and the crazy tinkle reached the ears of the listeners above the flapping of the tattered ceiling-cloth.

In the silence after the storm he glided from the more directly personal songs of Scotland, half humming them as he played, into the Evening Hymn.

"Sunday," said he, nodding his head.

"Go on. Don't apologise for it," said Spurstow.

Hummil laughed long and riotously. "Play it, by all means. You're full of surprises to-day. I didn't know you had such a gift of finished sarcasm. How does that thing go?"

Mottram took up the tune.

"Too slow by half. You miss the note of gratitude," said Hummil. "It ought to go to the 'Grasshopper's Polka'—this way." And he chanted, *prestissimo*—

> "'Glory to thee, my God, this night,
> For all the blessings of the light.'

That shows we really feel our blessings. How does it go on?—

> 'If in the night I sleepless lie,
> My soul with sacred thoughts supply;
> May no ill dreams disturb my rest,'—

Quicker, Mottram!—

> 'Or powers of darkness me molest!'"

"Bah! what an old hypocrite you are!"

"Don't be an ass," said Lowndes. "You are at full liberty to make fun of anything else you like, but leave that hymn alone. It's associated in my mind with the most sacred recollections——"

"Summer evenings in the country—stained-glass window—light going out, and you and she jamming your heads together over one hymnbook," said Mottram.

"Yes, and a fat old cockchafer hitting you in the eye when you walked home. Smell of hay, and a moon as big as a bandbox sitting on the top of a haycock, bats—roses—milk and midges," said Lowndes.

"Also mothers. I can just recollect my mother singing me to sleep with that when I was a little chap," said Spurstow.

The darkness had fallen on the room. They could hear Hummil squirming in his chair.

"Consequently," said he testily, "you sing it when you are seven fathom deep in Hell! It's an insult to the intelligence of the Deity to pretend we're anything but tortured rebels."

"Take *two* pills," said Spurstow; "that's tortured liver."

"The usually placid Hummil is in a vile bad temper. I'm sorry for his coolies to-morrow," said Lowndes, as the servants brought in the lights and prepared the table for dinner.

As they were settling into their places about the miserable goat-chops, and the smoked tapioca pudding, Spurstow took occasion to whisper to Mottram, "Well done, David!"

"Look after Saul, then," was the reply.

"What are you two whispering about?" said Hummil suspiciously.

"Only saying that you are a damned poor host. This fowl can't be cut," returned Spurstow with a sweet smile. "Call this a dinner?"

"I can't help it. You don't expect a banquet, do you?"

Throughout the meal Hummil contrived laboriously to insult directly and pointedly all his guests in succession, and at each insult Spurstow kicked the aggrieved persons under the table; but he dared not exchange a glance of intelligence with either of them. Hummil's face was white and pinched, while his eyes were unnaturally large. No man dreamed for a moment of resenting his savage personalities, but as soon as the meal was over they made haste to get away.

"Don't go. You're just getting amusing, you fellows. I hope I haven't said anything that annoyed you. You're such touchy devils." Then changing the note into one of almost abject entreaty, Hummil added, "I say, you surely aren't going?"

"In the language of the blessed Jorrocks, where I dines I sleeps," said Spurstow. "I want to have a look at your coolies to-morrow, if you don't mind. You can give me a place to lie down in, I suppose?"

The others pleaded the urgency of their several duties next day, and, saddling up, departed together, Hummil begging them to come next Sunday. As they jogged off, Lowndes unbosomed himself to Mottram—

". . . And I never felt so like kicking a man at his own table in my life. He said I cheated at whist, and reminded me I was in debt! 'Told you you were as good as a liar to your face! You aren't half indignant enough over it."

"Not I," said Mottram. "Poor devil! Did you ever know old Hummy behave like that before or within a hundred miles of it?"

"That's no excuse. Spurstow was hacking my shin all the time, so I kept a hand on myself. Else I should have——"

"No, you wouldn't. You'd have done as Hummy did about Jevins; judge no man this weather. By Jove! the buckle of my bridle is hot in my hand! Trot out a bit, and 'ware rat-holes."

Ten minutes' trotting jerked out of Lowndes one very sage remark when he pulled up, sweating from every pore—

"Good thing Spurstow's with him to-night."

"Ye-es. Good man, Spurstow. Our roads turn here. See you again next Sunday, if the sun doesn't bowl me over."

"S'pose so, unless old Timbersides' finance minister manages to dress some of my food. Good-night, and—God bless you!"

"What's wrong now?"

"Oh, nothing." Lowndes gathered up his whip, and, as he flicked Mottram's mare on the flank, added, "You're not a bad little chap—that's all." And the mare bolted half a mile across the sand, on the word.

In the assistant engineer's bungalow Spurstow and Hummil smoked the pipe of silence together, each narrowly watching the other. The capacity of a bachelor's establishment is as elastic as its arrangements are simple. A servant cleared away the dining-room table, brought in a couple of rude native bedsteads made of tape strung on a light wood frame, flung a square of cool Calcutta matting over each, set them side by side, pinned two towels to the punkah so that their fringes should just sweep clear of the sleeper's nose and mouth, and announced that the couches were ready.

The men flung themselves down, ordering the punkah-coolies by all the powers of Hell to pull. Every door and window was shut, for the outside air was that of an oven. The atmosphere within was only 104°, as the thermometer bore witness, and heavy with the foul smell of badly-trimmed kerosene lamps; and this stench, combined with that of native tobacco, baked brick, and dried earth, sends the heart of many a strong man down to his boots, for it is the smell of the Great Indian Empire when she turns herself for six months into a house of torment. Spurstow packed his pillows craftily so that he reclined rather than lay, his head at a safe elevation above his feet. It is not good to sleep on a low pillow in the hot weather if you happen to be of thick-necked build, for you may pass with lively snores and gugglings from natural sleep into the deep slumber of heat-apoplexy.

"Pack your pillows," said the doctor sharply, as he saw Hummil preparing to lie down at full length.

The night-light was trimmed, the shadow of the punkah wavered across the room, and the "*flick*" of the punkah-towel and the soft whine of the rope through the wall-hole followed it. Then the punkah flagged, almost ceased. The sweat poured from Spurstow's brow. Should he go out and harangue the coolie? It started forward again with a savage jerk, and a pin came out of the towels. When this was replaced, a tomtom in the coolie-lines began to beat with the steady throb of a swollen artery inside some brain-fevered skull. Spurstow turned on his side and swore gently. There was no movement on Hummil's part. The man had composed himself as rigidly as a corpse, his hands clinched at his sides. The respiration was too hurried for any suspicion of sleep.

Spurstow looked at the set face. The jaws were clinched, and there was a pucker round the quivering eyelids.

"He's holding himself as tightly as ever he can," thought Spurstow. "What in the world is the matter with him?—Hummil!"

"Yes," in a thick constrained voice.

"Can't you get to sleep?"

"No."

"Head hot? Throat feeling bulgy? or how?"

"Neither, thanks. I don't sleep much, you know."

"Feel pretty bad?"

"Pretty bad, thanks. There is a tomtom outside, isn't there? I thought it was my head at first. . . . Oh, Spurstow, for pity's sake give me something that will put me asleep—sound asleep—if it's only for six hours!" He sprang up, trembling from head to foot. "I haven't been able to sleep naturally for days, and I can't stand it!—I can't stand it!"

"Poor old chap!"

"That's no use. Give me something to make me sleep. I tell you I'm nearly mad. I don't know what I say half my time. For three weeks I've had to think and spell out every word that has come through my lips before I dared say it. Isn't that enough to drive a man mad? I can't see things correctly now, and I've lost my sense of touch. My skin aches—my skin aches! Make me sleep. Oh, Spurstow, for the love of God make me sleep sound. It isn't enough merely to let me dream. Let me sleep!"

"All right, old man, all right. Go slow; you aren't half as bad as you think."

The flood-gates of reserve once broken, Hummil was clinging to him like a frightened child. "You're pinching my arm to pieces."

"I'll break your neck if you don't do something for me. No, I didn't mean that. Don't be angry, old fellow." He wiped the sweat off himself as he fought to regain composure. "I'm a bit restless and off my oats, and perhaps you could recommend some sort of sleeping mixture—bromide of potassium."

"Bromide of skittles! Why didn't you tell me this before? Let go of my arm, and I'll see if there's anything in my cigarette-case to suit your complaint." Spurstow hunted among his day-clothes, turned up the lamp, opened a little silver cigarette-case, and advanced on the expectant Hummil with the daintiest of fairy squirts.

"The last appeal of civilisation," said he, "and a thing I hate to use. Hold out your arm. Well, your sleeplessness hasn't ruined your muscle; and what a thick hide it is! Might as well inject a buffalo subcutaneously. Now in a few minutes the morphia will begin working. Lie down and wait."

A smile of unalloyed and idiotic delight began to creep over Hummil's face. "I think," he whispered—"I think I'm going off now. Gad! it's positively heavenly! Spurstow, you must give me that case to keep; you——" The voice ceased as the head fell back.

"Not for a good deal," said Spurstow to the unconscious form. "And now, my friend, sleeplessness of your kind being very apt to relax the moral fibre in little matters of life and death, I'll just take the liberty of spiking your guns."

He paddled into Hummil's saddle-room in his bare feet and uncased a twelve-bore rifle, an express, and a revolver. Of the first he unscrewed the nipples and hid them in the bottom of a saddlery-case; of the second he abstracted the lever, kicking it behind a big wardrobe. The third he merely opened, and knocked the doll-head bolt of the grip up with the heel of a riding-boot.

"That's settled," he said, as he shook the sweat off his hands. "These little precautions will at least give you time to turn. You have too much sympathy with gun-room accidents."

And as he rose from his knees, the thick muffled voice of Hummil cried in the doorway, "You fool!"

Such tones they use who speak in the lucid intervals of delirium to their friends a little before they die.

Spurstow started, dropping the pistol. Hummil stood in the doorway, rocking with helpless laughter.

"That was awf'ly good of you, I'm sure," he said, very slowly, feeling for his words. "I don't intend to go out by my own hand at present. I say, Spurstow, that stuff won't work. What shall I do? What shall I do?" And panic terror stood in his eyes.

"Lie down and give it a chance. Lie down at once."

"I daren't. It will only take me half-way again, and I shan't be able to get away this time. Do you know it was all I could do to come out just now? Generally I am as quick as lightning; but you had clogged my feet. I was nearly caught."

"Oh, yes, I understand. Go and lie down."

"No, it isn't delirium; but it was an awfully mean trick to play on me. Do you know I might have died?"

As a sponge rubs a slate clean, so some power unknown to Spurstow had wiped out of Hummil's face all that stamped it for the face of a man, and he stood at the doorway in the expression of his lost innocence. He had slept back into terrified childhood.

"Is he going to die on the spot?" thought Spurstow. Then, aloud, "All right, my son. Come back to bed, and tell me all about it. You couldn't sleep; but what was all the rest of the nonsense?"

"A place—a place down there," said Hummil with simple sincerity. The drug was acting on him by waves, and he was flung from the fear of a strong man to the fright of a child as his nerves gathered sense or were dulled.

"Good God! I've been afraid of it for months past, Spurstow. It has made every night hell to me; and yet I'm not conscious of having done anything wrong."

"Be still, and I'll give you another dose. We'll stop your nightmares, you unutterable idiot!"

"Yes, but you must give me so much that I can't get away. You must make me quite sleepy—not just a little sleepy. It's so hard to run then."

"I know it; I know it. I've felt it myself. The symptoms are exactly as you describe."

"Oh, don't laugh at me, confound you! Before this awful sleeplessness came to me I've tried to rest on my elbow and put a spur in the bed to sting me when I fell back. Look!"

"By Jove! the man has been rowelled like a horse! Ridden by the nightmare with a vengeance! And we all thought him sensible enough. Heaven send us understanding! You like to talk, don't you?"

"Yes, sometimes. Not when I'm frightened. *Then* I want to run. Don't you?"

"Always. Before I give you your second dose try to tell me exactly what your trouble is."

Hummil spoke in broken whispers for nearly ten minutes,

whilst Spurstow looked into the pupils of his eyes and passed his hand before them once or twice.

At the end of the narrative the silver cigarette-case was produced, and the last words that Hummil said as he fell back for the second time were, "Put me quite to sleep; for if I'm caught I die—I die!"

"Yes, yes; we all do that sooner or later—thank Heaven who has set a term to our miseries," said Spurstow, settling the cushions under the head. "It occurs to me that unless I drink something I shall go out before my time. I've stopped sweating, and—I wear a seventeen-inch collar." He brewed himself scalding hot tea, which is an excellent remedy against heat-apoplexy if you take three or four cups of it in time. Then he watched the sleeper.

"A blind face that cries and can't wipe its eyes, a blind face that chases him down corridors! H'm! Decidedly, Hummil ought to go on leave as soon as possible; and, sane or otherwise, he undoubtedly did rowel himself most cruelly. Well, Heaven send us understanding!"

At mid-day Hummil rose, with an evil taste in his mouth, but an unclouded eye and a joyful heart.

"I was pretty bad last night, wasn't I?" said he.

"I have seen healthier men. You must have had a touch of the sun. Look here: if I write you a swingeing medical certificate will you apply for leave on the spot?"

"No."

"Why not? You want it."

"Yes, but I can hold on till the weather's a little cooler."

"Why should you, if you can get relieved on the spot?"

"Burkett is the only man who could be sent; and he's a born fool."

"Oh, never mind about the line. You aren't so important as all that. Wire for leave, if necessary."

Hummil looked very uncomfortable.

"I can hold on till the Rains," he said evasively.

"You can't. Wire to headquarters for Burkett."

"I won't. If you want to know why, particularly, Burkett is married, and his wife's just had a kid, and she's up at Simla, in the cool, and Burkett has a very nice billet that takes him into Simla from Saturday to Monday. That little woman isn't at all well. If Burkett was transferred she'd try to follow him. If she left the baby behind she'd fret herself to death. If she came—and Burkett's one of those selfish little beasts who are always talking about a wife's place being with her husband—she'd die. It's murder to bring a woman here just now. Burkett hasn't the physique of a rat. If he came here he'd go out; and I know she hasn't any money, and I'm pretty sure she'd go out too. I'm salted in a sort of way, and I'm not married. Wait till the Rains, and then Burkett can get thin down here. It'll do him heaps of good."

"Do you mean to say that you intend to face—what you have faced, till the Rains break?"

"Oh, it won't be so bad, now you've shown me a way out of it. I can always wire to you. Besides, now I've once got into the way of sleeping, it'll be all right. Anyhow, I shan't put in for leave. That's the long and the short of it."

"My great Scott! I thought all that sort of thing was dead and done with."

"Bosh! You'd do the same yourself. I feel a new man, thanks to that cigarette-case. You're going over to camp now, aren't you?"

"Yes; but I'll try to look you up every other day, if I can."

"I'm not bad enough for that. I don't want you to bother. Give the coolies gin and ketchup."

"Then you feel all right?"

"Fit to fight for my life, but not to stand out in the sun talking to you. Go along, old man, and bless you!"

Hummil turned on his heel to face the echoing desolation of his bungalow, and the first thing he saw standing in the verandah was the figure of himself. He had met a similar apparition once before, when he was suffering from overwork and the strain of the hot weather.

"This is bad—already," he said, rubbing his eyes. "If the thing slides away from me all in one piece, like a ghost, I shall know it is only my eyes and stomach that are out of order. If it walks—my head is going."

He approached the figure, which naturally kept at an unvarying distance from him, as is the use of all spectres that are born of overwork. It slid through the house and dissolved into swimming specks within the eyeball as soon as it reached the burning light of the garden. Hummil went about his business till even. When he came in to dinner he found himself sitting at the table. The vision rose and walked out hastily. Except that it cast no shadow it was in all respects real.

No living man knows what that week held for Hummil. An increase of the epidemic kept Spurstow in camp among the coolies, and all he could do was to telegraph to Mottram, bidding him go to the bungalow and sleep there. But Mottram was forty miles away from the nearest telegraph, and knew nothing of anything save the needs of the Survey till he met, early on Sunday morning, Lowndes and Spurstow heading towards Hummil's for the weekly gathering.

"Hope the poor chap's in a better temper," said the former, swinging himself off his horse at the door. "I suppose he isn't up yet."

"I'll just have a look at him," said the doctor. "If he's asleep there's no need to wake him."

And an instant later, by the tone of Spurstow's voice calling upon them to enter, the men knew what had happened. There was no need to wake him.

The punkah was still being pulled over the bed, but Hummil had departed this life at least three hours.

The body lay on its back, hands clinched by the side, as Spurstow had seen it lying seven nights previously. In the staring eyes was written terror beyond the expression of any pen.

Mottram, who had entered behind Lowndes, bent over the dead and touched the forehead lightly with his lips. "Oh, you lucky, lucky devil!" he whispered.

But Lowndes had seen the eyes, and withdrew shuddering to the other side of the room.

"Poor chap! poor old chap! And the last time I met him I was angry. Spurstow, we should have watched him. Has he——?"

Deftly Spurstow continued his investigations, ending by a search round the room.

"No, he hasn't," he snapped. "There's no trace of anything. Call the servants."

They came, eight or ten of them, whispering and peering over each other's shoulders.

"When did your Sahib go to bed?" said Spurstow.

"At eleven or ten, we think," said Hummil's personal servant.

"He was well then? But how should you know?"

"He was not ill, as far as our comprehension extended. But he had slept very little for three nights. This I know, because I saw him walking much, and specially in the heart of the night."

As Spurstow was arranging the sheet, a big straight-necked hunting-spur tumbled on the ground. The doctor groaned. The personal servant peeped at the body.

"What do you think, Chuma?" said Spurstow, catching the look on the dark face.

"Heaven-born, in my poor opinion, this that was my master has descended into the Dark Places, and there has been caught because he was not able to escape with sufficient speed. We have the spur for evidence that he fought with Fear. Thus have I seen men of my race do with thorns when a spell was laid upon them to overtake them in their sleeping hours and they dared not sleep."

"Chuma, you're a mud-head. Go out and prepare seals to be set on the Sahib's property."

"God has made the Heaven-born. God has made me. Who are we, to inquire into the dispensations of God? I will bid the other servants hold aloof while you are reckoning the tale of the Sahib's property. They are all thieves, and would steal."

"As far as I can make out, he died from—oh, anything; stoppage of the heart's action, heat-apoplexy, or some other visitation," said Spurstow to his companions. "We must make an inventory of his effects, and so on."

"He was scared to death," insisted Lowndes. "Look at those eyes! For pity's sake don't let him be buried with them open!"

"Whatever it was, he's clear of all the trouble now," said Mottram softly.

Spurstow was peering into the open eyes.

"Come here," said he. "Can you see anything there?"

"I can't face it!" whimpered Lowndes. "Cover up the face! Is there any fear on earth that can turn a man into that likeness? It's ghastly. Oh, Spurstow, cover it up!"

"No fear—on earth," said Spurstow. Mottram leaned over his shoulder and looked intently.

"I see nothing except some grey blurs in the pupil. There can be nothing there, you know."

"Even so. Well, let's think. It'll take half a day to knock up any sort of coffin; and he must have died at midnight. Lowndes, old man, go out and tell the coolies to break ground next to Jevins's grave. Mottram, go round the house with Chuma and see that the seals are put on things. Send a couple of men to me here, and I'll arrange."

The strong-armed servants when they returned to their own kind told a strange story of the doctor Sahib vainly trying to call their master back to life by magic arts—to wit, the holding of a little green box that clicked to each of the dead man's eyes, and of a bewildered muttering on the part of the doctor Sahib, who took the little green box away with him.

The resonant hammering of a coffin-lid is no pleasant thing to hear, but those who have experience maintain that much more terrible is the soft swish of the bed-linen, the reeving and unreeving of the bed-tapes, when he who has fallen by the roadside is apparelled for burial, sinking gradually as the tapes are tied over, till the swaddled shape touches the floor and there is no protest against the indignity of hasty disposal.

At the last moment Lowndes was seized with scruples of conscience. "Ought you to read the service—from beginning to end?" said he to Spurstow.

"I intend to. You're my senior as a civilian. You can take it if you like."

"I didn't mean that for a moment. I only thought if we could get a chaplain from somewhere—I'm willing to ride anywhere—and give poor Hummil a better chance. That's all."

"Bosh!" said Spurstow, as he framed his lips to the tremendous words that stand at the head of the burial service.

After breakfast they smoked a pipe in silence to the memory of the dead. Then Spurstow said absently—

"'Tisn't in medical science."

"What?"

"Things in a dead man's eye."

"For goodness' sake leave that horror alone!" said

Lowndes. "I've seen a native die of pure fright when a tiger chivied him. I know what killed Hummil."

"The deuce you do! I'm going to try to see." And the doctor retreated into the bathroom with a Kodak camera. After a few minutes there was the sound of something being hammered to pieces, and he emerged, very white indeed.

"Have you got a picture?" said Mottram. "What does the thing look like?"

"It was impossible, of course. You needn't look, Mottram. I've torn up the films. There was nothing there. It was impossible."

"That," said Lowndes, very distinctly, watching the shaking hand striving to relight the pipe, "is a damned lie."

Mottram laughed uneasily. "Spurstow's right," he said. "We're all in such a state now that we'd believe anything. For pity's sake let's try to be rational."

There was no further speech for a long time. The hot wind whistled without, and the dry trees sobbed. Presently the daily train, winking brass, burnished steel, and spouting steam, pulled up panting in the intense glare. "We'd better go on on that," said Spurstow. "Go back to work. I've written my certificate. We can't do any more good here, and work'll keep our wits together. Come on."

No one moved. It is not pleasant to face railway journeys at mid-day in June. Spurstow gathered up his hat and whip, and, turning in the doorway, said:

"There may be Heaven—there must be Hell.
Meantime, there is our life here. We-ell?"

Neither Mottram nor Lowndes had any answer to the question.

Ghost and Horror Stories from Fontana

The Fontana Book of Great Horror Stories
Edited by Christine Bernard
The 5th Fontana Book of Great Horror Stories
The 6th Fontana Book of Great Horror Stories
The 7th Fontana Book of Great Horror Stories
The 8th Fontana Book of Great Horror Stories
The 9th Fontana Book of Great Horror Stories
Edited by Mary Danby

The world's most chilling horror stories, including classics from the past, famous modern tales, and original stories by new writers.

The Fontana Book of Great Ghost Stories
The 3rd Fontana Book of Great Ghost Stories
The 4th Fontana Book of Great Ghost Stories
The 5th Fontana Book of Great Ghost Stories
The 6th Fontana Book of Great Ghost Stories
The 7th Fontana Book of Great Ghost Stories
The 8th Fontana Book of Great Ghost Stories
Edited by Robert Aickman
The 9th Fontana Book of Great Ghost Stories
The 10th Fontana Book of Great Ghost Stories
The 11th Fontana Book of Great Ghost Stories
The 12th Fontana Book of Great Ghost Stories
Edited by R. Chetwynd-Hayes

Stories of the dead—and the not-quite-so-dead, by some of the most imaginative writers of occult stories.

Lord Halifax's Ghost Book
Lord Halifax's own collection of unbelievable—but true—happenings in the world of ghosts.

Fontana Tales of Terror

Stories to chill your blood from every corner of the globe. Along with tidbits of haunting history and strange happenings never yet explained—for the truth is often even more hair-raising than the imaginary.

Gaslight Tales of Terror
Tales of Terror from Outer Space
Cornish Tales of Terror
Welsh Tales of Terror
Edited by R. Chetwynd-Hayes

London Tales of Terror
Edited by Jacquelyn Visick

Scottish Tales of Terror
Edited by Angus Campbell

European Tales of Terror
Sea Tales of Terror
Edited by J. J. Strating

Irish Tales of Terror
Edited by Jim McGarry

Fontana also publishes

Frighteners
Frighteners 2
Edited by Mary Danby

Fontana Books

Victoria Holt

The supreme writer of the 'gothic' romance, a compulsive storyteller whose gripping novels of the darker face of love have thrilled millions all over the world.

The House of a Thousand Lanterns

Bride of Pendorric

The Curse of the Kings

King of the Castle

Kirkland Revels

The Legend of the Seventh Virgin

Menfreya

Mistress of Mellyn

On the Night of the Seventh Moon

The Queen's Confession

The Secret Woman

The Shadow of the Lynx

The Shivering Sands

Fontana Books